The Language of the Lake

The Language of the Lake

On the Water's Edge Tahoe Trilogy

KATHY BOYD FELLURE

July 3, 2024

Kathy Boyd Fellure

For Carin, Wonderful today to meet you enjoy your vacation

The Language of the Lake
© 2018 by Kathy Boyd Fellure

Scripture quotations marked KJV are taken from the Holy Bible, King James Version, Cambridge, 1769.

Published in association with Books & Such Literary Management, 52 Mission Circle, Suite 122, PMB 170, Santa Rosa, CA 95409-5370 www.booksandsuch.com

Interior Artwork by Donna Plant
Author bio picture by Hidden Hills Photography
Edited by Kathy Ide
Cover design by Kim Van Meter
Snooks Candies used by permission of Jim Snook

Print ISBN-13: 978-1978167377

Dedication

To my husband Joe.
And
in loving memory of Kathleen Flanagan Kresa,
my children's book illustrator and friend.
For the Baby Boomer generation.

Part One

Summer ~ Shades of Blue

*I*n Tahoe's early days, the Washoe Indians peacefully inhabited its abundant shores with respect for the land, the lake, and one other.

The turn of the last century ushered in Tahoe's Gilded Age, when the world-rich descended upon luxurious mansions and stylish resorts that dotted the north, south, east, and west shores. Many privileged rode in on Pullman Sleeper train cars from Oakland, California piers embarking on a twelve-hour journey into Truckee. From there, porters loaded steamer trunks and the summer elite on trains on the last hour-long leg of the trek into Tahoe City. Lazy and endless were the summers as steamboats ferried wealthy vacationers to dine and gamble at the fashionable Tahoe Tavern Hotel and Casino, dance in elaborate ballrooms, and visit other resorts around the lake.

This illustrious past led the way for many in the mid-1900s to lease land from the United States government and build on choice, rugged, property. These Tahoe pioneers put in a full work week at their regular jobs in various cities and towns, then traveled up the mountain to spend the weekend clearing the land to build summer cabins. It was back-breaking, hard work that held the promise of a future vacation/retirement homes on the shores and mountainside of the majestic Sierra Nevada Mountain Range. Within these neighborhoods lifetime friendships grew from diverse backgrounds, and middle-class America began to populate, cultivate, and relish the—Lake of the Sky.

Chapter One

Sometimes the lake speaks sorrowfully because of the years of drought when its shores were laid bare. Rocks cut the tender bottoms of my feet when I ran across the endless sand. My toes were thirsty for that first mushy mix of glistening granules and cold water. My feet sank deep into silt, and transparent water rose and tickled my tan legs. Even in years of drought, I could still swim. I had to go farther and farther out, way past where I was told, as a child, never to go alone.

—Emily Maxwell Taylor, diary entry

My feet kicked off the lake's sand as I propelled my way to the thin line of the watery surface—one last breath away. Gasping and choking, I splashed, spreading my arms out for balance. Buoys bobbed far behind me. Not a single boat was in sight. I measured the distance of each stroke by the ache in my screaming muscles.

Treading water, I scanned the perimeter. My mental image of David had disappeared into the dusk of night. I blinked and saw Olivia blowing out sixteen candles, flickers of light vanquished by exhaled air, leaving narrow wisps of rising smoke.

Chills jolted through my body, the cold penetrating to the marrow of my bones. I welcomed the intensity.

The farther I swam, eyes open or closed, the more David's sullen face flashed before me. I squinted, trying to obscure the visions from the past: Sarah and Olivia sitting at the dining room table after eating a stone cold prime rib meal. We had waited an hour for my husband to arrive before picking at our food that night.

Clenching my teeth, I sliced through the water, right arm, left arm, without breaking stride turning my head side to side. My heart sped and thrashed about in my chest. A rush of warmth flushed through my body, pumping adrenaline with each memory. I increased my speed, kicking harder, faster.

David had shown up in time for birthday cake and sat at the head of the table. Apologizing for the late drive home from the college, his eyes looked down on the congealed dinner.

"That's okay Dad," Olivia managed. "You're here in time for dessert."

Before he could respond, a shrill ring of the phone beckoned from the kitchen. The girls and I simultaneously turned to him, remaining silent in the stifling, summer heat.

I dove under the surface, down three, five, maybe eight feet, and swam inches above the silt. Crystal clear water surrounded me like an otherworld cocoon. I wanted to be encapsulated, insulated. Still my husband's eager face appeared ahead of me, his anticipation emerging as he hurried to pick up the receiver. I met Olivia's gaze. She knew. We all knew. He'd be leaving us again.

I somersaulted underwater, all life momentarily muffled, contained, until pressure surged and my ears popped. I vaulted and resurfaced. Sucking in air, I headed back to the cabin's shoreline, taking in and spewing out gulps of water. My legs stiffened and cramped as I drew in short, shallow breaths. My fingers clawed inward. A sharp pain shot through my side, doubling me over face-first into the water. I moaned, pressing hard into the repeated stab and struggling to keep my head up.

I fumbled to wipe away the watery blur of a silver-and-bright-red boat moving closer to me. As the skiff neared, I recognized Doc, his face stern, brow creased with concern.

He didn't mince words. "Wasn't sure you'd make it back."

"Might have misjudged the distance a bit." I conceded, trying to catch my breath.

Grabbing hold of his extended hand, I slid over the side of the boat, dragging my calves and thighs like pillars of stone. Without saying another word, Doc pulled off his sweatshirt and draped it across my shivering shoulders. I flipped the flannel hood over my drenched mop and zipped up to my neck.

The oars smacked against the water in a disapproving manner the entire ride.

Doc stood, feet anchored and legs braced, to tie up at Pine Cove. "Every time you dive into these waters and swim out toward the center of the lake, you scare your Nana right out of her cabin and over to mine." He sat beside me on the boat's middle bench, cupped his hands over my blue-tinged fingers, and rubbed them together until feeling returned. When he started to let go, I held on a moment longer.

Doc Walter's hands were strong, capable of mending the broken and bleeding patients who showed up at his door. He had a healing touch.

He motioned toward the smoke spiraling upward from the cabin chimney. "You get yourself inside, into some dry clothes, and warm up in front of that fire your Nana has going."

I stood and took two steps onto the damp pier before my rubbery legs collapsed. I landed with a thud on the wooden dock.

"You come in first thing in the morning for your annual check-up. First thing, Em." Doc admonished. Then he untied the rope and headed home.

I sat on the deck and watched him row off in perfect rhythm.

"Come back." I whispered. Unexpected tears streamed down my cheeks as he vanished around the bend where red fir and Jeffrey pines stood guard against the darkening clouds.

I sat immobile, knees drawn to my chest, rocking back and forth, teetering on the edge of the creaking weather-beaten planks. Swaying, holding myself against the billowing winds sweeping in from the south shore, I could not breathe, could not think.

A hefty gust threatened to sweep me back into the choppy waters below. I edged over to the nearest pier post. Goose bumps prickled across my arms and legs. I tilted my head toward the sliver of light radiating from the crescent moon—searching, hoping. Storm clouds were moving in at an alarming rate. Too soon the overshadowing shades of gray and black would prevail. I staggered to my feet.

Out of the corner of my eye, I observed a luminescent trail streaming across the lake connecting my swim out and back in again. Little pieces of my heart floated there in an unbroken pattern. Before it would have been of paramount importance to me to pick up the pieces, however many, and take them with me. They always fit back together later, like a jigsaw puzzle, one thousand tiny shapes that completed a picture when correctly assembled.

I walked across the pier and down the rickety, slick steps to the massive slab of rock at the base of the dock that bordered the shoreline.

"Emily?" A familiar voice jarred me. "Emily, are you okay?"

Startled, I glanced up into the slice of moonlight drifting down through the pine boughs. Silver beams cascaded like a stairway from a hidden door.

"Em, its Jack. Are you okay?" He moved closer, twigs snapping under his over-sized jogging shoes. His trademark goofy grin exposed perfect, too white teeth.

And there he stood. My childhood friend turned foe. "Jack?" I wiped my eyes. "Where did you come from?"

"I was over at Nana's, knew you were arriving today, and thought you might want to say hello. I'm happy you'll be here for the summer." Jack reached out to me. Beside him, Hemingway barked a curious greeting. His chocolate Lab bolted, then trotted back.

"Top of my to-do list." I fingered a check mark in the air and dashed past him, inadvertently stumbling over my own two feet. Without skipping a beat, I grabbed onto a low-lying tree branch to steady myself, but not before stubbing my toes on a prickly pine cone.

"Are your toes bleeding?" He stooped down to take a look, Hemingway's wagging tail beating against his pant leg.

"What are you doing?" I swatted at his hand before landing flat on my rear.

Hem's bark progressed to a low guttural growl. "Just trying to help." Jack pulled back, and offered his hand.

I sat there looking up at all six-feet-two-inches of him, and that stupid long hair. "Why don't you get a haircut?"

"What?"

"Get some new clothes while you're at it. Don't you own anything besides jeans and flannel shirts? It's the 1990s. Jack, get with it!" Ignoring his hand, I stood and hobbled a few feet.

Jack caught up to me. "I was kind of hoping we could start off as friends this year."

"Well, that would be a new approach for you." I petted his dog's head. "Good boy, Hemingway." I liked Jack's pet much more than I liked him. Hemingway was better looking, less maintenance, and more faithful.

"I'm sorry about your husband," he called out as I marched off in the opposite direction. "And sorry I missed David's funeral." Hemingway barked as if in agreement with his master and ran ahead leading the way to the path.

"Come." Jack whistled three sharp notes. When his dog obeyed, they both and retreated back toward the water's edge.

I trounced up the slope, trying to hide my newly acquired limp.

The barking continued for a moment or two, then faded in a pleading sort of way.

Rain pelted down. A rogue cloudburst, soaked Doc's sweatshirt and weighed down my steps up the last stretch of pebbly beach. Home—familiar, shelter, comfort, safety. My tears mingled with raindrops on my cheeks.

I unlatched the wooden gate and crunched barefoot through pine needle and cone debris to the deck stairway, up to the back screen door. It was unlocked, as usual. The porch light strobed as the door slapped hard against the warped casing behind me.

Through the kitchen window curtains, Nana smiled and waved to Jack. Hand on one hip, she chided. "You have never treated that boy right, Emily."

"And you have always been in love with him." I teased, then slouched in a chair at the kitchen table, picking at the dirt stuck to the drops of blood caked between my toes.

"Why, I do believe you're right about that. So you'd better hurry up and reel in the line before he falls in love with me—or some other gal, if that's possible."

"Well I guess I missed that crucial point as he dated one pretty girl after another with hardly a breath in between." I sniffled, then sneezed.

"Emily, Jack just wants to be friends. Can't you manage a polite response when he addresses you?" She closed the lace curtains with a firm tug.

Grinding my teeth, I managed a thin smile as the muscles in my neck tensed.

Nana handed me a thick cotton towel and thermal long underwear. "I drew a hot bath. You go have yourself a nice long soak." She ushered me dripping across the stone kitchen floor to the bathroom, and cracked the door wide enough for the steaming air to waft out.

The chills hit hard and fast. "Okay." My teeth chattered the moment I opened my mouth to speak. "Cold. Water. Tonight." The shivers set in, shaking me to the core.

"Honey, get out of those wet clothes. Leave them on the floor. I'll get to them later." Nana closed the door.

I perched on the rim of the antique porcelain tub. Its brass claw feet had etched grooves into the hardwood floor. I did just as my grandmother said: left sweatshirt, swimsuit, and towel in a jumbled heap, then eased my achy body in heavenly warm water until all but my head was immersed. The lavender and mineral bath salts she'd added brought soothing, tingling relief. Strong, heady essence of the medicinal plant flooded the small room with a pleasant aroma, enticing me to yield to its natural lulling abilities.

I closed my eyes, imagining myself far away across an ocean in ancestral England. Unending fields of lush lavender waved in the wind, a salutatory greeting. I responded with silence until the water grew cool.

Nana gave the door a firm rap. "Careful you don't fall asleep in there."

I sat up straight. "I'm about to dry off. Be out in a minute or two."

"Okay, honey. Come sit by the fire a spell with me." Nana's voice drifted off, her mild Southern accent lingering, sweetening the gap between her world and mine.

After patting dry and slipping into my thermals, I wiped steam off the mirror with my sleeve. My hair was a tangled mess and the looking glass did me no favors. I struggled to comb through stringy blond strands that fought back with every stroke. I gave a quick thought to chopping it off and going with the trendy feathered, short crop.

Taking further inventory of the reflection before me became more disparaging. Long johns hung loose on my previously tone, fit body. I flexed. "Ugh." My eyes had a dull glaze to them, not the usual sparkling sapphire Nana claimed was the same hue as the deepest waters of Lake Tahoe. Laugh lines and crows' feet were the price I now paid for all the years of slathering myself in innumerable coatings of cocoa butter or baby oil to bake at an elevation of six thousand feet every summer.

"Well, at least I still like my nose," I mused aloud, satisfied to zero in on my lone asset. I had inherited my mother's not-too-Roman nose, with a definable dent at the tip. It gave me character.

I switched off the bathroom light and padded in the dark over kitchen cobblestones, eager to warm my feet on the massive wool rug overtaking the cold hardwood floor. The wood-paneled living room was a cozy temperature. A fire blazed hot, crackling and popping from a river rock hearth. Nana knew better than anyone how to build a fire and stoke it to keep the logs burning.

My robe and slippers sat in a neat pile at the foot of the brown sofa.

I wrapped myself in the red-and-green fleece robe imprinted with a herd of antlered deer, then wiggled my toes down into fur-trimmed moccasins. Stretching out on the loveseat opposite Nana, I relaxed.

"You going to be okay, child?" Her eyebrows rose in a questioning arc.

"Sure." Squirming to find a comfortable position, I shifted a couple of pillows under my head. "The drive up from Sacramento took three hours. Bumper-to-bumper traffic all the way up through Auburn. I used to buzz up here after work on a Friday in an hour and a half. Now tourists bottleneck coming into Tahoe City, sometimes snaking all the way back to River Ranch." I grumbled, exhaustion settling, taxing the last of my resolve.

Legs elevated, Nana reclined, bundled in a blanket. "I do miss the early days, the quiet of small-town life when all the townsfolk knew each other by name. Last year they chopped down the towering pine in the middle of the highway, in front of Rosie's Café."

Her lament was a shared sentiment among the year-round locals. "That was a sad loss. I guess one car too many ran into it. Seven years of drought didn't help either. I loved that old tree." I twisted both ends of the waist tie on my robe. "Nana, where were you when I got here?"

"Finishing up some business in Reno. Doc was going to take me, but this past week he's been dealing with an outbreak of some new flu strain that's hitting the locals. So Jack was my designated chauffer for the day." Nana trained her eyes on me. There would be no reprieve tonight for my lack of manners dealing with Jack Conner.

"How about some tea?" I forced myself out of the comfortable old couch and headed toward the kitchen.

"Do you need any help?" Nana called.

"I can manage."

Despite my declaration of independence, Nana joined me in the kitchen.

While I pulled out china cups from the cabinets, she filled the copper teapot with tap water from an immense farm sink that dwarfed her shrinking frame. Since summer in 1955, when my twin brother and I were ceremoniously christened in it, Nana has called it her, "baby bathin' sink."

While my ninety-one-year-old grandmother bustled about in the kitchen. I grabbed some floral napkins and a box of loose leaf Earl Grey from a cupboard. When the kettle whistled orders, she whisked it off the burner and filled the ceramic pot to the brim, tea steeping in a battered aluminum ball. She pointed toward a large wooden tray filled with all her proper tea accompaniments, and we ventured back to our seats. Before I plunked the cumbersome load on the coffee table between us, Nana buckled on the sofa.

"Now, honey, I could have hauled that out here. I'm not a helpless old woman you know. She erupted in breathy laughter. "My, wherever did you find those napkins?"

"I know your best hiding places. All pretty paper goods are in the top cupboard to the left, I should get on my tippy-toes to reach it. You stash the Snooks Candies in the bottom center drawer, under the sea of Jell-O boxes that are older than I am. Our favorite apricot tea is in back of the tin bread box on top of the Frigidaire."

"Goodness, I have no secrets from you anymore." Nana shuffled into a pair of ratty slippers she kept under the sofa. "When a woman meets her Maker, she should be able to take a secret or two to the grave that only they know."

"Well, if you have any left, divulge to your heart's content. I wouldn't want to hold you back from a major revelation that could set your soul free." I fanned my arms out, "Have at it."

"I might surprise you." She poured each of us a cup of tea, the heavy Brown Betty ceramic pot hit the tray with a clunk, almost slipping out of her hand. "Tea is served." Nana rubbed her wrists. "I knew you discovered the Snooks some years ago. I just never let on."

"I suspected as much. You always left the marzipan and mochas. I respectfully never touched your caramels. There is an unspoken code of honor when it comes to one's chocolates." I tipped a milky stream from the creamer into my cup, pinched a sugar cube from the crystal bowl, and plopped it into the strong brew.

"Here's to a couple of gals who know the tales these four walls have whispered over the decades and promise never to forget." Nana lifted her chintz bone china cup and carefully tapped mine. "Cheers."

I toasted in agreement and we sipped in mutual reverence.

Nana released a deep sigh. At first I thought she was tired, but then I realized she was remembering. I wondered what images overlapped as she brought them together in her mind on a stage where only she remained of the original cast of characters. She was dwindling away, by pounds and ounces. Her once-shiny silver hair had thinned and now fluffed a soft snowy white. Feathery wisps escaped the salon-coifed crown framing her delicate features. There was still a smooth, creamy texture to her skin that defied time in testimony to her years of shielding from the sun, instead of baking in it. An opaque film glossed over her once-twinkling eyes that Papa had always referred to as *Tahoe blues*. She sat gracefully poised in her oversized pink gingham nightgown. You could fit two Nanas under all that flannel.

I sipped tea, the hot liquid thawing out my throat. Getting low, I topped off my cup. Nana had barely touched hers.

She opened the dented tin of her homemade shortbread cookies, perfect for dipping. The fire crackled so hot that when I got up to warm my hands, I had to step away.

I drank the sugary-sweet last drops from my cup. Sometimes that final sip was too much for me, all the cane granules having settled to the bottom. Tonight, I craved the rush.

"Are your girls going to come for a visit soon?" Nana perked up.

"No. They told me it'll be a while. They're working lots of overtime." I so didn't want to be the bearer of such disappointing news.

"Oh." She sank deeper in the cushion.

"They're lucky to have jobs. Many of their friends can't find openings anywhere but fast food places." Their work wasn't the only reason I'd chosen not to invite my young-adult daughters to come with me. Nana would have picked up on the tension between them right away. Sarah got snippy whenever Olivia mentioned her father, which was about every three seconds. One grieving and one angry daughter did not make for great traveling companions.

"You up for a couple games of checkers?" Nana lifted the board out of the locker trunk next to her.

"Sure." I shoved the tray out of the way and made room.

She filled me in on the lake news and the goings-on in our cove while she beat me five straight games. I was not used to losing. My competitive spirit conceding defeat, I declined a sixth challenge.

"Would you like another biscuit?" I popped the lid off the tin.

"Child, you have as many as you like. I'm a little tuckered out. Think I may turn in early."

"You okay?" I set my cup down.

"When you get to be my age, tired just sort of creeps up and taps you on the shoulder. There isn't any point to putting up a fuss or next thing you know you wake up in the morning right where you were sitting the night before, with a crick in your neck that sets your day lopsided from the get-go." Nana ambled over my way. "You sleep in some in the morning and catch up on your rest."

I kissed her right cheek and patted the left. "Night, Nana. I love you."

"Love you too."

She strolled over to her and Papa's bedroom down the hallway, not even turning on the light before I heard her settle into the bed.

The fire had burned down, oak logs now reduced to glowing embers, but still radiating enough heat to keep me curled up on the sofa for a while. Twirling tresses of my air-dried hair repeatedly around my finger, I gave a bit of thought as to how I would spend the entire summer here. I was used to the activity back in the city. Was I was capable of "taking it easy," as my boss described the purpose of this company-imposed grief-sabbatical? He'd made it clear: take it, or I'd lose my job.

At least it was with pay. Due to the depletion of the life insurance policy David neglected to mention before his death, money was an issue for me for the first time since I'd married. I doubted he thought I would discover he'd borrowed against it, because he certainly wasn't planning on me having to use it so soon.

Ever since David died, my brain had gone on vacation. I'd made enough mistakes to warrant time off, maybe a couple of weeks. But an entire summer?

As much as I loved it here, what would I do with all that time? Nana didn't own a television. I'd encouraged her to try one after Papa died, to keep her company. But she insisted she had no need of "that thief of time" in her home. She listened to Giants ball games and news on an old transistor radio and 33 and 78 RPM record albums on a hi-fi stereo. On rare occasions, we'd go next door to Doc's and pop in a VHS to watch a movie or take in a sitcom on his TV.

To be honest, summers on the lake without television growing up was the main reason my creative imagination knew no bounds. As Papa used to say, "Who can sit inside watching the boob tube with the lake calling?"

When I called Nana to complain about not having a choice in the matter of taking time off work, she put in her request right away. "Come spend the summer with me, just like the old days." She'd insisted in that authoritative twang I never could resist.

The girls were thrilled when I mentioned her suggestion to them. Too thrilled, if you ask me, but I wasn't up for a summer of them bickering on a daily basis. Sarah was barely speaking to me when I left. The issue between us was widening a divide and causing friction we'd never experienced before. We stood on polar-opposite sides of a fence when it came to the subject of telling Livie about her father. I understood how difficult it was for Sarah when her sister talked non-stop about David. Couldn't she see that was how Olivia chose to deal with his sudden death? She'd been Daddy's girl all her life. She had no idea about her father's affair.

I forced myself off the couch and walked over to the sliding glass door beside the fireplace. The rain had subsided. I tugged the handle to the left until the door glided open, letting the cooler temperature flow in.

My feet instinctively led me out on the saturated deck, a flood of brilliant starlight now shining through the dispersing clouds. I inhaled deeply. The rain had purified the skies. A thick seasoning of pungent pine and smoky chimney residue hung heavy in the crisp air. Its intoxicating scent drifted in waves from the string of cabins and mixed conifer forest over the lake. This familiar scent I knew well and loved.

I propped myself against the deck railing and gazed out across the iridescent expanse illuminated by the vivid wedge of moonlight and the intensity of millions of stars. There was a dark beauty to this night, with a radiant beam of hope that rejuvenated my weary heart and held promise of penitent offerings.

I lifted my arms heavenward and stretched them wide open, uttering unspoken prayers far out into the universe. Longing for a calming presence, I searched the sky for some sign of acknowledgement, some tangible glimpse of God's existence, an attentive response.

The night stood utterly still before me.

Gradually I drew in my arms, clutched my robe tight, and stepped back inside the comfort of the cabin. I closed the sliding door and turned the lock until it clicked.

After flipping off the light switch on the wall beside me, I found my way in the dark to the coffee table. I gripped the tea tray handles and carried it to the kitchen table.

For a second or two I thought about emptying the teapot, but decided to head upstairs to bed instead. The little nightlight Nana left at the foot of the stairway cast just enough of a glow to guide my way up the hardwood steps. At the top platform, I veered left and entered my old room.

Scattering my slippers and robe on the chilly floor, I bounded into a bed flowing in welcoming layers of flannel sheets, thermal blankets, a chenille comforter, and a sea of fluffy, down pillows. I nestled deep, burrowed in, and pulled the covers up over my chin to seal in my body heat.

Dread of another long, sleepless night replaying my life's shortcomings on a reel-to-reel movie encompassed me, but I fell into a dreamy state of semi-consciousness.

I saw my brother clearer than I had in decades: rosy-cheeked, tow-headed Eddie toddling carefree across the glistening sands along the cabin-dotted shoreline. Gleefully he frolicked about, clapping his little hands as his resonant, melodious laughter bridged the infinite space between the two of us. Fleetingly he glanced my way, looking at me with my own eyes. Then he was gone.

Chapter Two

The first time I saw Lake Tahoe as a child, I thought God himself came down from heaven to swim in it on his summer vacation. Many times I wanted to ask a grown-up if they thought so too, but I never did.

—Emily's thoughts at age eight

*D*oc Walters was waiting for me in his office when I walked in. If I hadn't shown up, he would have just come next door to fetch me.

The place was empty. I was glad about that. I knew a reprimand was Doc's first order of business. He wouldn't waste time shooting the breeze with an old friend who had come home for the summer. He motioned me into the exam room and left the door open.

"Emily Maxwell Taylor." Doc paused until my gaze focused straight on him. "Whatever were you thinking last night? You hadn't been in the lake long enough to acclimate for a solo night swim. Your soul-searching adventures are going to end in tragedy one day if you don't pull yourself together."

I hopped up on the table before Doc could say another word and held out my wrist for him to take my pulse. "You can check my heart and blood pressure too. I'm sure you'll find that I'm very much alive and well."

"Em, please, I know things have been rough on you since David's death." Doc's voice softened. "What has it been now, six months?"

"Exactly." I looked away, not wanting him to see how close I was to breaking down.

"Have the tears all dried up, or are you holding out?" Doc checked my ears.

Oh, how I wanted to tell him the truth. "I need to move ahead. Life is easier that way." My voice cracked.

"Oh, really?"

He wasn't any more convinced than I was, but it sounded like a plan and allowed me time to regroup. The blood pressure cuff squeezed tight. "115 over 68."

My former personal trainer would be pleased.

"You still working out?"

"Religiously." The gym offered both a diversion from grief and a challenge.

Doc pressed the stethoscope over my blouse and listened to my heart, checking both my chest and my back. Breathe in, hold your breath, breathe out, and repeat. No talking. That part was fine with me. He finished the exam in fifteen minutes.

He handed me a lab slip. "Remember to fast from eight o'clock the night before."

"I know the routine." I grabbed a red sucker out of the *Good Boys & Girls* candy jar as I headed for the door. The handle inches from my grasp, I hesitated. "Thanks for helping me last night, Doc."

"You're welcome." He patted my shoulder and escorted me out into the waiting room. Mrs. Walker sat in a chair with baby Brianna in her lap, while her two-year-old, Bobby, pulled all the toys out of the wooden chest.

When the screen door shut behind me, the baby started to cry.

Trying to make a quick getaway, I nearly bowled over a teenage girl on the path between our cabins. After making a quick apology, but I turned around just in time to see Doc pick up scarlet-faced, screaming Brianna and hold her against his chest. Her yellow sun-bonnet disappeared under his nurturing hand while he patiently rocked her in his arms as if he had all the time in the world. Tenderness filled his voice as he caressed her forehead. "Hush, hush, little one. Hush, hush now."

I thought of Doc's own baby girl. The one he couldn't save, who came later in life than he'd hoped. Like my brother, she did not stay for long.

Lumbering pines shaded the footpath I strolled aimlessly until I parked myself on a granite boulder and kicked at the pebbles near the manzanita bushes.

Doc looked at life different than I did. He saw people at their worst: sick, tired, scared, betrayed. They often arrived late, neglected to cancel appointments with the requested twenty-four hour notice, but expected him to squeeze them in on his lunch break if illness befell unexpectedly. And he accommodated them.

He did not charge for visits when patients had no money. Annie used to keep a separate ledger and logged those appointments under "Will Pay Later." Most folks eventually paid, but some couldn't.

Doc put casts on broken bones and sutured open wounds that sometimes left scars that would never heal. He was able to reach past the pain of a guarded heart with a listening ear or brush away tears that were sometimes the only form of communication a patient could manage.

He visited the dying in their homes when hospice was contacted, and he traveled to Washoe Medical Hospital in Reno to check on new babies or visit the elderly no one else went to see. Until she passed away, Annie was always there by his side.

As far as I knew, he had never been sued.

Doc could have made a lot more money. Neither he nor Annie cared much about the paycheck. Living in the middle of an affluent town and in a country saturated in materialism, they'd found the contentment that eluded me.

The one thing they did desire was a child. They had prayed for years, waiting expectantly with a joyful anticipation I though foolish. When they entered their forties, I was pretty sure the answer to their prayers was an emphatic *no*.

In 1973, the year of my high school graduation, little Isabella Grace arrived. Everyone in town showered the new parents with gifts: handmade patchwork quilts, afghan blankets crocheted in variegated rows of pastel lavender, pink, and green, and bundles of stark-white cloth diapers. The baby's armoire was jam-packed with intricately embroidered and smocked dresses from the local boutiques.

Isabella never used the nursey Doc and Annie had lovingly prepared for her. They kept her in a bassinet at their bedside for the one brief week she lived with her parents.

She was born early with immature lungs and an infection her little body was too weak to fight. When it became clear she would not survive surgery, Doc and Annie brought her home. There would be no more needles, tape, tubes, monitors, incubators or painful tests.

Doc brought the white wicker rocking chair into their bedroom. He and Annie spent hours cradling Isabella in their arms, singing bittersweet lullabies and whispering the depths of their love into her tiny ears. They rested with Isabella snuggled between them in bed, counted her fingers and toes. Maybe they prayed for a miracle.

On a breezy summer morning while Annie was rocking Isabella, she simply fell limp while her mother held her. Annie kept rocking until Doc gathered his dead daughter into his arms. He lifted her upon his chest—just as he did the Walker baby this morning.

By chance I witnessed Isabella's death as I stood in the bedroom doorway with freshly laundered and warmed-up soft pink blankets. There was nowhere to run from the fear that seized me or the sorrow so deep it hollowed out part of me next to the whole my brother left.

I have never understood the strength Doc and Annie found to go on without the bitterness of jaded hearts. Losing either one of my daughters would finish me off completely. My mama never was quite the same after Eddie died, and she still had me.

Doc and Annie had "adopted" Jack as a kid. Don't know why. He was no Isabella. Everything changed when he fell into the family tree.

Chapter Three

Every year that I can remember, I'd say hello to the lake when I first arrived for the summer. Nana does it too. Over time, I learned to listen, as well as to speak.

— Journal entry, June 1995

"*D*id you get a chance to say hello to the lake when you arrived yesterday?" Nana asked as she hand-dried the breakfast dishes and I wiped down the table.

She knew full well I dove into the water without my usual acknowledgement. Nana had spoken the lake's language fluently from my infancy throughout my near forty years on its shores. This was one of those times I should have let the lake do all the talking. She was probably the one who sent Doc to rescue me.

"I'm still working on my lake-listening skills," I responded.

"Good for you, honey. Keep those lines of communication open." She snatched her ancient straw bonnet off the coat rack, positioned it just so, and tied the faded blue fabric strips in a bow under her neck. "Are you driving my truck or your car into Tahoe City?"

"We can take my Explorer." She still had Papa's old Chevy for people to drive her around in, but I was more comfortable in my own car. I grabbed our purses off the bench seat of the hall tree as we exited the front door. "Maybe you should lock it, just this once."

"You've been living in the city too long," She watered her potted flowers and plants on the porch, then we headed to my car.

Nana refused to lock the cabin doors. She said we didn't have any thieves on the east, west, or north shores of Tahoe. Apparently the south shore did not attain such a high rating due to those fool-hardy casinos.

When I was a kid I never saw any reason to lock doors. But in the late sixties and early seventies, hippies hitchhiked around the lake, slept on the beaches, smoked pot, and did mushrooms, LSD, and other hallucinogenic drugs. I, like others who lived on the shore, found them in our backyards in the mornings, naked and snuggled together in a hammock or the sleeping bags they carried everywhere.

Nana struggled to understand the long-haired, stoned-out-of-their-minds hippies. She'd invite them to picnic on the deck and shared how she thought Jesus was better than drugs and free love. They scarfed down her fried chicken and cherry pie, and said Jesus was cool for her but not for them. I'd get so embarrassed and wish she'd just be quiet.

She never stuffed religion down their throats, just answered questions and offered to pray for them. No one turned down prayers. In fact, they confided in her. She never repeated a word. Over the years, several hippies became her friends and returned to let her know how life was going. They'd tell me my Nana was a groovy chick.

A lot of hippies ended up settling at Kings Beach after the unfortunate incident on Fanette Island at Emerald Bay. Most locals preferred to believe that hippies, probably smoking pot, burned down the teahouse. It couldn't possibly be the rumored brazen, drunken lot of sods who stripped the window frames bare and built a bonfire in the middle of the once-famous picturesque teahouse of Mrs. Lora J. Knight. Inebriated neighbors? Never.

Still Nana did not lock the doors. To me that encouraged Jack's obnoxious, overly-attentive behavior. For a season he was fine until the end of high school when he got possessive of me.

He didn't go off to college right away like most of the graduates. Instead he hung around during my junior and senior year.

The summer after graduation, I started locking my bedroom door. I had Doc install a doorknob with a lock and key. I only used it because Jack's new habit of entering unannounced made me uncomfortable. He ignored all my requests for more privacy.

Nana scoffed at me ... until the day Jack walked in on me getting into my bikini. He came into the house, found my bedroom door closed, and just opened it and waltzed in. He got a peek of my bare back and the full range of my fury.

He swears he thought I'd gone to Reno with Doc and the house was empty, so he came in to get a snack. But, as Nana pointed out, the food was in the kitchen, not my bedroom.

Jack went off to the University of Reno that fall and moved into the boarding house directly across from the campus. That same year, I was accepted at CSU in Sacramento. It hurt Nana and Doc that I didn't even apply at their old alma mater, like Jack did. I figured Jack had that covered.

I don't think he ever got over me changing our childhood plans to go to college together.

"Emily!" Nana's urgent voice pulled me out of my thoughts. I straightened out the vehicle when a Mercedes Benz sedan blasted past us, the driver laying on the horn.

Nana smiled and waved, mouthing an apology. The two teenage males in the car hollered a scathing barrage of obscenities. Nana actually blushed. The passenger hung out his window, continuing the tirade as they swerved into the Safeway parking lot.

"You can't tell what a person is thinking when they are hidden behind dark sunglasses," Nana muttered as we parked.

We got out of the car observing those boys escalating, aggressive behavior.

"I know exactly what those two are thinking." I was tempted to dish out a rebuttal just outside of my grandmother's hearing as we sauntered through the automatic door. I shuffled Nana off in the direction of the shopping carts so she wouldn't witness any possible response. Sweet little old ladies shouldn't be subjected to the full extent of what those rich-boy tourists were capable of. With Nana preoccupied adding her produce groceries to the cart, I searched out the weekly specials in dairy and meats.

"Emily Taylor. Why, you sweet young thing. When did you arrive on the mountain?"

Selma Sue Crumley cornered me by the first of the season's Bing cherries. She wedged her cart and pinned me in against the all those luscious little fruits in their green mesh baskets that would topple should I flinch an inch. This had to be a strategic attack mounted from the moment she'd laid eyes on me.

"She just got here." Nana liberated me without offering a smidgen of information to the old biddy. "We are in something of hurry, Selma. No time for chit-chat today."

Nana towed me in line behind her when I commented on Selma's outlandish floppy sunhat and directed me toward the cash registers.

"Making dinner for the boys tonight, Hannah?" Miss Crumbly asked as she scurried to catch up to my Nana's sudden Olympic stride.

More than a twinge of jealousy tainted her fake Southern-accented inquiry.

"Oh, salads are hardly a meal to satisfy hearty appetites."

Nana had exact change ready when the total rang out. "We can talk at church on Sunday. Bye for now." She pushed the cart out the door and into parking lot.

I loaded up our purchase as Nana belted herself in, reached over to insert my key in the ignition, and turned on the engine.

"When did you take the keys out of my purse?" I chuckled as I shifted into reverse, backed out, and slammed the gear into drive.

I drove off snickering. In the rear view mirror I saw Selma smooth out the rumpled linen jacket that puckered around her bloated waist. An irritated scowl etched deep in her dour face. After scanning the perimeter, she ushered her empty shopping cart back inside as fast as her chubby knee-high-stocking-clad legs could march.

"She still chasing Doc?" I laughed at the idea of Miss Saccharin-Sweet Single Selma thinking she could win over Doc's heart.

"That woman didn't wait one day after we laid Doc's beloved wife in the ground." Nana gazed out the window as I passed a small grove of aspen along the roadside. "I miss Annie. John and I lost our best friend in that boating accident." Nana sighed. "The Lord gives and the Lord takes away."

"He didn't have to take her." The irritation in my voice rippled in angry waves throughout my body. I hit the accelerator. "Both Sophia *and* Annie could have survived the accident." My right eyebrow twitched and I pressed my left foot against the floor.

"Let it go, little fish." Nana's voice softened and her eyes misted. "We don't need to pay Miss Selma any mind ... except in our prayers."

"You know she absolutely hates it when you call her that." I grinned. "You should call her Stalker-Gawker, like the rest of us here in town."

"That isn't proper or respectful."

"Jack has a few pet names for her that he has mastered over time. You should ask him at supper tonight. He'll be more than happy to rattle them off."

"He was raised with better manners than that."

That declaration abruptly ended our discussion. I was raring to go full blast, but she changed the subject to the evening menu.

My Nana is a wise lady who never offers the extent of information busy-bodies are apt to try to pry from the innocent. She simply does not participate in lengthy conversations. The kind where you kick yourself later for divulging facts you had no intention of sharing. Nana could hold her own, even with pros like Selma Sue Crumbly, who generally underestimate her meek nature for weakness. Nana says her secret is silent prayer. She just lets the intrusive meddler jabber away while she "listens." They don't know she is praying.

I have to admit her plan has worked flawlessly for over three-quarters of a century. She never gets any more worked up than I saw her today. Sometimes I get irritated when she quotes a Scripture like that "gives and takes away" line from the book of Job. I knew where it came from, just don't give a fig. That signals the end of a conversation for her, when I am just getting started.

Doc, Jack, Nana, and I settled in the living room with our cups of coffee and plates heavy laden with slices of pie topped with fresh whipped cream. Hemingway sat at Jack's feet. He didn't beg—he knew better. He waited attentively for anything that might fall to the ground. I saw Doc slip him a piece of meat he'd saved. Jack didn't notice.

"Supper was delicious, Nana." Jack patted his stomach. I stared in shock noticing he had the beginning of a pot belly. He instantly sucked it in and arched his back.

"Oh, Emily and I dished this up together. It took most of the afternoon after we returned from our excursion into town." Nana smiled pleasantly at Jack.

"Well, good job, Em. I didn't know you had it in you." Jack took a stab at the remaining pie I had left." I opened my mouth to give him as big a piece of my mind as the mammoth hunk of my dessert he was about to decimate.

Doc intervened. "You two gals sure do know the way to a man's heart. Hannah, did you marinate the steak strips this time?"

"Actually, Emily concocted a seasoned rub. It was quite something to watch her roll the meat in her hands, toss the pieces into the wok, then sprinkle in ground ginger and garlic with all the vegetables."

"It's a new recipe I got from one of my co-workers." I found my courteous voice.

"You should make it again soon." Jack asked, "is it okay to take leftovers home?"

"Certainly." Nana answered for me.

"Well, I know this is Hannah's original custard pie." Doc set his dish on the end table and poured a cup of coffee. The strong aroma from the freshly ground beans in the pot drifted my way and settled above like coffee-house percolated clouds.

I inhaled deep and long preferring the smell of coffee over the taste.

"We ran into Stalker-Gawker at the Safeway today."

"Good old, Starve-you-to-Death Seductive Selma?" I offered the bait and Jack chomped down on the hook like a prize salmon.

"She still has it bad for old Doc here. Every week she brings some nutritionally depleted, burned-beyond-recognition casserole by the office. Even the neighborhood dogs won't eat the stuff. Hemingway runs and hides when he smells it."

Hemingway put his paws over his ears and buried his head under Jack's legs.

"See? Even the dog knows." Jack laughed so hard he snorted. I laughed out loud. Nana did not seem to be as amused.

"We have to soak the charred Pyrex dish in potent solutions of fluids for days. The residue from that alone could bleach your intestines into the next century." Jack shuddered. "Who knows what it does to the pipes when we dump it down the drain?"

"She means well." Doc swallowed his last sip of coffee.

"I think she means to cook like that daily for you the rest of your natural life, Doc," I teased. This would be worth the chastisement that was sure to come when they went home this evening. I was on a roll and there wasn't any stopping me.

"Well, it won't be a long life if you take a bite of whatever is petrified in those molten cauldrons. The casseroles are always the same puke color and alien texture no matter what she says is in them. It's down-right scary." Jack kicked off his shoes and hunkered down in the sofa cushions.

"No one eats what she takes to any church function involving food." I added.

"Me-thinks the damsel desires to dish it up for Doc on the spot." Jack raised an eyebrow. "But I'm always in the way of any possible romantic interlude."

I watched everyone sigh as if they almost felt sorry for Selma.

Nana rose to clear the dishes but Doc suggested she rest. "The men will do the dishes since the women did all the cooking." He motioned for his partner to join him.

Jack bent over, slipped back into his running shoes, and stroked his patient pet, who was poised to accompany him to the savory smells still floating in the kitchen.

I reveled in the moment, knowing the excessive mess I'd left in there, despite Nana's efforts to mop up right behind me as I muddled about. Jack would be cleaning for a while because Doc was just as fastidious as Nana, who didn't believe one iota in "newfangled contraptions" like dishwashers.

I chugged the last dregs of the tepid liquid in my mug and handed it to Jack as he stumbled by, Hemingway on his heels sniffing. "Don't let the door hit your bum on the way out, Mr. Conner." I stretched out and resting my head and feet on the sofa's welcoming arms.

Jack grunted. Nana shook her head and waved her index finger sideways at me.

Soon the kitchen musical began with the clanging of dishes and silverware landing in the drip-drain dish holder. The faucet ran while Jack washed and scrubbed, and Doc dried and put away. I enjoyed the clear view from my comfy perch.

Nana had dozed off where she sat, covered from head to toe in an afghan she'd pulled from the quilt rack. Her breathing was so shallow, I almost called Doc in to check on her. I thought it better to let her rest.

Jack glared at me as he passed the doorway on his way to the oven to soak up the olive oil splatter I'd left.

"Wipe down the burner grates too," Doc instructed.

Jack, sleeves rolled up past his elbows, scrubber and sponge in hand, tackled the greasy stove-top, growled at me.

What did I ever see in that guy?

The childhood crush I had on him had soured long ago.

"But, Nana, none of the girls really like me. They're only coming to my party because Jack will be here." I huffed and stomped my feet.

"Now, Emily, your mama and I have worked hard to make your thirteenth birthday a special one. She made the invitations herself. It's just a fire-pit wiener roast, and the leftover fireworks from the Fourth will make a spectacular finale."

"They don't like me, not even Marsha, who used to be my best friend."

"Let your mama do this for you. It's important to her." Nana gave me the look that told me it was a done deal. There wasn't any point wasting my time whining. She was determined to let my mother give me something I didn't need, desire or wish to celebrate.

"Besides, isn't Jack your best friend?"

"Yeah. Guys make better friends because you don't have to compete with them. But he's the best-looking fox on the lake—and he knows it. He's going to spoil everything if it keeps going to his head." I grabbed a few marshmallows from the open bag and sulked off to brood on the porch swing.

Jack came up, but I ignored him.

"I got your birthday present this morning." He skipped two steps at a time, beaming, and sat next to me. After giving the swing a big push with one of his size twelve-and-a-half cowboy boots, he scooted close.

"Your feet better quit growing or you won't be able to buy shoes anywhere around these parts."

"Aren't you even curious what it is?" He completely ignored my tart attitude.

"I don't know anyone with feet as big as yours, Jack. Do they make zories in a size thirteen for men?"

"You can't tick me off today, Emily. It's your birthday. You're supposed to be happy. You know—a party, presents, people who love you hanging around baking you a cake, putting thirteen candles on it so you can blow them all out and make a wish." He kicked off again, higher this time.

"You and I both know those stupid girls are coming here to be around you, not me." The thought of watching them flirt and fuss over Jack like he was some rock star ticked me off.

"I'm here for *you*." Jack's voice took on a serious tone. "I don't care about those other girls."

Something in his tone made me uncomfortable. I twirled hair around my finger, tighter and tighter, until I noticed the doofy look on his face.

"What?"

"Your mom really poured herself into this for you. She walked those invites personally to every door, and actually chit-chatted with the neighbor ladies. You know how much she hates to do that."

"How nice of her to finally make an effort. I'm freaking thirteen. She sure has taken her sweet time." I rolled my eyes and let go a disgruntled jeer.

"She even talked with my mom, Em. She was down there over two hours."

"Are you sure?" I planted my feet and stopped the swing in mid-motion. To my knowledge, they'd never spoken before.

"Yep. I was there. I witnessed the entire conversation. She even mentioned Beddie." Jack watched for my reaction. He seemed to be weighing the wisdom of relaying this monumental piece of information.

"Well, that explains everything. She's thinking about him, not me. Probably wishing it was her son here today." I slumped back into the wooden seat. "Are you defending my mother?"

"No, Em. She talked about you the whole time. She only said his name once."

"What did she say, about Beddie?" I looked up at him, the pit of my stomach releasing a distasteful slow roll of acid.

"She wished he could see how beautiful you are." Jack stood, relayed her words in such a familiar manner. I could almost hear Mama's voice, tentative and grief stricken, full of raw emotion and Southern grit.

"Really?" I stood up so close to him, the rhythm in his chest converged with mine. It surprised me how fast my heart started pounding. My palms got clammy.

"Em." He put his arm around me. "I ..."

My knees began to buckle and a loud belch escaped my lips.

"I'm here!" Marsha Millford announced and stepped up behind us waving her glitter-and-sequined invitation as if she needed proof to be admitted on the premises. Which in my book, she did. "What's the surprise?" Her right foot edged against mine.

"What Jack got me for my birthday," I lied, not wanting her to clue into our unfinished discussion.

"A ... a ... a kayak. That's what I got you." Jack stepped back, obviously shaken. The clip of his boot heels clunked heavy on the porch boards.

"You got her a kayak?" Marsha repeated, flabbergasted as she moved in between us. "A brand new one?"

"Yes. I worked at the gas station weekends to earn the money. I got one for me too: a-two-for-one special." Jack rubbed his hands together and wiped them on his jeans.

"You got me a kayak?" I'd been begging for one for a year, but my parents would have no part of it, and neither would Nana. Jack would pay dearly for this infraction. Any points he'd previously scored with Mama were about to be rubbed out by a giant eraser of unimaginable proportions, and he knew it.

"Jack got Emily a kayak for her birthday!" Miss Blabbermouth shouted to a string of my scantily clad so-called friends walking up the path in a variety of cut-off jeans and halter bikini tops. They rushed Jack all at once, but not one of them got past Marsha. Not even me.

Mama made a big deal about each present I opened. Mostly make-up, which I didn't wear yet, record albums, which I played on my hi-fi, and a few halter tops I knew she'd never let me wear.

"Too skimpy" Mama crinkled her nose when I opened Marsha's present.

Jack spent the evening encircled by at least four or five girls at a time. He broke away a few times and sat beside me on the shore.

He made me a hot dog with mustard and relish, just the way I like it. But in five or ten minutes a group of girls would drag him off to swim or ask him to go out on the floats with them.

I made my wish, and sliced the cake. My mom had baked my favorite chocolate cake with coffee in the frosting. Marsha scooped huge slab of vanilla ice cream on my dish. She knew I didn't like anything melting on top. Jack took that plate to my dad, then gave me one with cake and extra frosting that he scraped off another piece and piled on the side.

While everyone disappeared to chow down, Jack sat the closest to me he'd ever dared to before. We let the water run up and over our bare toes and legs to the frayed edges of our cut-offs. Doc and my dad set off rockets that soared so high, we craned our necks until we fell on the sandy beach.

"The fireworks are spectacular." Jack gazed up into the night sky, mesmerized by the flashing colors bursting like lightning in every direction. "It's almost magical."

I found myself looking more at Jack than the fireworks.

Marsha tried to lure him away. First Nana called her over, then Annie came by, but my mama hauled her off to assist with the clean-up. Marsha never helped with any volunteer duty. She did that night.

Jack stayed with me until parents stopped by to pick up their teens. Some went home with neighbors. That was how it was back then.

Jack saw a shooting star and made a wish. I missed seeing it. When he saw a second one, he told me to turn at the precise second to catch a glimpse of it spiral across the sky. The interstellar body disappeared fast, like a missile with a long shimmering tail descending to the earth. Once a brilliance out in the cosmic universe, worlds away. I wondered where such a beautiful heavenly thing would crash and disintegrate as if it had never existed.

Jack named it after me—Emiline.

Chapter Four

Papa's legacy is the poetic and poignant way he photographed our childhood against the amber painted sunsets and watercolor hues of Tahoe. Even the early black and white snapshots would make you swear you could see the sapphire blue of the lake.

-Emily journal entry 1989

The bright, morning sunlight shone through my bedroom window, bidding me to scramble out of bed and see what the day had to offer. Still, the thought of the lake's cold water made me hibernate in my toasty cave.

Peeking at the wall clock, I realized I'd slept through breakfast and my usual break-of-dawn swim. So I snuggled between my flannel sheets, waiting for the initiative to get moving.

By nature, I am an early riser, and my lack of any "get-up-and-go" as Nana calls it, gave me pause to think.

For the first few years of my marriage, I'd attended to my demanding husband. Sarah made her entrance into our lives before our first wedding anniversary, followed not twelve months later by Olivia. I'd risen with the sun every day since.

Shortly after David died, I found two airline tickets for Paris tucked away in his dresser drawer under the silk tie I'd given him for Father's Day. Maybe the trip was going to be a surprise for our anniversary. Or perhaps he'd planned a vacation with his mistress. But no matter. They were mine now.

Since the tickets were nonrefundable, I should've used them. Made reservations at a chateau in Nice. Right this minute, I could be nibbling cheese and sipping champagne in Cambrai. But I ended up here at the lake. Like always.

I yanked the covers over my head and closed my eyes. My scattered thoughts escaped into dreams.

A remote shoreline dotted with glistening stones beckoned me as the water washed over the beach at midday. Beddie was bending over and examining pebbles, his little toes struggling to anchor the weight of his body. After careful inspection, each stone was individually stored in his bulging, shorts pockets.

The navy-blue sailor suit and cap looked adorable on him. His long stick legs were hidden under baggy trousers billowing in the breeze. From this distance he looked at least five years old instead of almost four.

When I came close, Beddie showed me a hand full of rocks. He added the treasures into the slit pocket openings at the sides of his shirt. After feigning interest, I sat on a sandy part of the beach, closer to the fence line, where tender young blades of green grass grew in abundant patches. I twirled rogue strands of blonde hair around my left finger as I sucked my right thumb. Occasionally, I stopped twirling and stuck my hand in the oversized pocket stitched across the front of my sailor dress, just to make sure my tiny baby doll was still sound asleep in there.

The sun bore down through a cloudless, azure sky. The lake shimmered brilliantly, almost blinding. My cheeks flamed, and the continual heat tempted me to rest my drowsy head.

When I opened my eyes, Nana was peering down at me. "Lunch is out on the deck."

I leapt off the bed, my sweat-soaked pajamas clinging to me like a second skin.

Nana made her way to the door. "You were talking in your sleep, Emily." Her face paled under the ribbons of sunlight flooding the room.

"What did I say?" I slipped into my jeans and a tank top.

"Beddie." You said it three times, just like when you were a little girl. I haven't heard you say your brother's name like that in years." She rested against the door, clutching her dress to her chest. "I always thought it was sweet how you blended 'brother' and 'Eddie.'"

"Eddie loved that nickname too."

For an instant, sadness glazed her eyes. But it left quickly. Nana never hung on to sorrow the way Mama did.

Nana lingered in the doorway, as if hoping I might talk about my brother's death. But my recall was still spotty. Bits and pieces of that summer he died remained lost in my childhood memory. I wasn't sure what was reality and what I might have filled in the gaps with over time.

I started having dreams about my brother after David's death. Clear pictures appeared in my mind, so vivid I would reach out and physically feel his soft skin. He always returned my touch. Aware that I was remembering what had happened, I didn't want to wake up. I was experiencing a deeper longing for him than I'd had since he left me. But the memories offered no definitive, additional information about his death. So what was the point?

"Emily." Nana hesitated. "Do you remember any more about—that day?"

"Not really," I lied. She remained at the doorway while I brushed my hair, deliberately taking my time. I caught a glimpse of her face in the oval mirror. Her mouth opened to speak, but she walked out of the room and down the stairway in silence. Eventually, the soft pad of her light footsteps completely faded.

Nana and I sat on the massive log at the edge of the shoreline. She'd hiked up her jeans, and cuffed each leg about half-way on her calves. Papa's old green plaid flannel shirt hung down almost to her knees, covering a cotton blouse neatly tucked in at the waist. Sunglasses dangled around her neck attached to a coral-colored cord she'd sewn herself. She peered out from under a worn straw hat riddled with peekaboo holes that has been around since I was born.

The walk from the cabin had exhausted her. We had to make little pit stops and let her catch her breath. She told me to walk on ahead but I wasn't going to leave her. We certainly weren't in a hurry.

The beach was peaceful with no mid-morning activity. Birds chirped their cheerful greetings and flew by in hopes of bread crumbs, peanuts, or any other of Nana's daily breakfast entrées.

"Your friends have followed you," I joked.

"This is actually late in the day for me. They'll fly home and find the birdseed I left on the board for them." She adjusted her hat, and coughed.

"Nana, have you become 'The Bird Lady of Tahoe?'"

"Tweet, tweet." She cheeped. "I rather like that term of endearment."

I picked up a smooth, flat stone and skipped it across the placid water, then handed a second one to Nana. She angled herself, and with one level movement, she skillfully sent it sailing in the air a good distance out. It lit on the water, and skipped out twice as far as mine. When it plopped into the lake, ripples flowed out from the center in an ever-widening circle.

"Your papa taught me how to do that." She grinned with pride.

I'd always envied my grandparents' marriage. The joy she relished this moment brought my papa's presence back into her life, as tangible as if he were sitting beside her.

"What do you see when you look out at the lake?" Her voice took on a serious tone.

I gazed across layer upon layer of azure, teal, and cerulean water, pondering her question. The surface was smooth as glass, undisturbed—a perfect mirror reflection of the crisp, blue sky moored above.

"Do you want the truth or what I think you'd like to hear?"

"Always the truth, Emily. Nothing else matters."

"I see something I can't attain. A distance too far. I could swim and swim and never get there," I barely whispered.

"Where?" Her quiet voice carried a steel density.

"The other side. For all the splendor and majesty of Tahoe spread out before me, that's all I can see. Even if I make it to the heart of the lake, I could never get back on my own." I instantly regretted the honesty of my reply.

The glint of a tear pooled in the corner of her eye. "Are you swimming toward the center or away from the shore?"

How could I say when I didn't know for sure myself? I fidgeted with the buttons on my blouse, pressing my fingertips over the textured circles.

"No matter how far out you get, you still have to come back. And what you left behind will be waiting for you. In the meantime, life is passing you by. Precious time is wasted."

She was right, that much I knew for sure.

"What do you see when you look out at the lake, Nana?"

"Waters bathed in grace, redeemed from the cascading mountaintop snow melt," she said in a calm, steady voice. She scooched off the log and looked from one end of the lake to the other. "Pine trees raising their branches heavenward in praise to the Creator who rooted them deeply in rich soil." Nana sat beside me again and waited until my vision drifted in direct alignment with hers. "I see the beauty of a holy God who saw fit to plant me here for a season."

"You see things I don't see, that's for sure." I stared down at my zories and wiggled my toes, fishing through the glimmering granules of clumpy sand until I dug a small pit. If it were bigger, I'd jump in and reside there.

"That's okay," she reassured me.

We'd come to this difference of opinion many times. She would go deep. I preferred surface level. "Nana, you know I love you. I just don't agree with your religion and I don't see God in everything like you do." I let go a mocking laugh and shook my head. "If he's out there, he's busy with someone other than me." I stood. "And what if he isn't out there? You've staked your whole life on what you believe. What if you're wrong?" I was sharper in my delivery than I intended to be.

"Oh, he's real. And if you listen, you'll hear him talking to you, calling you by name." Nana stroked the spot where I'd been sitting and urged me to reclaim my spot.

I sighed, "we're headed straight into one of our long discussions."

"Emily, don't you think it's time you finally lay David to rest?"

"Where did that come from?"

I saw strong determination in her eyes and knew the calm of the morning was about to be altered.

"What is left when both body and soul have been violated? I need to know!" I clenched my fists, shaken by the unexpected anger that rose within me. If she had the answer, I was more than willing to listen. Shoveling sand with my heels, I filled in and pounded over the hole until it blended in as if it had always been part of the shore.

"Emily, there is good and bad in every marriage. Give and take. Decisions are made that shape who we let ourselves become.

David's life was cut short without warning, and you two never had the chance to try to turn things around."

"Oh, he made his decision before the accident." My vocal chords strained until almost no sound pushed past my lips. "And it wasn't me."

"Let go of it, honey. Forgive him for the lost years. Rise above it and move on." Grasping the log with both hands, Nana swayed her weight against me, her head on my shoulder. With a measure of urgency she whispered in my ear. "Bitterness and unforgiveness are just as deadly as a hit-and-run by a drunk driver."

My back went rigid. I knew the comment was meant to sting, for my own good. Because it was true.

David and I had been going our separate ways for years. We'd put so much effort into our jobs, there wasn't any time or energy left for our marriage. We worked in different towns, had our own friends, and didn't have much in common. "I don't blame him for everything," I sniffled. "Just most of it."

Nana hugged me close. The tenderness in her embrace made it difficult for me to vent my rage on her. "All I was left with after David's funeral service was more emptiness than I already had." I choked back a flood of tears.

I closed my eyes and tried to picture David's face. I wanted to see him crystal clear, not slipping out of focus as if he were walking into a distant fog. It was an obscure fog that eluded me, kept me at bay, on the edge of my sanity. As the end had drawn near, it deceived me, subtly letting me think we had time, another day, another moment. I had taken so much for granted.

My lips trembled, salty tears nipping the tip of my tongue. I slowly pulled away from the shelter of Nana's arms. "I'm working on it." Bleary-eyed, I tried to focus.

"I know." She gave my shoulder a gentle squeeze.

Boats zoomed by, and their wakes rushed to the shoreline, sending waves that seemed to speak loud, high, and mighty in attitude. Commanding our attention by intruding in our private conversation.

Soon the neighborhood children came trickling onto the beach with goggles, sand pails and shovels, inner tubes, sun-brellas, and excited laughter. They ran up to my grandmother with hugs, kisses, and giggles, dragging her to wade in the lake with them. She willingly followed the munchkin tribe, her zories flapping until she stepped into the water.

Nana splashed and ducked like a kid herself, walking out up to her waist. One of the boys had a power squirt gun that he repeatedly reloaded from the endless source of liquid ammunition. Somehow, Nana finagled the toy from his fumbling hands and soon had her little friends swimming to deeper depths for cover.

I kicked off my zories and ran my toes through the warming sand, closed my eyes, and basked under the rising sun. I thought about the first time David kissed me. I was intoxicated with him by the time his lips found their way to mine. He always kissed my hair first, his fingers weaving through the length and thickness with a yearning that stirred desires in me I'd never known before. I wanted more. He murmured passionate possibilities in my ears. Then his lips enveloped mine in a fulfilling oneness I thought would bond us forever.

My eyes opened reluctantly to behold the empty space around me. I ran the palms of my hands over the smooth ridges in the log on both sides of me. Unoccupied seats of wind-swept bleached wood that stood the test of time … so far. I sat conspicuously by myself, resistant to the laughter and beckoning calls from the distant reaches of our secluded cove—an amphitheater of mirth and mischievous amusement I had neither the inclination nor the patience for.

Crossing my arms over my chest, I drew my knees up and under, squeezing my torso until the voices dissipated into the same mist that had enveloped David's shadowy form.

Nana waved for me to join her. She was chest deep now and moving slow. "Emily, I need a teammate."

And she did. The kiddos were closing in, having joined forces, and were about to overtake the little old woman from Lakeside Lane. I ran to the beach, dove into the nippy water, and swam to her side.

She handed me the lime green plastic shooter. I reloaded and blasted the hooligans back twenty feet. It was a temporary victory, but a victory none-the-less.

Chapter Five

Perched high in the barren treetoed high in the barren treetoed high in the barren treetops in Rubicon Bay, osprey occupy nests left by other birds. The birds soar the Tahoe skies in search of food for their babies whose beaked, wobbly heads crest the twigged rims, awaiting nourishment. The ritual takes place several times a day. This cycle of complete reliance, trust and intuitive provision continues until the day the chick is nudged out of the woven sanctuary of its nest to spread wings in flight. Whatever the distance, the bird will one day, instinctively return. That is the order of nature: steadfast, dependable, divinely ordained.

–Excerpt from one of Emily's books

How could Doc forget he was supposed to meet me for dinner? I hung up the phone after he never picked up and stormed out of Nana's house, down the pathway to his cabin.

Jack had been breathing down my neck for days, rehashing the entirety of our lives. That was the last thing on my agenda, listening to lame excuses for his irresponsible behavior and philandering. All because he was so devastated when I married David. And now he wanted to go SCUBA diving with me.

"Give me a break." I shoved tree branches out of my way.

Once I got to the deck stairs, I tromped up two-at-a-time. Maybe Doc could get Jack to back off. He'd listen to Doc. He certainly wasn't paying attention to anything I said. Jack was too busy talking to listen or he'd have gotten the message by now.

Nana insisted I be courteous.

"Being polite just got me asked out on a date," I fumed out loud.

Oddly, all lights were dimmed throughout Doc's cabin. Stranger still, the front door stood slightly ajar. Music drifted out to the porch. I stopped when I heard the familiar tune of Doc and Annie's song. I'd grown up hearing that melody float across the tops of the sugar pines that separated our homes.

I gulped down a huge intake of air and flattened myself against the back porch wall next to the door before Doc could see me.

Old Satchmo's gravelly voice rang out in the night, singing about trees of green and red roses for two lovers, and such a wonderful, romantic world.

Time after time I'd watched Doc and Annie dance under the soft glow of a moonlit sky across their deck, into the cabin, and out again in unbroken step. He led and she followed, keeping perfect time, her size-five ballet flats sometimes positioned on top of his shoes. He held her so close they seemed to meld into one person.

The first time I caught a glimpse of them gliding effortlessly, they didn't notice me as they spun their magic. I saw stardust sprinkling with every dip and twirl. They were newly expectant parents celebrating the long-awaited news by spinning an album on the hi-fi and dancing the night away. Annie's long chestnut hair flowed in the breeze as Doc waltzed on air. Louis Armstrong crooned about skies of blue and white clouds. I was smitten and couldn't take my eyes off them.

Annie's hair grayed, Doc's turned white, but the music played on in sweet harmony under starry summer nights and in winter storms.

When Isabella died, I didn't think they would ever be able to dance again, but they did.

I hadn't heard this record play since Annie was killed in the boating accident, seven years ago.

Inching closer, I raised my hand to knock, and the timeless melody began to play again. I stood to the side of the door, moving out of Doc's eyesight.

Evening sunlight fell on him as he swayed slowly across the floor, casting a full shadow. His eyes were closed, arms out-stretched and bent around the open air, as if his invisible partner fit perfectly in his embrace. He moved through the room in familiar rhythm, never missing a beat.

I tip-toed away and fell back against the wall as I caught my breath, my heart pounding, skipping beats. Verse by verse the song played through to the end. I slipped out of my hiding place to peek around the corner.

Doc paused. He wrapped his arms around his shoulders and held them as if someone were hugging him. I knew it was Annie. Eyes still closed, his head tilted up. Tears trickled down his cheeks.

The scratch of the needle skipped on the worn paper label, the arm bumping against the center spindle. The record cycled repeatedly on the phonograph. Doc resumed dancing.

Even in Doc's grief, he knew the depths of a pure love that sustained him, held him close, and comforted him when loneliness swept through without mercy.

I knew no such comfort.

This private moment was not meant for me to see. Trying to cross the deck without being heard, I maneuvered my way to the stairway. The instant my feet hit the dirt, I began to run. I had no idea where I was going, but I couldn't get there fast enough. I was a fraud. Not even a real person anymore. Part of me died with David and I didn't get in his mistress' sport car with them. Yet he took a part of me with him that I could not get back.

I was tormented by questions about David's infidelity. Were there others over the years? Did I know them? Were they prettier than me? Did our friends know? Was I a laughing stock, a joke?

Rushing down the side stairs to the pathway panting, I sought cover under the trees, all the way to the shore. Branches bristled across my jeans and needles poked at my bare arms. My feet kept running until I tumbled over a granite stone. A sharp pain pierced through my knee. I'd landed on a jagged edge, gashing flesh and ripping my jeans. Hobbling to the pier, I sank on the wooden planks, trying to catch my breath, pinching the wound together to stop the bleeding.

I rolled on my back and bent my leg in the air. The pain didn't lessen. Blood wasn't gushing, more oozing. I sat up and cupped my hand over my knee, applying pressure. This was going to require more than a Band-Aid.

I took another look at the gash. "Oh man, I need stitches." My stomach rolled. "You are such a mess," I yelled at myself.

I tried to stand, but it hurt too much. "Just when are you going to get your sorry life back together?" I slumped back down, feeling defeated, and succumbed to the awful truth.

I'd fallen completely apart after the funeral, and everyone but Nana thought I was so strong. I'd become an expert at hiding out, mostly at work, a safe place where I could present myself as I wanted others to perceive me. I feared if anyone knew the real me, hopelessly flawed, weak, and inadequate, they would reject me. I wouldn't add up to expectations. It was easier to wear an outer mask that appealed to those around me than to expose my inner self to certain scrutiny.

The cold night air numbed my fingers, but not my aching knee. "You have to go to Doc for help." I fought the idea. I was incapable of rationally processing much of anything at the moment. "Concentrate. Focus. Block David out." I shut my eyes tight and shook my head. "Go away!"

David permeated the air I was breathing. I'd suspected he was involved with another woman, but I never did anything about it until that ski trip from hell.

How could I let Olivia know that her beloved father was a lying cheat? Her delusions of David were far greater than mine. And I was still more than slightly unhinged from the revelation.

The full moon shone like a spotlight. "You are just as much a hypocrite as David." Blood seeped through my pant leg. When I shifted to my side, a sharp stab pierced down to the bone. I rolled over, closed my eyelids, and squeezed the wound tight. A woozy lightheadedness overcame me, and a child sang a different song on the hi-fi.

A memory of clear blue skies colored over the darkness, only a handful of cumulus clouds whipped across the horizon. A little blond-haired girl dances circles around a tree over-laden with an abundant harvest of ripe plums. Her soft shoulder-length curls flow in the breeze like spun cotton candy. Tan arms stretch out and sway in rhythm as she sings in perfect harmony, a sweet song her mother usually sang with her when they hung laundry together.

The whole world is in his hands.

Her dolly's clothes are mixed in, hanging with the family wash.

Ripples of pastel flutter outward in a wave and the child gathers her sundress in her hands twirling in delight. Bare feet sweep over tall blades of flowing grass. She pirouettes toward the neighbors freshly mowed lawn, moving beyond the white picket fence line where a wide open gate invites her to continue her ballet in the garden beyond. It is too much to resist. Flowers of every color and fragrance are beckoning in full bloom bursting forth in rows as vibrant as a setting sun in variegated hues of yellows, oranges, fuchsia, and fiery shades of red. The air is intense dripping with sweet jasmine nectar.

The woman hanging the laundry never notices the quiet that replaces the joyful singsong. She busies herself clamping the wooden pins on the corners of crisp white sheets, struggling against a persistently increasing wind. Rows of billowing sails surround her as she reaches in her apron pocket for another clothespin. Tall and excessively slender, her golden hair is piled on top her head in a tight, neat bun, only a few wisps dare blow in the breeze. Her blue eyes are dark and do not dance. She purses her thin lips, focused on finishing her chore.

The girl looks back for a hint of a smile, but there simply isn't the slightest emergence or hope of one. In silence the woman moves down the clothes line, a stark figure against the immaculate linens that flap, the only sound on the sloped hillside of lush emerald green.

Next door a hunched-over elderly woman follows behind the boisterous youngster, helping her pick bright pansies with happy painted faces, dependable hearty daisies, budding roses and blue forget-me-nots. Soon their bouquet is as fragrant as perfume in an exquisite crystal bottle.

The wrinkled old woman sends the child on her way with a loving peck on the cheek. She leans her gnarled wooden cane into the soft give of the earth. Before leaving the garden gate, the precocious child pulls a forget-me-not out and hands it to her friend who bends the stem and places it behind her ear, the delicate blue blooms resting on the downy pillow of her white hair. The wind is gentle against the little girl's skin as she curtsies, poses full-scale, toes pointed, and then skips back out the gate.

Each step is slow and cautious as the child nears the full clothesline. She guards her gift by shielding her hands around the fragile blooms. Her pace quickens and her eyes search. Hiding the bouquet behind her back, she approaches the figure hovered over an empty wicker basket, their eyes meeting as she proudly brings forth the fully bloomed floral arrangement.

"What have you done, Emily?" The woman indignantly demands an answer. "Where did you steal these from? Have you been over in old lady Michael's garden again? What am I going to do with you? You're seven years old now and you know better. I have told you over and over again, do not go over there uninvited." She seizes the bundle of flowers and tosses them into the blustery wind, scattering paintbrush splashes of color in every direction.

The child is silent, her eyes widen, tears well up, but she does not cry. She does not utter a sound.

Swiftly the woman raises her hand, delivering three consecutive spankings, each one more powerful than the first. "Go to your room Emily, there will be no supper for you this evening even if your father gets back from out of town."

Clasping the hem of her cotton dress, the child runs up the hill into a house, up the staircase, and throws herself on the bed. The house is empty, hauntingly still.

"Mama, what's wrong?" She hugs her dolly, burying her face. "Mama." Her sobs go unattended, unnoticed.

"Come back to me. I'm still here." She curls up into a ball, hugging the doll. Weeping. Tears stain her reddened cheeks. "I need you." She whimpers into the deep darkness of the night. "God, please help my mama. She misses Beddie."

Only sleep brings escape. There are no arms to hold her. No soothing words of reassurance, no comfort, no familiar voice telling her she is loved. The wind howls through the shingles on the roof, shaking them loose to fly away in the ensuing storm. Her prayers seem to go unanswered, as though even God has abandoned her.

A willowy shadow passes through the dimly lit doorway, stealth in movement. Long tresses of soft hair brush away the dried tears on the little girl's sleeping face. Pale, thin arms reach forward and with trembling hands, she draws her slumbering daughter close to her heaving chest. Her dark vacant eyes gaze out the bedroom window. Humming, she stares out into black pool of sky, framed by the edges of each window pane. Only when dawn breaks does she gently lay her child down, pull the covers up, and tuck them loosely around her. "Emily, Mama was here," she whispers in her ear. The child stirs, eyes fluttering. She clutches her mother's lace sleeve, holding on until her fingers slip away, one by one, and a sleepy haze of exhaustion outweighs her desire to awaken.

Standing in the doorway, her mother's white flowing nightgown catches the first light of day. She closes the door and moves like a ghost down the hall to her other world. She presses a pansy between the pages of a book on her dresser, then floats to her bed as if walking on air. Her head touches lightly on the fluff of pillows, and she seeks the sleep that eludes her at night yet welcomes her in the daylight of wishful dreams.

"Where are you, God?" I shook my fist at the air. "Nana says I should pray to you. You never answered any of my prayers when was a little girl. Why should you start now?" The wind moaned across the lake. Waves rippled and foamed around the pier. Chilled air pushed up through the thin slices of space between the creaking boards under me.

I rolled over to the edge of the dock and looked deep down into the waters. What did I think was going to happen? Lightning? Thunder? Maybe an angel or two would descend from the heavens and swoop me into their arms or wings or whatever and carry me away to an imaginary celestial kingdom.

I tried to shut down the pain and think things out. Pull loose ends together.

Woozy and lightheaded, I needed to get help before I passed out.

My daddy used to say that secrets are dangerous things. They own you body and soul, play tricks on your mind, whisper behind your back, holding you captive in invisible bondage. My secrets are making me ill. I was pretty sure Doc had zeroed in on that from day one. I knew Nana didn't agree with me, keeping this from Olivia. She believed I should tell her the truth and let her sort through it like Sarah and I had.

How could David do this to his daughters? He always put himself first.

And Jack would just love to hear all about how David betrayed me. Then Jack could make his move on the pitiful abandoned widow.

So much for the all-knowing God of the universe.

Get help.

Water sloshed against the pier posts, a near-freezing spay across the wood. I limped off the deck, rubbing my throbbing knee.

Doc's lights now burned bright. I knew he would tend to my cut. I hobbled my way up the sandy beach, my knee screaming in pain with each footstep, back to his porch.

I knocked on the open door. "You there, Doc?"

"That you, Emily? Been wondering when you were coming. I made split pea soup—good heavens girl, you get right in here." Doc took one look at me, swung the screen door open, and motioned me inside.

"I fell," I whined, planting myself on the ottoman inside the doorway. "Can you patch me up?"

"Come in the treatment room with me. Lean against my shoulder." He reached under my arm, supporting me as he led me into the office and flipped on the light switch.

"What happened? You been running out there in the dark?" Doc shifted my weight to help me sit up on the table.

"Ran down to the beach." I grimaced.

"I'm going to have to cut through those jeans so I can see if you need any stitches. Looks like the cut might be pretty deep." He turned and washed his hands in the sink.

"This is my best pair of designer jeans," I protested when he started snipping away.

"Make them into cut-off shorts. Isn't that what you gals are wearing these days?"

He cut the denim material well above my knee. There, I've done half the work for you." He held up one pant leg. Your Nana can wash these and use them for patches."

"Oh, my brand new jeans," I complained.

He carefully probed around. "Oh yeah, you're going to need at least three or four stitches, maybe more."

"Stupid rock."

"So it is the rock's fault?"

Doc grabbed a basin and some peroxide. He gave me a quick head-to-toe assessment. "Did you hit your head too?"

"No."

He placed a towel under my leg and poured the peroxide over the wound.

"Ouch, that really burns." I tensed up and pressed my upper teeth on my lower lip.

"Got to flush out the bacteria. I'm going to give you a shot to numb the area before I start sewing. It has to go right into the cut."

"I know."

Scoot back against the wall." Doc grabbed a pillow from the rack under the table, and cushioned it behind me.

"This is going to sting. Tell me if you start to feel faint." He drew from a vile into the syringe and bent my knee at a precise angle before injecting several places into the wound.

"Don't tense up, Em."

I focused on the gold star taped on the ceiling to draw children's attention away from things like this, and tried to relax taking in and exhaling slow, deep breaths.

"Don't think I've ever patched up your knee before."

"Yup, this is a first."

Doc pulled out a sterilized needle kit from the top drawer under the sink. "Have to give the anesthetic some time to go to work. You want to tell me what happened?" He arched an eyebrow as he opened the zip-lock bag.

"I fell."

"Why?"

"I wasn't watching where I was going."

"Where were you going?"

"Here, for dinner."

"Your Nana phoned after you left. You forgot the bread pudding she baked.

That was quite a while ago. She brought it over herself. We were both worried about you."

"I walked to the pier first, needed some time alone.

I fidgeted with the stethoscope dangling from a metal rack on the wall. "Do you think it's been long enough now?"

"No."

Paper crinkled underneath me as I wiggled toward one side of the table trying to get comfortable.

"You want to talk about it?"

"Not really. Maybe later." My stomach rumbled. "Let's get this over with and have some soup."

"Okay." Doc rolled his stool next to me and pulled up the tray table.

I lay back and he moved my leg into position.

"Okay Doc." I wanted to tell him about my AIDS test but the words remained under lock and key. I trusted him for wise advice if the results came back positive.

I'm terrified. I'm angry. My brain has shut down.

He threaded thin, black, nylon-coated wire through the eye of a curved stainless steel needle. There wasn't any pain, just sensations of pulling and a little pressure. Five stitches later, I sat up. The perfect opportunity to share, but I couldn't speak the words out loud. Not even to him.

"How about an episode of *Perry Mason* with that bowl of soup?" Doc guided me over to the chair and ottoman in the family room and stuffed pillows under my leg.

"'The Case of the Sleepwalker's Niece,'" I suggested. "It was an early episode with the short-lived character 'Jackson' as Perry's assistant, before private detective Paul Drake came on the scene full time. I loved Paul. He had it all together. Jackson never did."

"We'll start with your pick and end with mine, 'The Case of the Sulky Girl.'"

I grunted.

Doc called my nana to let her know I was there, safe, and wouldn't be home for a while. Then he pulled out two VHS tapes from his collection.

I shifted my hips, trying to find a pain-free position, hoping to forget about my troubles for the night. Doc slid the video into the VCR and handed me the remote control.

When I noticed a vase of pink roses on the coffee table, it dawned on me that tomorrow was the anniversary of Annie's death. How could I have forgotten?

A card stood open beside the flowers. It was signed "Sophia."

That must have been Sophia I'd passed on the path the day before. I hadn't recognized her all grown up—a stunning, leggy sixteen-year-old with model potential.

"Keep that leg elevated. You'll be sore in the morning, but you won't have to worry about popping any stitches when you walk. All the suturing is above the kneecap."

Doc relaxed in his recliner, pulled the hand lever, and raised the footrest. "You comfortable? Could you use a blanket?"

"I'm good." I thumb-tapped the remote buttons until dramatic theme music filled both the courtroom on television and the stillness between our chairs. Perry faced the audience and shot me a knowing glance. A chill ran down my spine. When hiding secrets, watching a 'who-dun-it?' is probably not a wise course of action. Doc was sharp, that's for sure. *Murder She Wrote* was probably next: amateur sleuth Jessica Fletcher, a substitute English teacher in quaint Cabot Cove, Maine, would see right through me. Raymond Burr or Angela Lansbury—either way I was a goner.

Part Two

Autumn ~ Azure Shore Soliloquy

Sometimes the waves of the lake get choppy. The wind whips them up in a fury as they peak and foam, crashing into the shore with such force they seem to roar. The language of the lake is not always an easy thing to master. You must be a diligent student, practicing each lesson learned. Sometimes the lake speaks sternly, calling you to attention, reprimanding you for daring to think you can sail as far out as you desire, to the very center. Suddenly you realize the winds have set your course. You steer the helm starboard, buffeted by menacing waves, battered by a mighty force, praying for mercy. When you reach your destination, you tie up at the pier having developed a keener sense of hearing and a deeper respect for the language the lake speaks.

Chapter Six

Annie

What is the measure of one's life? If it is true it is not so much in how they die but rather how they lived, why do some survive when others perish? Is it divinely ordained, or by accident, or can we go back and alter the timeline of destiny? I need to know.

-Emily journal entry 1988

"No, Doc, not today. Not ever." Anger rose in me as I moved under the shadow of a nearby pine. "He deserved what he got, a life sentence."

"I think it might help you to move on if you came with me to visit the young man." Doc held open the passenger door to his truck.

I closed the door, just like every other time we'd argued about this. "How can you go see him?"

"How can I not? I've forgiven him. You should too." He got in, belted up, and pulled out of his driveway.

I dropped to the ground and sat cross-legged on the dirt. "Forgive him? I don't think so." I had every right to be glad that selfish boy was locked up for the rest of his life. He'd changed so many lives in just minutes. "Spoiled, drunken, brat!"

I watched Annie stand on the edge of the dock and give Doc a light peck on the cheek. She turned for another, and he obliged. Then they loaded their eight-year-old neighbor Sophia onboard the *Martha*. Brilliant hues of cobalt and azure water spread out in shimmering layers across the lake under the clear, blue early-afternoon sky.

Doc untied the ropes and tossed them in as Sophia sat clutching both hands along the side of the rocking boat.

I slipped out of my zories after Annie boarded, and handed her the picnic basket Nana and I had packed. She tucked it under a seat, and got right to work going through her usual pre-boating check list.

"I can still go with you two. Doc will be fine in Reno without me." I flipped up my blouse and flashed a new coral one-piece swimsuit, strutting as if on a fashion runway. "I need a day on the water, off land. Please."

Sophia's green eyes widened in hopeful anticipation, auburn curls bouncing. "Can Emmy come around the lake with us?" She continued holding on, white-knuckle tight to the boat while trying to look cool at the same time.

I figured I had a chance with her pleading on my behalf.

"Not today." Annie told Sophia firmly. "Emily's going with John." She turned to me.

"He needs a hand picking up all those medical supplies. It'll take hours making so many stops." Annie turned on the engine. The motor spit and sputtered, before roaring full blast.

"Emmy will come next time." The deafening reverberation drowned out her voice. Annie zipped off, hat securely strapped under her chin, gray hair flowing behind her.

Doc and I stood shading our eyes from the glaring sunlight, watching them shrink from view toward the other pin-dot boats out in the middle of the lake. Annie looped back around before setting her course out toward the horizon.

"Guess we'd best get up to the truck and on our way." Doc glanced over his shoulder one more time. "I want to be here when they get back."

"I'm ready if you are." Slipping back into my zories, I tucked my blouse back into my jeans and started up toward the stretch on Highway 28 where the old Ford was parked. I hustled ahead, making Doc hurry to keep up with me.

"You might want to change into a pair of closed-toe shoes." Doc wasn't suggesting, he was telling me.

"I have a pair in the truck bed. What are we going to unload?"

"Annie made a couple dozen baby quilts for the hospital nursery and the unwed teenagers." He was panting, just a step behind me now.

"When did she sew all those?"

"She makes time here and there. She enjoys picking out the fabric. Says the young mothers won't have a spare moment once they take their babies home." Doc ushered me to the passenger side and opened the door.

"Ah, come on Doc, let me drive for a change. Give you a chance to relax." I pressed against the door panel, batted my eyes, and worked up a perfect pout face.

"I will be relaxed if I drive." He strode to the driver's door without giving my persuasive antics a cursory glance.

"Hmph."

I flicked on the radio as I sat in my seat. Music blared, but Doc didn't complain. Gazing out the window at passing traffic, I wondered how my girls were doing at junior cheerleading camp. They'd surprised David and me by both making the squad their first time out, and they were beyond ecstatic. David was off at a

California State Professor conference. I always ended up at the cabin like a homing pigeon.

"I want to go over Mt. Rose on the way to Washoe Medical." Doc's voice pulled me out of my self-analysis.

"That's fine." I enjoyed the mountain pass, especially during winter when the slopes were capped in a blanket of fresh powder. Riding the tram up to the mountaintop and skiing downhill held a seductive appeal.

Annie explained to Sophia once again, why they always wore a life jacket. "They keep us safe, even if we fall into the water. You'll float until someone comes along and scoops you up, sweetie. Just be still and wait."

"I can swim good, Miss Annie," Sophia grumbled, tugging on the straps. She fidgeted with the bright orange dual pillows protecting her chest. "No one can see my new swimsuit!"

Annie laughed. "You remind me of Emmy when she was your age." Annie turned the key to shut down the motor. "Now we won't have to shout at each other over that loud-mouth engine. How about some lunch?"

"Well, I am hungry."

"Let's see what we've got." She opened the picnic basket. "We have turkey sandwiches, carrots, and fruit salad. Want to share a sandwich?"

Sophia nodded. Annie handed her a triangular half.

Sophia chattered between bites. "Sally Thomas told me that third grade is going to be harder than second grade. Mr. Whitmore gives three-hour homework assignments every day. And girls can't wear dresses, only jeans and tee-shirts or sweatshirts."

"Summer just started. You don't need to worry about next year yet. Splash around the beach for a couple of months first."

"A girl has to be prepared," Sophia stated with sophisticated certainty as she lifted her head in a classic profile pose, nose pointed upward. The ruby red polish on her finger and toenails were a perfect match to the designer bikini obscured beneath the billowing fluorescent-orange life preserver.

"Having once been a third grader myself, and being fairly knowledgeable about social gatherings, I wonder what you'd think about fire-pit weenie roasts with s'mores?"

"That stuff is okay, so long as no one at school finds out." Sophia gobbled down the last of her fruit salad and licked her fingers.

"I see. It just so happens that Doc and I are roasting hot dogs and marshmallows in the fireplace tonight. He might even bring out a chocolate bar and graham crackers."

"Can I come? Please?"

"I think that can be arranged."

Abandoning all pretense, Sophia clapped her hands. "You and Doc and Emily are my favorite old people in the whole world!"

Annie chuckled. Emily would be appalled to know she'd been included as a senior citizen.

"It's time we head back home." Annie put their leftovers into the basket, then tightened the strap on her lifejacket. She stood and flipped on the ignition.

Two boats loaded with teenage water skiers zoomed by a few yards off. They'd made several passes during lunch, but nothing this close. By this time of day, the kids were probably down to the bottom of several bottles of their parents' most expensive hard liquor.

Seeing the incoming wake from the motorboats, Annie hollered, "Hold on, Sophia!" She shifted into gear, but the engine stalled. Annie clicked the key off, then on. The engine boomed to life. She turned starboard, trying to avoid another pass by the reckless kids.

One of the silver speedboats raced directly alongside the *Martha*, spewing four-foot-high waves into it, and splashing icy-cold water all over both occupants.

"Slow down!" Annie shouted.

Where was the other speedboat?

"Hey, they don't have lifejackets on." Sophia screamed, shaking a fist in the air as she slid down the drenched seat.

"Sophia. Hold on with both hands!"

A speeder rammed the rear of the boat. The kids backed off, then bumped the stern again. A third thrust hit even harder. Annie steered as straight and steady as she could to keep from tipping over.

She caught a glimpse of the boat in her rearview mirror as it crept alongside. Half a dozen teenage boys egged each other on.

After a jolting clip, they slowed down and backed off, laughing and shouting while passing around a bottle of booze.

Sophia sobbed hysterically.

"Hold on, sweetie." Annie stretched to reach and comfort her little shipmate, but Sophia was buffeted from one end of the bench to the other every time the boat hit.

The other silver speeder that had been shadowing a close parallel to the *Martha*, backed off, way off.

Annie swallowed hard, gripped the wheel, and made a quick scan of the area. No boats were anywhere near, most clustered nearer the south shore.

"Annie!" Sophia's terrorized scream alerted her to turn in time to see the speedboat inches from center stern, coming in fast. "Lord," she prayed, "help Sophia."

The impact propelled the *Martha* into the air. Gravity pulled her back into the water. Annie's body flew up and down with it. As it capsized, her head smacked against the *Martha's* hull, knocking her unconscious.

Sophia bobbed and shivered, screaming, frozen with fear. She inched her way around, hand over hand along the exposed side of the *Martha*.

"Annie, where are you?" Sophia looked around the side of the boat where she landed. "Somebody help us," she cried, "Annie, I'm scared." She supported her head against the hull, her hands grasping for anything to hold on to. Fingers slipping, legs kicking, Sophia whimpered, "Come and get me, Annie."

Crying, she let her arms relax out to the sides, and waited for Annie to come to her. When no one came, she swam and searched on the other side of the boat where she found Annie floating face down. "Annie!"

Grabbing handfuls of gray hair, Sophia struggled to lift Annie's face out of the water. No matter how hard she tried, she couldn't.

"Annie, wake up!"

A speeder pulled alongside. One of the boys started to jump in, but his friend behind the wheel took off, knocking him back down beside another teen who was vomiting everywhere.

"Forget her," the driver shouted. "She's dead and the kid can ID us."

The resulting wake repeatedly batted Sophia up against the boat as she spit out water, coughing. Annie drifted away.

Doc and I had just finished the supply deliveries at Washoe Medical Center, and were heading toward the maternity lounge to drop off Annie's boxes, when a call came in at the nurses' desk. I overheard Annie's name mentioned and figured they were waiting on our delivery down the hall.

The head nurse called two doctors over, but not Doc. They huddled amid whispers and shot looks our way. I wondered if Doc had heard too, but he didn't say anything and led the way to the lounge where we sat with our boxes waiting for someone to return to the maternity nurse's station.

A surgeon padded down the long, empty corridor toward us, his paper booties crunching against the shiny tile floors. His face looked grim—just the way Doc looked when he had to tell a visitor about a loved one's passing. I figured he must want Doc to help him break the news to the family of one of Doc's patients who didn't make it through surgery. He had several on the schedule today and had stopped in to see a few of them when we'd first arrived.

Dr. Zimmerman sat beside Doc, then put his arm on his shoulder. "John, there's been a boating accident." He drew in a deep breath, and held it before exhaling. "Annie's gone, my friend."

I gasped out loud, not sure what I heard was real.

Doc's face went ashen and his hands trembled. "What happened?"

"A couple witnessed the incident from their cabin. After calling the Coast Guard, they boated out and found Sophia floating next to Annie, holding her hand, telling her not to worry because they were both wearing life jackets. They couldn't get Sophia to leave Annie so the husband got in the water with her."

I tried to comprehend his words. Boating accident. Annie is dead.

"Matthew Hendricks, was one of the first responders on the scene."

Doc nodded. "Matt's a good medic. Been my patient since birth."

"He swam off with Sophia, repeatedly assuring her that the other medics were bringing Annie to you."

"What happened to the boat?" Doc asked.

"Teenagers rammed it. It flew in the air and landed capsized. They were near Meek's Bay."

I should have gone with them. My heart pounded wildly.

How can Doc be so calm? I tried to fight back tears, but it was useless.

"After repeated attempts at CPR failed, the medics brought Annie ashore. Her neck was broken. She never regained consciousness."

"How is Sophia?"

"Scared, but okay." Zimmerman folded his hands on his knees, eyes facing the floor. "I am so sorry. Annie was a special lady, loved by many of us here."

"Thank you." Doc barely whispered.

The surgeon stood when his beeper flashed red. "I have to get to the operating room." He turned to me. "Will you be staying with John?"

"Yes." A catch in my throat garbled my answer.

Doc doubled over and heaved deep sobs. I wrapped an arm around his back and shoulder. He shook in my embrace.

No words of comfort came to me to help ease his pain. I rocked in motion with him, tears streaming down my cheeks.

Nurses trickled over, one at a time, murmuring sympathetic words. When a small group of them sat and cried with Doc, I got up to go call Nana on the payphone across the hall. I stared at the empty chairs in the lounge. It crossed my mind that is was a good thing no expectant fathers were there waiting for babies to be born. What a strange thing to think about.

I wept as I told Nana about the boating accident and Annie's death.

"Dear Annie. What will John do without her?"

She had no way to get to the hospital because Jack was on a cruise in Alaska. I offered to come and get her as soon as I could break away. She was crying when I hung up.

Soon after I rejoined Doc, a policeman approached. "John Walters?"

"Yes."

"Sir, I am so sorry for your loss. The Coast Guard caught up with the speeders on their way to the south shore. Half a dozen empty bottles of whiskey and rum were discovered in the hull of the boats. Seven high school seniors on a Southern California football team were charged with being drunk beyond the legal limit. An eighth boy had alcohol poisoning so severe it landed him in intensive care."

"Were any of them arrested?" I yelled.

"Not yet. We haven't determined who was driving."

I turned away so Doc would not see the anger rising in me. It was all I could do to keep my mouth shut.

Doc stood and took the man's hand between his. "Thank you for your help." He walked right past the cardboard boxes of baby quilts, and headed for the main entrance.

I rushed to join him, and asked for his keys. He looked at me, his eyes blood-shot, then handed me his keychain. When we reached the truck, he got in the passenger side.

"I need to go to the morgue." His chest shuddered. "Can you take me?"

My body cringed at the thought of seeing Annie dead. How could he bear to view her like that? But Doc knew the routine for these situations. He'd had to accompany family to the morgue many times.

"Yes."

When dawn broke the following day, Nana and I went next door and knocked for quite some time to no response. We let ourselves in and found Doc in his chair, asleep, still dressed in the clothes he had on the day before. He was clutching Annie's favorite patch-work quilt. We didn't disturb him.

The phone answering machine blinked, signaling an incoming message. Nana pushed the button. "Dad, I'm catching the next plane out of here." Jack faltered, "I am so sorry I wasn't there with you. I'll be home as soon as I can."

It took Jack a few days to get back from his Alaskan cruise. He called from Anchorage, Seattle, and Sacramento.

When he arrived, he rented out his apartment in Carnelian Bay for the next twelve months and moved in with Doc. He gave up his bachelor social life. I was surprised by the sacrifices Jack made to help Doc through one of the hardest years of his life.

Doc was lonely for Annie, but his faith remained strong. Losing her in such a senseless, destructive way destroyed any religious beliefs I had left. No matter how many times I questioned *why?* there weren't any answers.

I have not managed to be as forgiving as Doc. How he still makes regular prison visits to the unrepentant, arrogant driver of the boat is beyond me. The boy's own family rarely goes, and all his friends turned on him to get their sentences reduced. Jack goes with Doc on his visitations. That to me, is the biggest mystery of all.

Chapter Seven

There is another forest about three hundred feet below
the surface of the lake. The evidence lies in the silent
depths. Once tall trees are but stumps. I wonder what
story they could tell? What language the people of that
time spoke? Why it disappeared?

-Journal entry, historical research, Emily

Nana was pretty miffed at me for not letting her know I'd
injured my knee. It was barely a scratch compared to my
dare-devil teenage years. I only had to keep the stitches dry for a
week. I lasted five and a half days. Doc did a good patch-up job.

Accidentally coming upon him in the midst of his intimate
moment had made me feel, for the first time, like an intruder in
his life. He rarely talked about Annie's death. He sure loved to talk
nonstop about the way she lived, though.

I never sit in Annie's chair when I'm over there. It isn't that
it bothers him. It bothers me. Whenever I look at that chair, I see
her rocking away, quilting or crocheting baby blankets. Her basket
for skeins of yarn and fabric swatches nests next to it. Neither Doc
nor Jack ever sits there either.

During my boring five-and-a-half days that I couldn't swim
laps in the lake because of my stitches, I frequented the bookstore
in Tahoe City. George had really built up the stock over the years

and created quite a little haven. Hence the name: Lake Cottage Book Haven. Very appropriate.

He had my Robert Frost, Emily Dickinson, and the brand-new Pat Conroy novel, *Beach Music*. I figured that'd last me until at least next week.

Jack backed off on pushing me to go SCUBA diving. How lucky did I get with that one?

Although I do wonder where that extra set of equipment he showed me in his office came from. Your average guy might have a spare pair of fins, a mask, and an air tank lying around. But not a suit that looked to be exactly my size.

I'm taking Nana to Reno tomorrow. She says she has a hankering to go by the Realtor's office and make a run by the Boatworks Mall in Tahoe City and stop at Snooks Candies for chocolates.

As fiercely independent as she is, I marvel that she never got her driver's license. She used to walk or ride her bicycle almost everywhere. But it's seven miles into Tahoe City. Doc and Jack take her to church on Sundays and then wait for her to do her weekly marketing.

I'd go stir crazy being so cabin bound.

These days, though, that's about the extent of her venturing into town except for visitations with Doc at the hospital, and the Hollister House she renamed the "Old Folks Home for Wise Ones." It's a shameful institution where families dump their drooling, dementia-riddled, rejected relatives who have become a burden in their twilight years. Most never return to visit, not even on holidays.

She and Doc sit with the residents, comb their hair, brush their teeth, and spoon-feed blank faces that are incapable of showing the slightest hint of gratitude or any interaction. They do everything for these intentionally forgotten shut-ins ... except diapering. There are regulations about that.

Sometimes Jack accompanies them—or so Nana tells me.

They keep asking me to go with them, but I'm not comfortable in those places. The noxious odor of urine and vomit just about knocks me off my feet the minute I open the door.

I'll never let Nana end up in a place like that. Doc either.

I did help Nana sew a couple dozen bibs during my stitch-recovery period. Thick terry cloth on one side, to absorb spills, and primary colors in 100 percent cotton on the other. She says the folks love the cheerfulness of bright colors over pastels. I swear I saw the denim that Doc cut off my jeans on a couple of those bibs. My brand-new Tommy Hilfiger's became designer bibs for the senior sippie-cup social society.

Nana and I played Scrabble out on the deck after lunch today. She's good with words. She and Papa used to play every Thursday after he retired from the law office of Bartlett, Baker & Butterworth. It was a pretty even match this time, and I don't think she let me win. I scored big points at the end of the game with *xylophone*, 24 points, and *queen*, 14 points with a dark blue square triple on the Q giving me an extra twenty points. Nana got caught holding a ten-point Z.

Before supper I grabbed a stack of magazines from the den, which I'd found by digging around behind the old radio cabinet. Nana has saved some vintage issues of *Look, Life,* and *The Saturday Evening Post.* There were even a couple of *McCall's* and *Ladies Home Journal* magazines. I sat on the floor against the wall, to flip through them. At first I was just passing time, but then I came across an F. Scott Fitzgerald short story, and another by Sinclair Lewis. All pure treasures in my opinion.

The advertisements were a hoot.

"In 1940, become fit & slim by taking Bile Beans."

"Men wouldn't look at me because I was too skinny. Now that I've gained ten pounds this new easy way, I have all the dates I want."

"Queen Bess corset, skirt supporter."

How long have women let themselves be merchandise for the merchants?

Good old dependable Betty Crocker showed readers in 1950 how to bake a red velvet cake with Gold Medal Flour. I remember the day I discovered that Betty wasn't a real person. Where did all those yummy recipes and boxed cake mixes come from? Advertising ... the creative mill for fabrication with a deceptive spin that has an irresistibly seductive appeal to the masses. In other words, brainwashing.

"Emily, did you hear me?" Nana nudged my shoulder.

"Sorry. I've been time traveling." I closed the *Look* magazine on my lap and placed it on top on the lopsided stack at my feet.

"Doc just called to invite us over to watch one of those new VDF movies. Do you want to go? I finished baking the muffins for morning breakfast." She shook off her apron and hung it on the hallway hook. "I'm free to go."

"It's VHS, Nana." I grinned after thinking twice whether or not to correct her.

"That's what I said, isn't it?" She grabbed our sweaters off a hat rack hook and handed me mine. "It looks like it's going to be a nippy night. We might need these for the walk home."

I slipped my arm through a sleeve. "Do you know what movie Doc has in mind?"

"He checked out something from the video store called *Shadowlands*. Do you know anything about that one?"

"I do. It's about the author C. S. Lewis. It takes place in England. Doc has chosen wisely." I buttoned midway down and tugged on the hem.

"Have you already seen it?" She headed for the back door.

"Yeah, at the theatre, when it was first released in America last year. It premiered two years ago in England."

"Why, I've never heard of it before."

"That's not surprising. You're not a regular movie-go-er and you don't have a television to catch the previews on."

"I have my transistor radio." She shook her hips sideways and did a little dip-curtsey-thingy. "And I get around."

"Yes, you do. Let's not be late for Doc's movie theatre." I chuckled.

"He has the popcorn popping on the stovetop. He asked if we'd like butter and salt. I said yes." She danced another couple of hipster steps to the door. "And Cokes in glass bottles."

"This is more of a box-of-tissues movie than a popcorn flick."

She gave me a concerned look. "There isn't any nudity or cursing, is there?"

"Doc would never pick a movie that would bother you in the slightest way."

"Very true." She resumed her jolly jive-jig and invited me to dance with her. I declined but said I would save a spot on my dance card.

So this was the big smash-bang end to my week on the lake. Seven days of Scrabble, magazines, books, and an invitation to feed blended foods to senior citizens at the rest home. And oh yes, I helped sew three dozen dribble-and-drool bibs for those same seniors. And to think I'd been complaining about going diving, which involved snorkeling, swimming, boating, and sunbathing.

I opened the back screen door for Nana and couldn't help but wonder how I was going to survive the entire summer hanging out with this jet-set crowd.

Chapter Eight

The lake listens when you speak. My voice carries and settles on the surface of the water, resting there before descending to the depths. There words remain in darkness that becomes light. Conversations ride on the waves. What words did I choose? Truth, lies, arguments. Imagine the clamor, boats, hang gliders, water-skis, SCUBA divers, paddle wheels, metal, aluminum, wood. And wafting among and above them, words. Hallowed words. The lake beckons. "Come talk with me," it says. "Swim and hear." The water is crystal clear at morning dew, as I sit on the shore. And listen.

—Em, journal entry, conversation with the lake

Nana and I sat at the kitchen table to relax after folding and putting away the week's laundry.

"Jack's going hiking at Yosemite with his longtime partner in crime and bachelor buddy Jake McAllister." I told Nana.

"Yes, I know. And Doc will be in Reno for a medical conference. So—I invited my great-granddaughters to come for a visit on Sunday."

I gulped. The last time I'd seen my daughters was when I left to come here. Sarah had lectured me about keeping this insidious secret about her father from Olivia. Because of the mounting tension between us, Olivia had assumed Sarah was upset with her for some unknown reason. They avoided each other at the Sacramento house, each one inhabiting an opposite end.

"I suggested we have a barbecue on the back deck." Nana tucked her hands into her apron pockets. "I told the girls to bring their young men, swimsuits, and a fresh fruit pie from Ikeda's in Auburn."

"Lovely." At least we'd be free of Jack's incessant badgering and annoying jokes for the entirety of the upcoming visitation. Nana would have the girls all to herself to dote on to her heart's content. And I'd get another chance to chat with Brice and Todd. Oh, goody. Knowing how much Nana yearned to see my daughters, I kept my concerns to myself.

Sunday dawned cold and overcast. It was the kind of morning when your breath hangs frostily in the air so long it can practically speak back to you. Olivia and her boyfriend Todd arrived first.

Todd drove his newly restored 1969 hunter green Ford Mustang: spit-polished chrome, hand-waxed and buffed exterior, leather seats, and original license plate, the gleaming metal defying dust as he pulled into the dirt and gravel driveway.

Standing with Nana at the dual-pane front window, I half expected the wild horse emblem to gallop off the hood, kick up its hooves, neigh, and charge us.

"I had a boyfriend in college who drove a car just like that," I said.

"Was he a nice young man?" Nana asked, her eyes glued to the driveway.

"No, he was not. He couldn't formulate complete sentences. His car was red."

We watched Olivia and Todd unload the trunk. She took the pie box and left him to bring in her tote bag. They murmured to each other until they spotted us staring out the window. We grinned and waved, a good old-fashioned welcome-to-the-lake greeting. Todd gave us a thumbs-up and smiled a ridiculous I'm-not-worthy-of-your-daughter grin. Olivia rolled her eyes.

Sarah pulled in right behind them, her passenger seat empty. Where was her violin-playing musician? She rushed out of the car, totally ignoring her sister. She bypassed me proceeding directly to Nana and gave her a long, enthusiastic hug.

Great, they're already quarreling. What is it now?

Olivia and Todd barreled in behind Sarah and went straight to Nana too.

No hugs for Mom. I already felt like the expendable interloper.

Nana embraced Olivia, then turned to Todd. "Are you going to introduce me to your new, fine-looking beau?"

Todd, ever the charmer, took my grandmother's hand, held it to his lips, and made a lengthy production of kissing it. Such a tawdry imitation of a reputable, Southern gentleman. I wanted to gag. He'd used the same routine on me the first time I met him.

Nana didn't gush the least bit at his fawning gesture, but Todd was so pleased with himself he didn't take notice.

I heaved a disgruntled moan and walked away before a profusion of words I was certain to regret issued forth from my mouth. I suppressed the urge to deliver an opinionated barrage of my daughter's latest questionable choice of male companionship and offered a courteous, yet impersonal handshake. "Welcome to the lake." It was a bona fide salutation, even if I didn't mean it.

"Nice place you got here, Nana," Todd said, taking in the surroundings.

"So where's Brice?" Olivia asked her sister, a snippet of sarcasm in her tone.

"We had a slight disagreement when I went to pick him up this morning." Sarah avoided eye contact.

"Is he not coming at all?" Olivia persisted.

"No, he's not!" Sarah brushed by her sister and marched into the living room.

"What happened since I saw you two yesterday at the beach?" Olivia demanded, clipping Sarah's heels all the way behind her.

"I decided we need to take a break from each other for a while, that's all." She pulled a slightly bent envelope from her purse and offered it to Nana. "He asked me to give this to you."

She opened it and pulled out a greeting card bearing a photograph of a renaissance floral bouquet in a vintage Limoges vase. Nana read out loud, "With gratefulness for your hospitality." She handed it to me. It was signed in elegant cursive penmanship, "Sincerely, Brice Winston."

Nana displayed it on the fireplace mantle, a place of honor reserved for the special intimate remembrances from family and close friends. "This took thoughtful foresight," she stated. "I am sorry things did not work out for you two today, Sarah. I so enjoyed his company during your last visit."

Todd took the pie from Olivia and shoved it into my grandmother's hands.

"It's cherry. Livie said that's your favorite."

"Actually, it's my favorite," I said, taking the Ikeda dessert. "But Nana is fond of all fresh-fruit pies."

"When are we going for a swim?" Todd unfastened the only two buttons holding his slip of a shirt together, then tossed it on the rocker.

"You're welcome to go on down to the beach for a dip anytime. It's quite cold this early in the day before the sun has warmed up the water," Nana cautioned.

"It takes a while to acclimate."

"I can take it." He strutted through the room and out the back door.

The rest of us settled deep in the sofa cushions for a leisurely chat.

Olivia filled Nana in on her summer life-guarding at Folsom Lake, proudly mentioning how she had saved a drowning child. "He'd stayed in too long. Suffering from both heat stress and exhaustion. I noticed him struggling, and by the time I reached him, he'd gone under."

She relayed the rest of the story with detailed emphasis on the gratitude of the distraught, non-swimmer parents who had watched helplessly from the beach.

"It's just part of our job," Sarah snipped, her arms crossed.

I was so proud of Olivia.

"You are both little fish like your mama." Nana beamed. "She practically has gills and fins." She chuckled, then tried to suppress a coughing episode. She labored to catch her breath, the rattle and wheeze in her chest making a worrisome racket. "Please excuse me for a moment. Got to clear the old windpipes," she sputtered, heading for the bathroom.

"Is Nana okay?" Sarah asked after the door closed.

"She's getting up in years, girls. At ninety-one, any exertion is taxing. Even laughter." I found myself disconcerted by my own words.

"Does she need any help?" Olivia rose from her seat.

"She'll let us know if there's something she wants us to do." I frowned. "Nana wouldn't want you girls to spend the day fretting."

"Can we help by preparing the food?" Sarah pulled her hair up in a ponytail and wrapped an elastic band around it from her wrist. "I can grill lunch. I barbecue at home all the time."

"Take her up on it, Mom. She skewers a mean kabob and has been known to fire-roast a rack of ribs to perfection at beach parties." Livie finally managed to say something civil about her sister.

Sarah hurried to the kitchen, where she slammed pots and pans around. I followed her. She furiously sliced and diced onions, assorted vegetables, garlic, and herbs that were about to succumb to a rather violent, minced end. Hammering away with the meat tenderizer on the cutting board, she pulverized the chicken breasts into what appeared to be fleshy flattened pancakes.

Noticing Olivia looking out the back window with a pensive expression, I joined her.

"He's not so bad, Mom." She winced as I pulled the curtain back. Todd stood shivering, arms wrapped tight around his torso, his low-hanging cut-off jeans soaked.

"Please tell me he brought a change of clothes."

"Does Nana still have spare pants and shirts in the bench seat?"

"Nothing that will fit that boy," I balked.

We looked at him out there, squatting and huddled down into as tight a ball as he could form, facing away from the cabin. Livie looked at me, hard at first. Her resolve evaporated, she hung her head and butted it twice against the wood-paneled wall.

"You have to admit, he could use a friend right now," I said.

Nana wandered in, holding a beach towel for our guest. She gave it to Olivia. "Be nice to that boy. He's already learned a hard lesson from the lake."

"Don't worry, Nana, I'm benevolent at heart." Livie snagged the towel and exited.

"She's not going to dump him when they get back to town, is she?" Nana peeked through the window.

"I'd wager there's a good likelihood of that."

Nana went to check on the lunch massacre, and I watched Olivia hand Todd the towel. After he dried off and wrapped himself in the soggy blanket of terry cloth, he made advances toward Olivia that she fended off. He followed her back up the pine cone-littered incline, offering what sounded like explanations and apologies. She trudged ahead of him without answering. He lagged behind, stumbling barefoot over chips of slate rock and fallen twigs, weaving and hopping from one foot to the other until he reached the deck steps.

I let the curtain flutter back in place.

Olivia ushered him straight back to the bathroom.

The day would not be a total loss. Once Olivia saw the light, it'd be a swift, automatic shifting of gears to the next step. She'd figure him out by the evening. Todd would not be coming back for another visit, and that would be a relief.

He came out wearing his chest-baring slip of a shirt and a pair of pants someone had left from about twenty years ago, a polyester-hopsack blend. His thighs were squeezed so tight, I didn't think he'd be able to sit. Somehow, he made it work, like a model on the side of a bus that catches your eye. The kind you crane your neck to get a look-see as it flashes by.

Nana threw his drenched jeans in the washer.

Olivia took him back to the bathroom to blow-dry his thick, layered hair. From the laughter that filtered out the semi-closed door, I suspected he thought he'd redeemed himself. But I knew better. Olivia was merely making sure he was presentable to Nana. Or at least marginally suitable.

The girls began setting the dining room table. Olivia laid the napkins and silverware on the right side of each plate.

"You're doing it wrong." Sarah bundled them all up and replaced them on the left.

"They can go on either side. It's a matter of choice." Olivia put every stick of flatware right back where she had originally placed it.

"Girls, please!" I raised my voice in exasperation and flapped my arms about in a failed attempt to initiate a temporary peace.

We took our seats at the table. Todd grabbed a forkful chicken off the platter in the center and popped it into his mouth. Olivia kicked him under the table. He groaned and yanked his hand back.

Nana bowed her head, closed her eyes, and said grace in a quiet voice. Conversation after that was slow starting. Both girls seemed to have nothing to say.

Everyone filled their plates and ate in silence.

The basil-and-garlic chicken breasts, rolled around an herb cream cheese filling that Sarah had sautéed in olive oil, melted in my mouth. The chopped vegetable medley was perfect for toddlers transitioning from jars of puree to grown-up chunky food. The veggies looked like what the seniors ate at Hollister House.

"What kind of chicken is this? I've never had it before. It's like a Swedish crepe thing." Todd finished off what was left in front of him.

"Just something I made up," Sarah answered.

"Wow, you make up your own recipes like a professional chef?" Todd nudged Olivia. "That is so cool."

Olivia nudged him right back. No comment.

"So," Todd said to Nana, "you live here by yourself year-round. Wow. Not bad for an old woman." He heaped a third helping on his plate before any of us had a chance for seconds.

Nana moved the carving knife out of Sarah's reach under the pretense of only wanting half a chicken roll. She left it neatly tucked under the rim of her plate.

Sarah poked at her roasted potato, repeatedly piercing holes in it with her fork.

"Hey, can I stop by with a few of my snowboard buds when the powder's good?"

As he spoke, Todd sucked in a sliver of chicken wedged half out of the corner of his lips before he swallowed.

Sarah nearly choked on her sip of iced tea. What audacity to ask for an overnighter!

"You are welcome here anytime, young man."

"You're cool." Todd gave Nana another thumbs-up.

She returned the gesture.

An image flashed in my mind of half a dozen teenagers draped across the living room floor, covered with Nana's quilts and afghans. A blonde snow bunny was neatly tucked under Todd's arms and legs. Boards and boots lay strewn throughout the hallway in puddles of melted snow amidst crushed beer cans and crinkled-up potato chip bags.

I gasped out loud.

As surely as Todd would show up, Nana would graciously accommodate him and his frozen band of ski bums. I could only hope they would have the common sense to bring sleeping bags and a change of clothes. Of course this would be long after he and Olivia had broken up. Now that Todd knew the precise location of my grandmother's cabin, it would be open-season all winter long.

As Sarah and Olivia did the dishes, steam rose, fogging up the window. Nana kept a watchful eye on them from her sofa. The girls squabbled, the rush of water steadily running from the faucet, obscuring the escalating volume as one washed and the other dried.

Nana told Todd, "Doing dishes by hand is a bonding activity. These new-fangled electric dishwashers that are supposed to make life easier actually rob us of intimate opportunities to share our lives." She relaxed into the sofa cushions, a content smile spread across her face.

I wasn't so sure. Maybe when they were little girls, but not today.

While Todd and Nana struck up a conversation about vintage cars, I strained to hear the discussion in the kitchen, got up and walked to hang out in the doorway.

Olivia swiped at a couple of strands of hair stuck to her forehead with a slippery, sudsy yellow glove. "What happened? I know you like him, a lot."

"I need some time to myself, to think."

"About what?"

"Things."

"Come on, give it up. What things?"

"I don't want to talk about it right now." Sarah grabbed a plate off the dish rack.

"You're just jealous because I have Todd!"

"What?"

"You heard me." Olivia tossed a pan into the dishwater. Suds bubbled out in waves onto the counter, overflowing to the floor.

"Don't be an idiot. He's just like Dad!"

"What's wrong with that?"

"You always pick guys like Dad."

"What is wrong with you?" Olivia slammed off the faucet and faced her sister.

I rushed in, hoping to quell the storm. "Girls, you're going to upset Nana. Stop bickering, now!"

"Sure, Mom, anything you say." Sarah threw the towel on the table and stormed out.

"Why is she so mad at me?" Olivia's mouth twisted. Her knuckles ghost white, gripped the lip of the kitchen sink. She bent over and sopped up the water off the floor with a towel.

Frazzled, I left the room to be sure Sarah didn't take off.

"It's always good to have music in the home." Nana told Todd. "It balances the emotions of the heart and head."

"Uh-huh." His head flipped back and forth, torn between surveillance of the heated battle in the kitchen, and continuing to schmoose Nana.

I flounced in the recliner, flipped up the footrest and folded my arms across my chest. Sarah sat opposite me, leering in my direction.

"Emily, why don't you play a few songs on the piano?" Nana suggested.

I sprang up, eager for a diversion. I ran my hand across the grain of the walnut-stained Kimball upright, then lifted and pushed back the fallboard over the slightly yellow-tinged ivory keys. The edges were brittle, the centers worn from both age and extensive use. I caressed the first keys my fingers lit upon with gentle, slow strokes. Sitting on the tapestry-covered bench,

I positioned my feet on the dull brass pedals and lightly pumped the damper and una corda.

"Can you play Beethoven's '*Für Elise*'?" Nana requested.

The beautiful chords breathed a life of their own, filling the room with a pleasantness that remained after the last note wistfully settled. I turned and noted Olivia had joined us, sitting in the chair across from her sister.

Friction permeated the air as my two ice queens' animosity frosted a minus-zero chill.

The quiet lull was broken by Nana's request for her favorite hymn, "The Little Brown Church in the Vale."

I loved William Pitts' old country spiritual and knew it by heart.

As I began playing, Todd stood, pressed a hand against his chest, and sang along in a perfectly pitched baritone about the old country church from childhood. Stunned, I faltered, then continued to play, trying to hold the notes to match his pace.

Nana joined in the refrain, then Todd sang the next verse solo. His voice, strong and rich, smoothed over every treble and clef note. Nana rejoined in the final verse, her soprano tone harmonizing as if the two of them hadn't missed a single choir practice in all their years singing at Sunday service.

I finished playing and let Todd sing the final refrain a cappella. The melody transported me to Pitt's vision of that wooded area in a lush valley formed by the Cedar River in Bradford, Iowa, and the church that had been built there. For a moment, I escaped to that serene place.

"Why, thank you, Todd," Nana said. "That was beautiful."

He shrugged. "I used to sing in the church choir."

Dumbfounded, I swallowed and said nothing. Had I misjudged him?

I played several more old hymns and Todd sang every one flawlessly.

"Thank you, Todd. You have a gifted voice." I meant it too.

Nana yawned. "Time for my Sunday nap." She went to the laundry room and returned with Todd's jeans. After he left to change into them, she retreated to the chaise lounge on the deck.

I knew she wouldn't sleep, though. She always read her Bible this time of day.

My girls joined her and I followed as far as the doorway.

Instead of letting Nana read, they asked questions about things they never discussed with me, making me wonder how well I knew my own daughters.

I listened, holding my tongue. Olivia talked about her father, her hope that he was in heaven. She didn't sound sure.

That caught me off guard. I was certain Olivia thought David was perfect. Sarah shot daggers my way when her sister grew quiet.

When Todd came back in his shorts, Nana sent them all on down to the beach.

"The water should have warmed by now." She stared into the noon sun.

Todd grabbed a handful of towels from the pile on the picnic table. He and my daughters scurried off.

"Don't you want to join them?" Nana asked.

"No, I'll stay here with you. Let them have their moment." I sat in the other chaise, raised my red painted toenails straight above me, and wiggled each one.

I watched my girls wade into the water up to their waists, splashing and thrashing around. Todd ran whooping and hollering. He swooped Olivia into his arms, ran deeper into the water, and threw her up in the air like she didn't weigh an ounce. She shrieked, caught in the thrill, and went back for more.

"I expect he's at Folsom Lake a lot when she's life guarding," I mumbled.

"Of course he is. Smart boy too, keeping an eye on his pretty young lady and staying fit at the same time." Nana sighed. "There's more to that fellow than meets the eye."

"Guess you'll be seeing him when the first snow falls," I teased.

"That would actually be a pleasure. I enjoy these youngsters. They are full of life."

She motioned toward Sarah, who swam to the pier, climbed the ladder, untied the ropes on the *Martha* and made a quick jaunt outside the cove, her wakes churning the calm water.

I hoped the lake listened to her while she was out there.

When the kids returned to the cabin, they gathered their belongings and took them out to the cars.

In the middle of the driveway, Todd picked up Nana and spun her around, then planted a big kiss right on her lips.

Olivia laughed when he deposited Nana back on solid ground.

"Sakes alive, it is good to get a bit dizzy every now and then." Nana teetered a bit until I looped an arm under her and reeled her close.

After Todd and Olivia drove off, Nana handed Sarah a small package wrapped in brown paper and tied with string. "Open it when you get home." Then she slipped her a folded-up manila envelope. "This one is for Olivia, when she is alone."

Sarah thanked her, then Nana went to the cabin to take that nap.

As Sarah strode to her car, I rushed over to her.

She halted at the driver's door.

"Why didn't Brice come today?"

She gripped the door handle. "We had a disagreement."

"Is it serious?"

"You tell me!"

"I don't understand."

"I told him I was going to tell Olivia about Dad today. Brice said you were right, to wait, she isn't ready yet."

"I see."

"Really, Mom? Exactly when will she be ready?" Sarah opened the door.

"I don't know. But today would have been a mistake."

"Every time I bring it up, it's too soon." My daughter turned her back to me, got in the car, and turned on the ignition. "She has a right to know the truth." Sarah spoke in angry, clipped words, her voice raspy but firm. She slammed her door and sped off at the same time. A dirt cloud billowed, then settled behind her.

Chapter Nine

I held my breath. Dare I let it disappear into the morning mist? Undefined syllables only I understood strained to escape my trembling lips. Who would hear? Who would care? I dove deep under the chilly, blue waters until the searing pain in my lungs drove me up.

-Emily, conversation in the lake

*J*sat at my favorite booth at The Station, nibbling mindlessly on potato skins and intermittently sipping an iced tea.

Jack arrived right on time.

"Don't you drink beer anymore?" He slid across from me and snatched an appetizer off my plate.

"Don't you ever ask first?" I wanted to slap his hand, but he popped it into his mouth and lifted a second one, slouching back in the padded bench, out of my reach. "I know Doc and Annie taught you how to say *please*."

"The Station makes these better than anyone else on the lake." He motioned for the waitress and she sauntered over, tugging the hem of her ridiculously short skirt.

"You want the usual Jack?" she whispered just loud enough for me to hear.

"Thanks, Janie." Jack cocked a half smile and winked. "Could you bring me a beer now, instead of with the meal?"

"Sure, anything you want, sugar. Does your lady friend want a refill?" She never turned an inch in my direction.

"Sure, bring Emily a pitcher," he murmured in a sexy tone I hadn't heard for years.

The waitress glanced over her shoulder and gave me the stink-eye, turned back around, and lowered her exposed cleavage smack in Jack's face before she left, satisfied she'd marked her territory.

"I thought we were just snacking while we talked. I don't have time to wait on steak for you."

"So you do remember."

"I've grilled your steak and onions enough times over the years to tell the demons in hell just how to rake it over the coal—and you with it!" I grabbed my purse and keys and started vamoosing sideways out of the booth.

"Come on, let's get down to business." He stuck out his foot, blocking my exit.

"Okay, so cut to the chase." I shoved my purse back against the wall, keeping the keys in my hand as I positioned myself directly across from him.

"Look, I just thought you should know how many times I've driven Nana into Reno to see her specialist and a lawyer. Doc and I handle all the general practitioner stuff at this end, but."

"What are you saying?" My shoulders slumped. Specialist. It had to be her heart. I grew quiet when the waitress returned with Jack's drink.

"Here you go, Jack." She placed the open bottle within his reach.

"Thank you." He waited for her to leave before continuing. "She has leaky heart valves, Em. Plural. Her last echo cardiogram wasn't good." Jack took my hand, keys clinking. "Do you understand what I'm telling you?"

"This," I cleared my throat, "this is an office visit, isn't it?" A low hum buzzed in my head and got stuck somewhere between my ears. The din of the restaurant faded as the facade of faces around me warped into a vortex far away. Jack was saying something else. I wondered if it was important. Maybe detailed medical jargon, more descriptive than "leaky." I knew that was for my personal benefit. Simple, plain, and crystal clear, old friend to old friend, as if I had actually allowed him the courtesy of civil conversation.

"Are you going to be okay? You're squeezing kind of tight there, Em."

"I'm sorry. Didn't realize I was." Jack shook his hand in mid-air after I released my grip. I dropped my keys. "How long?"

"Let's just say it's a good thing you came for the summer. I think she needs you right now more than you need her."

No wisecracks or irritating jokes. I didn't know what to do with this version of Jack. He looked kind of lost, unnaturally subdued. Jack was never quiet. I believed he was incapable of attentive silence outside of his doctor's office.

Coffee cups jangled as the waitress brewed a pot of freshly ground beans. I sipped my iced tea and dipped the lemon slice into the glass. The thought of Nana not being around never had occurred to me before. She was always there, anticipating needs with plenty of her "pluck and vigor."

"How could I be so selfish not to notice?" The words escaped, leaving me wide open.

"I think we're all a little guilty there." He swished the remnants of amber gold hops in his bottle before he lifted it high, examining the liquid contents. "She doesn't have long. Actually, she's living on borrowed time already."

"Really? Borrowed from who? Or is it whom?" All of a sudden I felt trapped. I wanted to flee. Anywhere was better than where I sat, listening to this news.

"I guess from the God she loves so much. But I don't see him helping her." He pursed his lips on the rim of the bottle, but set it back down without drinking a single drop.

"What will I do without her?" I stared out the window at the passing blur of cars. I tried desperately to hold in any show of emotion in front of him.

"I don't know, Em." His voice cracked, barely audible. "But she doesn't have a lot of time for you to figure that out."

I bit my lower lip until my teeth pressed in so hard it hurt. "How long?" I asked again. Maybe if I kept asking Jack would say something different.

"A couple of weeks, maybe a couple of months." He hung his head and clasped his hands together. "You need to know she has filed a Do Not Resuscitate order. "

I wanted to tell Jack I appreciated him telling me. Hard as I tried to verbalize a sentence, nothing came out of my mouth. Emotion and reaction hit a road block. All life-giving flow was restricted in the valves of my heart chamber. Was this how Nana struggled to breathe day to day?

Jack's eyes were red and watery. For all our troubles, there was never any question about the depth of his love for Nana. "I'm sorry, so sorry." He pushed the beer aside and cupped his hands together in the middle of the table.

I laid my head on top of his hands. Tears began to trickle.

Jack gently pulled out one hand and placed it on my head.

The waitress's apron appeared at my eye level. She grunted something, then the apron was gone. Ceramic plates pinging on the metal warming counter broke the momentary sound barrier. Ice clinked in a glass across from me, a patron asking the waitress to come and refill his iced tea.

Janie's voice bellowed from the direction of the grill, "Sure, sugar, anything you want. I'll bring you an entire pitcher. Jack, do you want me to get that plate for you now, or should I leave it under the heat lamps a little longer?"

Jack didn't answer.

She bristled by our table and converged on the guy in the booth across from us, pouring tea past the top of his glass. It splashed and ice cubes bounced to the floor.

She gasped. "Oh, dear, what have I done? Let me get a towel and mop this up for you." She grabbed the plastic pitcher.

"You did that on purpose!" He bumped the table as he stood to dry off his saturated Hawaiian shirt and shorts.

"I assure you, I did not," she hissed through her teeth like a snake taunting its prey before devouring it whole. Then she turned our way. "Can I bring your steak now, Mr. Conner?" The pitcher of tea landed on the tabletop, barely missing my head.

"We'll take it to go," Jack answered crossly.

"But I kept it warm for you."

"I said to go!" He flashed a scowl.

The strain between the two of them seemed to me to be more involved than changing an in-house order to take out.

"Fred," the waitress shouted, "make that last order to go." Then she turned to the soggy patron. "This meal is on me. I'm so sorry about your shirt." She pulled a towel out of her apron pocket, rubbed the shirt, and dabbed his khakis.

"Well, thank you for comping my meal," he responded sounding somewhat astounded.

"I's the least I can do." When she bent forward to wipe his table, her skirt raised like a flag. After grabbing a Styrofoam to-go container, she whisked my remaining potato skins away and dumped them in the box. I took it and stood to leave.

Jack escorted me to the register, paid for my appetizers, our drinks, and his meal, which the cook brought over to the cashier. He opened the door for me. "We can go sit across the street at the beach and eat if you'd like."

"I'm not really hungry. Can we take it back to the cabin?"

"Sure." He reversed direction toward the parking lot.

"We can eat at the kitchen table. Nana's out with Doc in Reno. But you probably already knew that." I realized he and Doc must have partnered in this planned intervention.

"The kitchen's fine." He opened the driver's door for me. "I'll follow you home. You okay to drive?" His voice transitioned back into physician mode.

"Yes. I'll be fine." I caught my breath. "Thank you for being honest with me."

"I'm here if you need someone, Em. So is Doc." Jack didn't close the door until I buckled up and turned the key in the ignition.

I watched him jump into his Jeep, then I pulled out into traffic. I drove slowly until Jack caught up. Tears flowed and as hard as I tried to concentrate on the road ahead of me.

Nana is dying. Life will never be the same without her.

Chapter Ten

Jack

Language is more than speech. One can speak clearly and definitively without being understood. Sometimes it's the things we don't say that speak the loudest. Often we utter careless words that wound to the core of another's soul, never knowing the depth of the carnage we have inflicted.
  —Something Nana said to me a while back.

The last patient left early, so I had an entire hour to myself for lunch. I checked out my office window to see if Em was still on the beach. She hadn't budged. I stumbled out of my work clothes and into my swimming trunks, snatched a towel and adjusted my sunglasses. I made a quick dash for the door before the phone rang or any patients showed up early.

"Want to go for swim?" I didn't have to urge Hem off of his bed. He leaped through the door ahead of me and ran straight to the water, his webbed-paw, built-in fins, ready to get some action.

I hoped Emily would notice my dog hit the waves, but she never looked my way. Hemingway was already in the water and he wouldn't be back for as long as I'd let him get his doggy paddle laps in.

It was now or never. I walked to where she was camped out on the beach.

I stood in front of Emily, casting my silhouette over her. "I haven't seen my biological parents in over a decade. My mother never moved back from Paris, and my father is now married to his third child bride, Kiki. They live in Maine." I blurted out a fairly recent summary of my overtly dysfunctional family history.

"Why are you telling me this now, Jack?" Emily squinted up at me blocking the sunlight with her hand.

"Don't talk about it much, every once in a while with Doc when we have a slow day." I spread out my beach towel and situated myself next to her, then adjusted my Ray-Ban's. "If we're going to be friends again, I thought I should share some of the things you don't know about me."

"Okay."

"What you been thinking about?" I asked. "You've been stretched out on that old rag of a towel for at least an hour. That threadbare thing's been around since we were kids."

"About the day Annie died." Emily ran her hand over the multi-striped pattern and smoothed out the pebbly lumps underneath. Gritty sand still coated her feet from her swim. She smelled strangely alluring of suntan lotion and sweat. She dug her toes under inches of sand and looked out across the lake.

"Why think about that sad day?"

"I've always wondered how different things might have ended up if I had gone out with them. Maybe Annie would still be here." Emily continued sitting there staring out at the lake.

"Don't torture yourself like that," I brushed a few strands of her hair behind an ear and hoped she would keep talking.

"I wanted to go with them in the worst way. But I didn't want to contradict Annie in front of Sophia. I knew she wanted help for Doc, but I'd suited up intending to spend the day boating around the lake with them. Even packed a lunch for myself in the picnic basket." Her voice droned on, her eyes fixated towards the east shore.

"At least you were here to help Doc through the initial shock. Not off on some Alaskan fishing trip." I didn't think she'd actually heard what I just said.

What had spurred her to talk about this after seven years? In many ways, Emily remained a mystery to me. Every time I thought I'd figured out her out, she'd surprise me.

"I've gone over the *what ifs* in my head for years. I know I could have helped Annie. Sophia was too young and not a strong swimmer."

Emily's face clouded with desperation laced with a lethal dose of self-loathing. I knew that look well. I couldn't get her to look at me when she talked.

"How do you know we wouldn't have lost you too?"

She didn't answer my question but rattled on about the senseless waste of a life, the self-destructive behavior of the teenagers involved, and how they turned on each other like a pack of starving wolves. How Sophia has never truly been the same, struggling with survivor guilt to this day.

"Sophia stopped by to see Doc for the anniversary of the accident." I pushed my glasses up to rest on the bridge of my nose and crossed my legs.

"I know, I walked right past her and didn't recognize her." A beach ball rolled our direction. Emily tossed it back to a couple of kids playing beside us. Their laughter filled the warming air with pure exhilaration as they went right back to their dodge ball game.

I moved my toes as the water rushed up and lapped about our feet, soaking the edges of our towels before receding. The constant rhythmic motion was both soothing and cleansing, washing away sandy grit as each wave rippled in along the shoreline. Mesmerized, I studied the frothy capped rows farther out, rise and peak, then roll in with perfectly synchronized order. "I find comfort in Annie's faith."

"You're not going religious on me, are you?" She pulled off her wide-rimmed sunglasses to look straight into my tinted lenses.

"I'm just saying Annie wasn't afraid to die, that day or any other. Of course she loved being here with Doc, and us too. But I swear, she knew something I don't." I tossed a handful of stones out into the water. They splashed and plunked, breaking the flow, then the waves rolled in again in a reassuring pattern.

"Jackson Luke Conner, I do believe you have surprised me for the first time in years." A big grin broke across her face, spiked by a hint of natural delight.

"It's good to see you smile."

She laughed, snorting intermittently. I pulled back as she slumped on my shoulder, then buckled over, giggling like an inebriated barfly.

"I'm sorry, can't help it. Very inappropriate behavior, eh Jack. Look," she turned around and attempted to explain herself. "I'm trying to work through some things I've never really dealt with, Annie's death being one of them." She wiped absent tears from her eyes, and in record time the walls of the mighty fortress behind which she found refuge went up and her smile faded.

"I wonder what might have been different if I'd been there too. Maybe we can help each other out." I knew this was a risky suggestion, especially on the heels of her spontaneous outburst. But what was I waiting for?

"You were in Alaska, there wasn't anything you could have done. I, on the other hand, was standing right there on the dock, with one foot ready to board the boat."

"The one time Doc needed me, I was as far away as I could be."

"I just moped off with Doc like a petulant child." Her eyes were fraught with anguish, pleading for absolution.

THE LANGUAGE OF THE LAKE

I longed to say anything that would lift the self-imposed burden she'd taken on. "Annie would never have wanted you to do this to yourself. You've got to know that."

She rested on my arm. "Do you ever wish we were kids again? Life was so easy then." She pointed to the kids who were down in the water now, shrieking, splashing, and squealing without a care in the world.

I knew nothing I could say now would give her the healing answers she was searching out. From an early age, Emily faced the deaths of the people she loved. And it wasn't going to stop now.

I held her stroking her hair in slow, fluid movements, hoping to help her relax. For several minutes she was silent, breathing in heavy sighs. Her heart pounded fast against my shoulder. Fear does that, accelerates the heart rate at rapid pace. I see it all the time in my patients.

"Thanks, Jack."

Her cheeks has a reddish twinge, not quite sun burnt yet. Her heartbeat steadied over the next few minutes and her breathing pattern regulated. We sat there, listening to the waves roll in and out, the children's enthusiastic banter, and dogs barking, my Hemingway the ring leader. A cool breeze skimmed by.

She straightened and tossed her sunglasses aside. "I'm going out for a swim. Do you want to come?"

I peeled mine off too. "Yeah, I do." The massive body of water before us was irresistibly inviting. It seemed to roll without end, as blue as the cloudless sky.

I started to run, with Emily close behind. She caught up and we dove in when it was deep enough. We swam together for about half an hour, then I headed back to shore and sat on the beach to dry off. I'd have to scrub up and get back to work soon.

She went out, farther than she should have. Some people walk off grief, some drink it down. Emily swims it out. I watched her for a short time. She'd swim to the right, somersault, and swim to the left. She'd disappear underwater and surface past the buoys and backstroke toward the shore. As soon as she got remotely close to civilization, her feet kicked up and under she went again.

There was a distinct repetitive configuration to her solo journey: east, west, south and north. The distance in each direction varied but the pattern remained the same. Not north, south, east and west. Still, it formed a cross section, like a search grid. Above the water, under the water, as deep under as she could go, probably barely above the sandy bottom would be my guess.

I knew she wouldn't be coming back to chat with me. She was busy working things out. She didn't even need to talk with me earlier. She could have just as easily talked out loud to the dead span of air surrounding her. Then she wouldn't have had to deal with my conversation and questions slowing down her continual cycle of recycling.

Feeling foolish and angry, I gathered up my towel and headed to the office. Hemingway barked at me. He wasn't ready to come on dry land.

"Jack, where are you going?" Emily shouted.

I hadn't noticed her walk up behind me. "What do you care?"

"What's wrong with you?"

"You're what's wrong with me." I snapped my towel into the air twice, and bolted around to lock on her eyes.

"What did I do?"

I dug my feet in the sand and stood there. She looked at me like I was nuts. I know that's what she was thinking, that I was behaving like a little boy having a temper tantrum. Yep, that's what she'd tell herself alright. It's always irresponsible Jack's fault.

"Jack, we were getting along fine."

I don't think so. "Lunch is over. I have patients waiting." I heard her saying something about me needing to relax a little as I headed up the beach stairway and back toward the office. Hemingway bounded up from the lake.

She actually ran after me. Now if that wasn't a first. Emily coming after me instead of me going to her. Breathless, she caught me half-way up the path, panting and gasping.

"Wait! Jack. Please."

I spun around. She was dripping wet, her feet and zories encrusted in a layer of sand. Hemingway raced up behind her, and shook, spraying water everywhere.

"I didn't mean to upset you talking about Annie like that. I know how much you loved her. I'm sorry."

An Emily Maxwell Taylor apology was a rare occurrence, an earth-shattering event as a matter of fact. Too bad a couple of squirrels scampering across the path between us were my only witnesses.

It was the first time she had ever apologized to me. *Who was this?*

"I know you have to go back to work. I don't want to make you late." She turned to leave, then faced me and said, "Annie loved you, Jack."

The woman walking away from me wore her one-piece like a fashion model. There was a fluid grace and beauty to her every movement. Emily was unaware of her effect on men. That was part of what appealed to me. She never knew that the girls didn't like her when we were growing up because they were seething with jealousy. They wanted to be her. I regretted sleeping with most of those empty and easy women she once called her friends.

The scent of her tanning lotion lingered in the air, coating my senses, leaving me bound in willing captivity. What hypnotic power did she possess over me?

Those stupid squirrels blazed over my feet on their return trek across the path. I would almost swear they were laughing at me. Hemingway chased them up a tree.

One of my next patients shouted through the screen door of my office. Brother and sister Sherry and Sean McLaughlin took turns bellowing different orders at me and Hem. Pretty brazen for six and eight year olds.

"Are you coming inside, Mr. Conner?" Sherry asked.

I strolled through the door they held open for us, bare-chested in my swim trunks, beach towel wrapped around my waist. The women snickered, whispering. I hid behind my Ray-Bans and made a beeline for my office.

My dog scurried to the kids. "Good boy." Sean scratched behind his ears.

"Look," Sean lifted his shirt. "Almost all our chicken pox have fallen off." Marching a step behind, Hemingway followed, leaving wet prints on the floor.

"You picked yours off!" Sherry corrected her him. "Have you had chicken pox yet?" she tried to examine my chest.

I stepped back. "Yes, when I was about your age. Now, you two go to the waiting room and stay there with your mother until I call for you." I ushered them out the door and closed it, allowing only Hem, to enter.

"After all these years he's still smitten with Hannah Mae's granddaughter." Mable Parker's voice bore through the door loud and clear.

"I didn't know." Sarah McLaughlin answered. "He's something of a womanizer. But a great PA."

"What's a womanizer?" Sean asked.

"Be quiet," his mother hushed him.

"But you said Mr. Conner is a womanizer!" Sean hollered.

"You sit in that chair and don't say another word." Sarah yelled right back.

"You hear that, Hemingway?" I murmured. "My patients think I'm a womanizer, but a great PA." I grunted flippantly. "So, now I know the truth."

My faithful companion slunk to his oversized sheepskin bed, circled three times and flounced in the center, his front paws extending over the bulky edge.

"Womanizer." I threw my shirt over my head and forced my arms in the sleeves but it was sticking to my damp skin. "But, a great PA" I sat in my desk chair struggling to get my legs in my jeans over my trunks. Slipping into my shoes, I stubbed my big toe on the rug and blasted out an expletive that certainly barreled through to the next room with brusque clarity.

Hemingway sat on his haunches and barked a reprimand. And another.

"Wow. Mr. Conner said the s-word!" Sean called out.

"So?" Sherry retorted. "Daddy says it all the time."

"No, he doesn't." Sarah barked louder than Hemingway. "Both of you sit in those chairs and be still."

I stepped out to the frosty greeting of Mable's aghast expression and the McLaughlin children's displeasure at doing their time-out in the waiting room chairs.

"Hello, Jack," Sarah said. "Are you ready for the kids now?"

"Yes. I just need to wash up." I forced a smile. Hemingway trotted behind on my heels. "Good boy, stay." I pointed to his bone on the carpet, under the window by Mabel.

He looked pleadingly at me. "Go, sit."

"Come on, Hemmingway, come to Mama." Mabel reached out and snagged his collar. "We'll just sit here and chat until Mr. Conner is ready for me. Good doggie." She nudged then dragged him to her side, while articulately relaying a litany of her current aches and pains in detailed medical jargon most first year med students would envy. It was a long list.

I stood at the sink and washed my hands and arms. Sarah had shushed her children into silence and marched them into my office. When she closed the door, Hemingway let out a pathetic cry followed by a repeated succession of high pitched howls and yowls. Low moaning doggie pleas for deliverance went on and on.

"Is Mrs. Parker killing your dog?" Sean asked.

Chapter Eleven

Jack

The letters and syllables we learn as children are intended to teach us a myriad of words with which we can communicate and build relationships. Language involves listening. One person speaks and another listens. Some of us are more apt to verbalize than to sharpen our auditory skills. The silence between the sentences can be deafening, or respectfully allow time for reflection. Every time we open our mouths to talk, we make choices. Our words can encourage, condemn, compliment, flatter, deceive, educate, illuminate, manipulate, vindicate, honor, confuse, destroy, protect, annoy. Choose carefully when talking with your patients.

- Teaching conference for Physician's Assistants

"Doc, I don't think I've felt as exhausted as I do right this minute." I smacked closed a file on the desk in front of us, tossing my pen aside. I was done. The rest of the notations could wait until tomorrow. Our end-of-the-day file blitz in my office hit the wall.

"It was an unusually drawn-out afternoon. We never took a break, or lunch for that matter. Must be the backlash from the end of the school year. I'd rather keep busy, Jack. Lots of babies and children today with asthma, hay fever, the flu. Sure do hope there isn't another bug getting ready to made the rounds." Doc pushed his reading glasses up higher on his nose, and continued writing in the file he was working on.

I settled back in my chair and put my feet up on my stack of files. "I can't even remember who I've seen today. It's all one big haze. Doc, I seem to be losing my drive. My incentive to plug along is diminishing day by day. I used to be able to push myself to the limit and beyond. Now I watch the clock tick away the hours and count down to quitting time. I have to make myself focus in on a patient's face or my mind drifts and I realize I haven't heard a word they were saying."

Doc stopped, closed the file he was working on, and turned his chair in my direction. "It's called burn-out, son. I've been watching you for a while now and it seems to me you are having a difficult time concentrating. I'm concerned you have forgotten your initial motivation for becoming a physician's assistant. Do you remember why you chose this profession?"

"You are the reason I made this career choice. You encouraged me from day one when I was floundering about aimlessly in college. There wasn't anything that interested or challenged me like becoming a P A." I lowered my feet to the floor. "I love what I do, Doc. Why isn't it enough anymore?"

"You're the only one who knows the answer to that question. But I think it's been eating you up for a couple of years now." Doc sealed eye contact with me before I could glance away.

"I can't put my finger on any one thing that seems to be different. My feelings haven't changed about my work or my patients. I'm certainly not bored. There's too much information to keep abreast of. With the medical field advances and all the new technology and procedures, I can barely keep up."

A headache began throbbing in my right eye. Rubbing my temples, I tried to ease the pain away. "There just seems to be a lack of satisfaction. The sense of fulfillment has ebbed away. Some mornings," I pressed hard and held my fingers in place, "I have to drag myself out of bed to drive in here. I used to look forward to a day's work. I didn't care how long the hours got or what the day brought." I released when the pulsating dulled, bringing slight relief.

"How's your private life, if you don't mind me asking?"

"I'm not seeing anyone. Haven't for months. I wanted to be free to spend some time with Emily while she's here this summer." I cleared a thickening in my throat.

"So you made changes in anticipation of her visit?"

"I guess you could say that."

"Why?" His voice deepened.

"We have unfinished business that needs to be dealt with. You know that."

"Why can't you deal with it and continue your life the way it was before she arrived?" He reclined in his chair and slipped his glasses in his shirt pocket.

"Em would never pursue anything with me if I was involved with another woman."

"Did it ever occur to you the same principle may apply to your work? Perhaps you need to make some permanent changes in your private life too. Tone it down a bit. Find a sense of balance instead of always living on the edge. You have a wild side, Jack. You can't go on forever the way you have all these years. Are you going to go into your fifties and sixties sleeping around the way you do?"

"I have toned things down since Maggie's husband left her because of our affair. I never meant to break up their marriage. She and I had an understanding from the start.

Everything got out of control at the end. It was a mess." My chair creaked as I bent forward, cupping my head in my hands, resting my elbows on the hard, solid oak.

"Affairs have a way of going in that direction. Someone always ends up getting hurt. There is a ripple effect that reaches out and drags down unsuspecting innocents: the spouse, the children. Exposure is painful, humiliating, and sometimes very public."

"We tried to be discrete. For over a year no one suspected a thing." I shifted my eyes away toward the door hoping Doc would drop it, let this go.

"Wrong. I knew from the beginning. You have a pattern, Jack. Are you aware of that?" Doc's tone was firm but not harsh.

"What do you mean? I'm not attracted to the same kind of woman. I like variety." I squirmed in my chair.

"Son, you set out after impossible relationships every time. I may have used the word relationship too loosely here. With a married woman, you don't have to make any kind of a commitment." His piercing blue eyes penetrated deep. "You seek out women to have sex with, looking for a satisfaction that never seems to be quenched."

"Is that what you think of me? Apparently some of my patients would agree with you." I felt the need to defend myself. "I overheard Sherry McLaughlin say something similar yesterday." He didn't look surprised as I thought he would. "She said I am a good PA, but I'm a womanizer. She said it in front of her kids and Mable."

"I see you trying to fill a void that you haven't been able to fill in over twenty years of fooling around." He drew closer, his brow creased, "Even if you had married Emily, you would have cheated on her."

"You're wrong. I would never have cheated on Em." I shoved my stack of files until they toppled over the desk top and landed on the floor in a scattered heap.

"Just leave them there for now." Doc stretched over the middle of my desk and placed a hand on top of mine. "Even Emily can't fill that bottomless hole in your soul, Jack. She's plenty busy working things out for herself."

He squeezed my hand tight. "You are the best PA on all four shores. But do you want more out of life than just a job? Am I hitting home?"

"I don't know. To be honest, I am kind of lost these days." I clenched my palm closed.

Letting go, Doc sat back into the curve of his chair, running his hands back and forth over the wooden arms, gripping the oak claw ends.

"Partying isn't the fun it used to be. I'm the old guy now. No one knows me for who I am. Not even me." Shaking my head, I let my hair fall over my face like armor. "What am I missing?"

"Do you have peace inside, Jack?"

"I have no idea what that means."

"Do you want to?"

The setting sun cast a streak of light across Doc's face from the window in front of him. I studied his demeanor. He was beginning to show his years, mostly in the worn features weathered by lack of tending to himself. Though his eyes were filled with compassion, I wasn't sure I wanted to hear what might come next.

"Of course I do. Who in their right mind wouldn't? That can't be the answer."

"Is that at least in part what you are looking for?"

"Doc, I thought I had it all. A terrific job that I love. I earn good money. I have freedom to ski, kayak, backpack, hike, golf, hang glide. Whatever sports these mountains offer, I have given it a try. But none of those things matter anymore." I pinched my forehead, trying to ward off the returning headache.

"I have to be careful sleeping around with all the STD's and AID's out there. These younger women are reckless in a way I've never experienced before. You can't trust them to be straight with you about who they've been with."

"Have you considered the fact that you probably need to get tested as a precaution because of your lifestyle?" Doc spoke in a quiet tone.

"Do the math. You are long overdue. The figures are staggering today. This AIDS is the granddaddy of them all, Jack." His voice cracked.

"Yeah, Doc, I've done the math in my head. I don't like the sum I come up with either." Sweat beaded on the back of my neck.

"What are you going to do about it?"

"I suppose I should get tested sometime."

"Soon?" He moved in closer.

"Do you really think it's necessary to act quickly?" The clock ticked, seven p.m..

"How would you advise a patient who came to you with your track record?"

I glanced behind Doc at the bulletin board plastered with pictures of my patients. Some I had talked into these very tests. My shoulders sagged.

"Jack, I know you are interested in Emily. Would you sleep with her before you knew beyond a shadow of a doubt you aren't going to pass anything so devastating onto her? I know how you feel. You need to be responsible and face this head on. There are always consequences for our actions. Sometimes it takes time for things to catch up with us but, eventually it comes right back to us."

Doc gave me a few minutes to let it all soak in. He waited while I remained silent.

I straightened. "I know I would tell a patient to get tested and to do it before they had sex with anyone else. Sit tight. Wait until the results are back."

"Then heed your own advice, and we'll face whatever is ahead together. You know I'll be here for you."

"You and Annie always were."

"The numbers don't look good for me if you go by the law of averages." I hedged momentarily. "Write up the lab slip. I'll head to Reno first thing in the morning."

Doc went into his office and came back within seconds with a pad and his stamp. He checked off boxes down a column of the page. After he signed the bottom and stamped the top, he tore off it off and handed it to me.

"That was quick."

He patted my shoulder. "You will be glad to have this behind you. The truth sets you free, son." He pulled me up into a hug and held tight.

"I sure hope you're right." Fear ran through me, penetrating to my bones. It's different being on the receiving end of this medical dilemma. I'd written these slips and sent patients off without any more than a pat on the shoulder. When results came back positive, I tried to be empathetic, but I could read the instant fear in their faces, like a monstrous beast was about to devour them. Doc held on to me out of love.

"Thanks, Doc." Backing away, I realized I was shaking.

"We'll come through this together." His voice trembled but his eyes spoke volumes.

"I'm counting on it. Can you cover my first few patients?" I swallowed the lump in my throat and rung my hands together, trying to arrest the jitters.

"Done. Now, let's see if there's enough leftover pot roast, and throw in some extra potatoes and carrots. I'm as hungry as the bears that are dining at the neighborhood trash can delicatessens." He followed me into the kitchen and flicked on the light.

"Those old bears are getting bold these days. I hear they've been hitting some of the restaurants on a daily basis. They've figured out how to unlock the dumpsters. Mac was closing over at the pizza place in Carnelian Bay, and he surprised a Mama bear with two cubs." I grabbed a cast iron skillet off a hook over the stove. "There were still a few customers inside. He back-stepped all the way to the kitchen door, then hollered for everyone to get out." I chuckled, remembering Mac's sheepish face when he told me the story.

"I guess a hungry bear is as formidable as a hungry man." Doc took a container out of the fridge at the same time I tried to light a fire on the stove burner. My hand shook and one match after another burned down. Doc steadied my wrist until the flame caught with the last match from the box. A blue ring of fire and the strong smell of gas blasted my senses awry.

Chapter Twelve

Jack

Old friendships change. Sometimes one person out-grows the other or it's a mutual drifting apart. A strange uncomfortableness develops in the relationship, like peeling off clothing that shrank while you're wearing it. Jack's washed our laundry and ironed out the wrinkles. He put my favorite little black dress on a hanger in the hallway. The longer I walk by and look at it, the more I wonder if it will fit again.

- Journal entry, Emily Maxwell Taylor,

June 17, 1995

After Rosa finished cleaning and closed the door, I swung my swivel chair around and hoisted my feet up on the desk to give the old dogs the rest they deserved.

Doc chuckled. "Feeling it a little today, Jack?"

"I'm rethinking my plans to head into Tahoe City tonight. Maybe a hot bath instead of a night out." I kicked off my shoes and massaged my throbbing feet, then stretched around to rub out the ache in my lower back.

"You're welcome to spend the night in my guest room. I have a hospital fundraiser dinner to attend at Sunnyside. You want to tag along?" Doc stood, snatched his black corduroy sport coat off the back of his chair, and brushed back a tuft of silvery hair.

"I'll pass on the fundraiser, but take you up on the spare room."

"Okay." Doc gave my shoulder a squeeze on his way out the door. "Get some shut-eye. We have another jam-packed day tomorrow."

Too tired to move, I relaxed against the hard oak for support, and stared at the ceiling. After a minute or so, I raised my finger to my mouth and repeatedly strummed my lower lip, "Buumh, buumh, buumh..." Amused, I kept making sounds in varying tones and pitches. They echoed in the empty office, like a village idiot's one-man symphony.

"Putting your college degree to the test today?" Emily's voice alarmed me.

I swung my feet off the desk knocking a stack of mail to the carpet. "How long have you been standing there?"

"Oh, long enough." She laughed.

Scrambling to pull on my socks and shoes, I tripped over the wastebasket and smacked my head into the side of the solid oak secretary.

"Ouch!" I landed sprawled out, facing the tip of her spike-heeled, skin-tight boots.

My loyal pet ran up licked my ear, my hair, the inside of my left nostril.

"I thought you might like to grab dinner in town, but I see you need to visit the nurse first." Emily stooped down, and gathered up the envelopes.

Faded jeans hugged her fanny and thighs. Shiny white pearl buttons fastened in a straight row up a burgundy sweater to her chest, deceptively demure. Honey-blonde hair swept across her back, cascading in soft, gentle waves with her every movement.

"Dinner sounds great." Collecting myself and my wounded pride, I laced up my shoes, stood steady and ready to go. Hemingway wagged his tail and headed for the door. "Stay, boy."

"Really? Doc mentioned on his way out you were probably turning in early tonight after a soak in the tub." Emily smiled coyly as she replaced the mail on my desk.

"Better put some ice on that bump." She brushed her fingers over the swollen bulge developing on my sweaty forehead. Chanel perfume lingered lightly.

I'd given her a bottle years ago. I wondered why she used it tonight. "By the time we get to the restaurant, I'll be fine."

Noting her raised eyebrow, I went in the kitchen and tossed a few ice cubes into a baggie. "The Station's open. We could share soup and salad," I suggested, slipping into my jeans jacket and combing my fingers through my unruly mop of hair.

"Sounds good but I'm driving." She held out her hand for my keys.

Hemingway jumped up expectantly at the familiar sound of metal jingling.

"Go lie down on your bed, boy." I commanded. He slunk over and plopped down objecting with a pouting whine that wasn't going to get him anywhere tonight.

"You didn't damage this fine musical instrument when you tumbled did you?"

Emily took the key ring off my finger and held the porch door open. "Gentlemen first," she insisted, with all the charm of her Nana's Southern hospitality.

"No permanent finger injuries." I assured her in passing.

"Good, PA Conner. Your patients will be glad to know you can stay on schedule tomorrow." She led the way to my Jeep.

She was enjoying this way too much. I wondered what brought her over to begin with, especially in such good humor. But it didn't matter. I was about to have her all to myself for a nice long evening.

"Keep that ice pack in place for twenty minutes." She admonished when it slipped off to the side while I fumbled to fasten my seat belt.

"Yes, ma'am." The cold eventually numbed the throbbing pain in my head to a dull twinge.

"I like being behind the wheel with you in the passenger seat." Emily's eyes sparkled with that familiar mixture of mischief and fire I never could resist.

"You're in good spirits this evening." I winced as we jolted over a pothole.

"Yes, I am." She grinned all the way into town and right up to when we were escorted to our table. A quick scan of the restaurant indicated that Nancy was not on shift tonight.

I pondered the wisdom of pursuing the reason for her change of heart, but decided to let it go and enjoy the moment. We sipped wine by flickering candlelight, which cast a warm glow through the red hurricane glass sitting in the center of our table.

Hours of conversation over dinner blended the past decades. I'd been waiting for this, though I had no idea what I'd finally done to deserve it.

"You're a good man, Jack Conner." Emily's tone was smooth and silky, hushed by the clamor of voices crowding the restaurant.

"Is that the wine talking?" I half hoped it was, except Good Jack Man would be above such Neanderthal thinking. Which Jack was I tonight?

Her blue eyes narrowed. "No. I've been watching you, from our cabin window."

"Really? You're observing me?" I squirmed, edging toward the window.

"More like, noticing." She never broke her direct, infiltrating gaze.

"Are you stalking me, Emily. Not that I mind." I inhaled deeply, the winds of change were shifting and it appeared to be in my direction.

"You and Doc only close the screen door. Through the kitchen window Nana opens at dawn, I can hear everyone chatting as they come and go." She crinkled her nose and winked.

"Emily, have you been spying on me?" I winked right back and moved in closer. "I don't think you can hear anything from across the pathway, Emily." There had to be more to this than she was sharing.

"Just helping out an old friend with back-logged paperwork. You and Doc are several months behind, and I happen to have lots of free time to help in the file room." She sat against the wooden booth and took another slow sip of her Cabernet Sauvignon.

"When were you helping?" I raised my glass and swallowed the remaining cab.

"All last week, in the mornings. Jack, my intention isn't to upset you. I've always been Doc's patient. I've never known you as a professional. You're different at work. I watch your patients come and go. I can see how you interact with them while they're sitting in the waiting room and in your office. You take your time with each one. You listen. It reminds me of Doc."

She watched intently for my reaction, her face radiating shades of crimson in the elusive shadows of our secluded corner.

Obnoxious laughter rang out from the bar, making it harder to hear her responses.

Noisy customer banter was overwhelming our quiet conversation. I strained to pick up her words and pressed forward, still only able to discern bits and pieces between her sentences.

Holding out her glass for a refill, she dabbed the edge of her napkin at the outline of her mouth with her other hand.

I obliged and poured the last of the bottle. The band was setting up to play.

"You want to stay for a few dances?" My sore feet could handle slow dancing.

"I'd like that." She raised her glass for a toast. "To old friendships."

Only friendship? I frowned. "My glass is empty."

Em tipped most of her wine into my glass. She licked the overspill off the side of hers.

"And renewed beginnings." I clinked glasses and finished off the mellow wine just as the band's lead singer started belting out the ritual introductions starting with his girlfriend, Heather, the lead female vocalist.

"Hard Liners is one of my favorites." I shouted. "Perfect mix of rock and jazz."

Daryl Bannister opened the evening with "Foxy Lady," a worthy rendition of Jimi Hendrix's best. I gestured for Emily to head out with me to the dance floor. The lights dimmed as the drummer and lead guitarist started up.

She slid out of the booth, dancing before her feet hit the floor, all the way to center stage. Strangers crushed in, breathing hard in tempo with the music. Emily swayed in rhythm with the guitar, her body an instrument she played in sync with the band. I slipped my hands around her waist, trying to strum along with her. She broke free, eyes closed, enraptured in the steady beat, her arms gracefully following every riff, as if she were one with the music.

I two-step shuffled, and gyrated my hips in her direction as the throng of dancers encroached. Limbs thrashed in stuffy pockets of alcohol-soaked air.

Eric Clapton's "You Look Wonderful Tonight" was next. We'd last danced to this song in our more congenial days. I pulled Emily close. She hadn't slow-danced with me since the 70s. She fixed her eyes on mine and wrapped her arms around my neck, but left ample space between our bodies as we moved in our minuscule spot on the dance floor. Occasional jabs didn't deflect her trance-like gaze. She nestled her head on my chest. My heart thumped and pulsated madly.

When the next song blared, I led her off the floor. "Let's get out of here!" The stale and smoky room was stifling. I couldn't breathe.

"Sure." She crawled across the bench and retrieved her purse when six hard-core regulars claimed our table.

"Hi Jack." Jenna, one of my exes, sidled up to me. "You leaving already? The party's just getting started." She clamped her lips on mine before I could block her advance. I backed away from my too-friendly former girlfriend. Emily looked up from the booth and rolled her eyes.

"Hurry up Jack, the moon is full tonight." Emily tugged on my sleeve and guided me to the door. Jenna snagged the end of my shirt tail, but I yanked away and bolted out.

The instant rush of the cold, fresh air hit like a blast of winter.

"Nice change isn't it?" I hurried her away from the club.

We buttoned up our jackets and darted across the street to Commons Beach. She ran ahead to the wooden stairway. Em locked arms with me as resonant waves rushing up to the shoreline made their own music as we descended to the beach. We sat on a log a few feet from the water's edge, captivated by the allure of the rolling chorus.

An incandescent moon lit the sky, its reflection generating a shimmering pathway across the lake, a seemingly endless road to a distant world bejeweled in twinkling stars.

"Don't you wish you could hike that path?" Emily sounded serious.

She'd stunned me with her spontaneous question, like the Emily of our youth.

"You mean walk on water? I think someone else has already done that."

"I'd love to swim from one end of the lake to the other." She kicked at the mixture of sand and rocks. "Let's do it Jack. Let's hike that trail! We may never get another chance." She unzipped her boots and flung them across the sand.

"Now I know it's the wine talking."

"That night-light in the sky will never go out, we can make it." Em shed her jacket, jeans, and top, down to her trademark one-piece Speedo.

"I see you came prepared. I was always up for a dip in the lake, especially skinny-dipping. But we can't hike on top of the water. All the way across the lake. At night." What was going on in that head of hers? I picked up her clothes and tried to talk sense into her.

"Why not Jack? Because no one else has done it before? Let's be the first. Maybe they'll erect a monument to us in Tahoe City like they did to Dr. Church." She traipsed across the beach, then tip-toed into the water, strolling leisurely along the shore.

"The Father of Snow Surveying?" I stalled for time hoping the cold air would snap her back to reality.

"We need more heroes like him today. Ordinary people who do extraordinary things." She shivered, stuttering out her last word, beckoning me to join her.

"I can't believe I'm saying this, but why don't you get dressed? Let's leave the swim for a day we haven't both been drinking."

"That's not like you. I'll bet if it was one of your bimbettes out here, you'd jump in."

She yanked the clothes out of my hand and dressed in a flash yelling at me the entire time. I couldn't discern one sentence looped into the next—she was speaking so fast, her arms flying in the air between outbursts. Emily wears anger like a second skin and I have always found it to be another of her strangely attractive features. Maybe a swim wouldn't be so bad.

"At least walk along the shore with me." She barked like an old seal. "Come on, just roll up your jeans."

"If I didn't know better, I'd think you were doing drugs."

"Please." She planted herself on a granite rock and waited.

"Maybe a walk will clear your head." I perched beside her, slipped out of my shoes and socks, and wiggled my toes in the gritty sand.

Teenagers drinking from a shared paper bag headed our way from the Mackinaw condos.

Emily tossed my shoes a safe distance from the lake and led me along the inky flatness of the shallow shoreline.

The lake was freezing and invigorating. My spine tingled as her warm palm pressed against the cool skin of my hand. Goose bumps tickled the hair on my arms.

"Caught you off guard tonight, didn't I?" She bent over to pick up a skipping stone.

"You could say that."

The moonlight illuminated her features, her petite frame and those endless blue eyes I wanted to swim in. Frequent gusts of chilly wind blew in from the south shore, whipping and lashing long tresses of hair across her eyes.

"I heard you talking with Sally Pritchard and her little boys this morning. You were comforting, reassuring, caring. There's a side to you I know absolutely nothing about." She gazed at the moon as water lapped up the sides of her feet and ankles, thirsty for a taste, before receding into the vast waters. Soon the tide rolled right back again, just like me.

"You know, I've always been here. You pushed me away."

"I know. I got bitter the last few years David was alive, mad at myself for letting my girls see me wallow in misery, not brave enough to break away and face the uncertain. Not a very healthy example for them to follow." She turned and placed her fingers over my lips.

I grasped her hands gently. "You were dying inside, piece by piece. It was agonizing to watch."

"You lost respect for me, didn't you?"

"Every year I figured you'd pick up and go, but you stayed until your spark burned down and almost disappeared. I knew for years he'd been cheating on you. It takes one to know one. Maybe I should have told you." I couldn't quite look her in the eyes. Was it too late? Were we both too damaged?

"I wouldn't have listened to you. I was too ashamed to admit I'd given up, even to myself." A tear trickled down her cheek. She didn't wipe it away.

We turned around and headed back. A rogue wave came crashing in, drenching our pants up to the knees. The constant rush was soothing, like the slow strum of a guitar. Music to my ears, an irrepressible harmony that played on without end, like an unfinished song.

"I'm not the person you think me to be. I haven't been for a long time." Her voice drifted off as she stared out into space. "The stars look like they invaded the sky tonight, one planet at a time."

"I'll walk this road with you. If you let me."

"Be a friend to me first," she whispered.

"I've always been your friend. It's been a while since you've been mine." I grabbed our shoes and stowed them under an arm. She looked like that little five-year old girl she was when we first met. We took our time walking. At the foot of the stairway we paused at the same time.

"Things will be different tomorrow," Emily said.

"You mean you'll have a clear head and maybe you'll regret tonight?" I tried to hide my disappointment by making light of her statement.

"I won't regret tonight. But you have other friends."

I glanced sideways and dug my hands in my pockets.

"Jenna, Janie, Shelley."

"Those friends are in my past, Em." I cut her off before she could get any further down a litany of names. "I can't change the past." I hung my head, knowing the list was much longer than she could possibly imagine.

"Neither can I. David will always be a part of my life."

"Why did you pick David instead of me? That day our lives separated, both David and I were at the regatta, offered you champagne, danced with you, sat at your table. Was it because he came in first in the race and I was second ?" I asked.

"You men all think alike. It had nothing to do with the race." She raised her voice. "Just before David crossed the finish line, Marsha Milford told me you'd spent the week before I came up at her place. You'd told me you were in Reno at a medical convention. She slithered up alongside me. I was pretty sure that forked tongue of hers was telling the truth before it rolled back. I hoped she would choke on it. No such luck. You lived with her for over a year after that regatta and never told me. I had to hear it on the street."

After all these years hearing why she'd chosen David over me stung. I exhaled a deep breath, straightened my shoulders and looked up the stairs to the highway. This wasn't going to be easy.

"I was a different person then. I never meant to hurt you. I figured you didn't know because she left for Hollywood, then Paris, Rome, and died in that plane crash covering a story in Africa. I would never do anything like that now." I paced my steps with hers up to the platform.

"If there's anything else I should know, tell me now. No surprises later."

"I wouldn't know where to begin." I figured it was all over. "The two decades you were married raising daughters, I partied. If not for Doc and Annie, I would have kept wasting my life like my parents did." I realized I had nothing to offer her. No stability other than my job.

"Well, Jack. We have to start somewhere, so this is day one." She headed up. "Just walk beside me and let's see how we do."

I kept time with her the rest of the way to the top.

The wine had worn off, fatigue set in, and my bump had gone down, so I drove back to the cabins and she talked. I listened and rolled down my window to let the brisk night air keep me alert. For the first time since out teens, I had hope.

We sat in the jeep parked in front of Doc's the night of sharing our confessions. We shed old baggage, dumped some non-essentials and decided to travel light in the future. I was good for short flights, not ready for cross-country or overseas yet. We both came with an accumulation of luggage and most of it had been sitting on a turn style, waiting to be reclaimed for an extended period of time. My claim check dangled from an elastic band, attached to the handle of my suitcase. I wasn't exactly sure where my next flight was going. Would it be a one-way or a round trip ticket?

Emily hugged me before she went inside. A hug, not a kiss. But it was enough of a new beginning for me. Would it be for her?

Chapter Thirteen

Emily

Brokenness is painful. None of us would willingly accept suffering if given a choice. Sometimes you'll find shards of glass along the lake's shoreline. Those of us who live here step carefully, scouting the sandy beach for a glint in the sunlight. Children run out with wild abandon and they are usually the ones cut by slivers of beer and soda bottles. Mommies doctor their little ones and after tears are wiped away, the children will venture out more cautiously across the beach. It doesn't keep them from jumping into the water and playing the day away with just a bandage to remind them that glass cuts, and it can cut deep.

–Doc's advice to Emily when she was a teenager.

I checked my make-up in bathroom mirror, combed my hair and gathered it in a clip before wandering into the kitchen where Nana sat waiting for me.

"You still in your pajamas?" She seemed surprised.

"Well, you are dressed early this sunny morning. Is the picnic basket already packed?" I tore a sprig of grapes out of the fruit bowl in the center of the table.

"I asked Doc and Jack to boat along with us today." She nudged me to finish getting ready, offering me jeans and a cotton blouse that smelled to be fresh off the clothesline.

I took the pile and inhaled a whiff as I bunched the clothes up under my nose. "Thanks, Nana." I glanced out the window. "Why isn't the *Martha* at the dock?"

"We'll be going out in Jack's boat, *The Tempest*. He's driving up to the pier. I didn't give him much notice this morning but he didn't seem to mind at all. Is something going on there, Emily?" Nana fussed with her scarf, tying it snug around her neck.

"I invited him out to dinner last night and we danced a few steps at The Station."

"I see … " She motioned for me to join her at the table.

"What?" I knew a chat was coming.

"Emily, do you remember much about Helen or Zack Conner?"

"Neither of Jack's parents ever gave me the time of day." I fidgeted in my chair, uncomfortable with her question. "I don't think they liked me."

"That alone should tell you something. That boy has been in love with you from the first time you two pelted snowballs at each other. How old were you, five?" She folded her hands into a neat pile in her lap, a river of blue veins more visible than flesh.

"I was five and he was seven." I tittered with satisfaction. "I won that first battle."

"He let you win." Nana's laugh had a somewhat irritating ring. "There wasn't a boy in the neighborhood who could stand against Jack Conner. They all tumbled down the hill trying. Papa and I watched you two through the kitchen window. Jack threw that snowball fight. He knew from the beginning how much you needed to win." Her usual congenial manners had somewhat slipped.

"No way. I won when he ran into a tree and fell. He just lay there while I fired away, until I sat on his back and claimed my victory."

"Hmmm. He couldn't get up?" She stifled a laugh that rattled out, a deep cough.

"Well, I guess he could have. Wait a minute, that faker has been bamboozling me from the beginning. Why did he let me think I won? What mockery."

"Emily, Jack's parents never cared about anyone but themselves. I've never met two more self-absorbed people. You, on the other hand, cared deeply from the beginning. Whether you were throwing snowballs, or learning to love. You give it everything. How could he not have been besotted with you?" Her eyes misted up.

"Why do you think he was always at Doc and Annie's? Jack needed to be loved up anyway he could." Nana took in a deep breath, and waited a few seconds before ex-haling. "I'm not excusing his years of philandering, filling that void big as a black hole."

A twinge of guilt filtered through my surfacing memories. "I used to be so jealous. Jack tagged along to everything." Though a part of me had always felt sorry for him.

"Jack's really Doc and Annie's son. They raised that boy from the first day he wandered down the road and landed at their doorstep after school. There were no parents at his home, and it was snowing hard. He had no key to let himself in his house. Annie took him in, fed him the first homemade meal he'd probably had in years. The Conner's wined and dined in fine restaurants, on TV dinners, or sometimes on nothing but alcohol. It was always feast or famine."

"Jack never said a word of this to me." I felt confounded by my own insensitivity.

"Of course not. He was ashamed. Children blame themselves and shoulder the burden of responsibility." Nana strained to keep her voice from cracking. "Usually the finger is pointed directly at the innocent, especially when alcohol and drugs are involved. Jack's folks hit him with a double whammy. Helen drank and Zachary used both illegal and prescription drugs."

"How do you know that?" I asked.

"Zack would periodically pester Doc and Annie for unnecessary prescriptions and any alcohol in the house. Then they would come over here. Always when the well ran dry at their place."

I hugged my clothes to my chest and drew in a deep sigh. "No wonder he was drawn to a family environment."

"Doc and Annie loved Jack and offered him a home. I never once heard either of them criticize or condemn his parents to him. Jack was hungry for love and discipline. He soaked it all up." Nana was cut off in mid-sentence by a knock at the door.

"Are you ladies ready to go?" Doc stood at the back screen.

"Just about." Nana beckoned him to enter. "Could you carry the thermos and basket on down? Emily and I will be right behind you."

"Certainly." Doc scooped up everything and was out the door in a flash. I swear I saw him wink.

Nana picked up where she'd left off. She fanned her hands in front of her on the table. "John raised that boy with all the love he showered on Isabella, and no less than he would have devoted to a flesh-and-blood son of his own."

"I remember Annie talking to Helen one day about adopting Jack. He was about ten. His parents had left him alone for over a week and Annie was beside herself. I understand now what Annie meant when she said Jack would never end up in 'the system.'"

"That was the Colorado ski trip after Zachary won big at the south shore casinos. That poor boy waited three whole days in the dead of winter before he bundled up and walked to Doc and Annie's. He arrived ahead of one of the biggest blizzards we'd had in years."

I always expected so much of Jack and credited him for little. Any affection I ever showed him was conditional.

"Every human being needs to be loved. We wither and die from the inside out without giving or receiving love." She rose from her chair, slightly tilting my way before steading where she stood.

"That is one of the truest statements I've ever heard."

"Come on. You get dressed and let's go have a nice afternoon together."

Doc took over the wheel of The Tempest and Jack came and sat behind me on the bench. We headed to Cave Rock on the east shore after our picnic. I loved this part of the lake. Turquoise water tinted the shallow, sandy shoreline. Cobalt blue defined the deeper waters with a wide swath of a lighter shade of azure the closer we got to the area just this side of the buoys.

"Remember when we used to race kayaks here as teenagers?" Jack shouted in my ear over the ruckus of passing speed boats.

"Yeah." I warmed inside remembering some of the best times in my life.

His hand lit gentle on the nape of my neck, his knees stalwart against my back.

I tried not to let on how much his touch moved me within. I'd held back each time he'd reached out to me during the picnic. He wasn't invasive, more tentative. But he was definitely sending signals, and waiting for some kind of a red or green light response.

We were on the last leg of the jaunt on our way home after going around the lake. The water glistened periwinkle blue, calm and stilled save for a waffle pattern imprinted on the surface, floating untouched until boats altered the stamp of perfection. I closed my eyes and inhaled vanilla and butterscotch, imagining the sweet scents from the Ponderosa pine trunks could drift on the mild breeze, all the way to our boat.

Tourists jetted about in droves on the Lake of the Sky, but it didn't bother me like it usually did when they engulfed the basin.

Jack ran his fingers through my hair.

I reclined against his legs. It was a natural reaction leaving me more, and more relaxed as the hours circling the lake neared an end.

The sun disappeared, playing behind a puff of cotton clouds. Jack sat beside me, cupped my chin in his timorous hand, and kissed me long on my lips. Doc sped up as he rounded the cove. The force of gravity pushed Jack against me until Doc pulled out of the turn and straightened out the boat. I didn't mind. In fact, I kind of liked the spontaneity of the moment. We finished the outing chatting like in the old days, nothing held back now. Jack mentioned his plans to go on an African safari next summer.

He remembers. That was all I talked about in my senior year of high school. I was so envious when Marsha Millford later went to Uganda to cover a story for one of the magazines for which she wrote. She died on the return flight. They published the piece with her own photography as a special memorial in her honor. She'd had a professional photographer with her, but they used her pictures instead.

"Have you charted out where you'll go?" I asked.

"Maybe you can help me research the best way to spend a month there."

"An entire month? What a dream."

"Jeff from Dr. Jennings' practice on the west shore can fill-in for me at work. I've already checked to be sure he's available next July."

"So it's pretty much a done deal?" *Don't start pulling back like you always do.*

"Except for charting out my itinerary. They offer pre-planned trips, but you have the option of compiling your own." Jack stared beyond the mountains.

I knew what he was saying, without saying it. It was open for me to consider and he knew I was interested, but wasn't going to push. This was a possible future for us. A lot could happen between now and then. "Jackson Luke, how will you astonish me next?"

We were heading up the Nevada side of the lake back into California. The rock formations molded spectacular clusters, both massive and diminutive. From Zephyr Cove, Sand Harbor, to Speedboat Beach, all up the east to the north shore. Being out on the water is different than looking at the lake from the shore. Only a part of Tahoe can be experienced from the beaches, a one-dimensional glimpse. The granite boulders under the transparent water bespoke a story of their own, tales of long ago, submerged in volcanic history.

My skin soaked up the rays of sunlight, the warmth a pleasant sensation. A spray of water washed inside the boat from a wake that an inexperienced boater, splashed before speeding off, driving way too close. Doused by the cold intrusion, I normally would have responded with loud words of indignation. Not today. I sat through the assault with calm acquiescence that startled me.

Surrounded by changing hues of blue, we were now in some of the deepest waters near the Cal/Neva border. Jack and I never got out the skis. Home was not far around the bend. I wanted this to last, this space in time, this unexpected bliss.

Doc guided The Tempest along Pine Cove pier and docked the boat. He and Nana had been unusually silent. Quite pleased with themselves those two conspirators.

One boat ride does not equal a reconciled friendship. Though Jack's kiss aroused a part of me I thought no longer existed, awakened spirit and soul, stirred life.

Chapter Fourteen

Water has a cleansing quality. When I swim in Tahoe, it washes over and through me in a way that I can't explain. I am keenly aware there is something more to it, something pure and reviving. Something I want and need.

- Emily, journal entry, summer 1980

"No, Sarah, don't say anything yet. She isn't ready. Give her more time." I raised my voice in frustration after repeating the same sentences for the third time.

"It's been over half a year, Mom. I'm lying keeping this secret." Stone, cold silence was followed by the usual click and dead tone.

I gripped the receiver. "Lying, cheating husband!" I slammed the handle on the black phone cradle hard enough to make it shake.

"Did Sarah call you?" Nana's voice didn't sound reprimanding, but a tone of disapproval rang in her words.

"No, I called her this time. She doesn't always pick up when I phone and hasn't been returning my messages." I wanted to scream but managed to hold back a rush of emotions running amuck. I considered redialing, but what was the use?

"Let's go sit a spell on the deck. I washed some grapes we can nibble on before breakfast." Nana's warm hand smoothed over my death grip on the kitchen step-stool before she walked out the screen door. I swatted repeatedly at the dangling coiled telephone cord, batting it against the wall before it could strike back at me like a biting snake. I had no more tears. The well dried up and left me barren. Taking in a deep breath, I followed Nana to the deck.

Patient and unruffled, Nana waited, fluffed up with a mountain of pillows in chaise lounge facing the lake. I padded barefoot across squeaky wooden planks and wriggled in the chaise next to her. Examining the Pink Profusion color I'd chosen for my pedicure the previous day, I stretched my legs and raised my feet on a pillow Nana offered me.

It was uncommonly warm for eight o'clock in the morning. I welcomed the penetrating rays of sunlight and lazed about to absorb every degree of heat. One of the best parts of summer here is the moderate temperatures on land and lake. No 115-degree Sacramento bake, sizzle, and fry.

Nana poured a tall glass of sun tea from a heavy crystal pitcher. She handed it to me with great strain, her bony arm trembling, and poured herself another.

"Will the girls come up for a weekend visit?" She inquired while stirring in a pinch of sugar. Ice clinked against the inside of her glass until she set the long silver spoon down on a folded orange cloth napkin.

"If they can pry themselves away from their boyfriends for any period of time, I expect they may choose to grace us with their presence. Sarah is dating Brice again."

"How wonderful. A soloist and a violinist. The girls are doing well for themselves." She sipped her tea, then pressed a dainty white lace handkerchief to her mouth. "It's lovely to have a musician and a singer in the family again."

"Trust me, Nana, there's more. I'd fill you in but that would spoil the beginning of this sunshiny day." I took a long sip of tea to avoid any further discussion, and so I didn't have to answer questions.

"How are the girls coping with their father's death?"

"They seem to have made their peace, each in their own way."

"I imagine they confide in each other. It's good for them to be together this summer, works things out some." Nana revelled in the serene sapphire expanse spread out before us. "Time is a tough teacher."

"Our conversations are guarded. Sarah says sometimes she can hear Olivia crying through the bedroom walls at night. I suppose it's harder on them living in the house while they're working back in town. I packed up most of David's things and donated them to charity before coming here after the girls picked what they wanted to keep." I would have tossed all of it in a huge dumpster and sent his garbage to the local refuse station, but I declined to mention that fact.

"What did Sarah choose?"

"Not much. Olivia loaded up a trunk." I didn't mention any more specifics.

"Pain can't be avoided for long. It may subside for a while, but eventually it comes back stronger than before. It's best to deal with it head on." Nana reached out to me, but my chair was about a foot too far.

"I know you agree with Sarah, but Olivia isn't ready to hear the truth about her father. It will destroy her. She idolized David. Not that he deserved any of her devotion."

I kicked at the edge of the wicker lounge with my heel.

"How will she feel when she finds out the two of you knew, and didn't tell her?"

"It's too soon," I insisted, twisting to the right, then to the left in the chair. I scooched up and tucked my legs to my chest.

Nana didn't say a word in reply, she sipped her tea until she reached the residue of herbs at the bottom of her glass and swallowed every last drop.

Steller's jays swooped by, squawking as their blue wings spread out over the table top in a fly-by attempt to steal a grape or two.

I'd heard them in the trees planning their attack as they moved in closer, limb by limb, from the higher branches.

"Noisy, annoying birds," I muttered, shooing them away, knowing full well they'd be returning until they got what they wanted.

"I'll put some bread crumbs out on the feeder ledge for them. They're letting me know it's late this morning and they're getting a little too demanding for their blue-birdie britches." Nana tried to get out of the chair with considerable difficulty. The more she tried to push herself up and out, the deeper she sank.

"Do you need a hand?" When she started falling back into the chair cushions yet again, I rose and pulled her up. She stood still, laboring to catch her breath. An alarming wheezing rattled in her chest, and the closer I drew near, the louder it sounded.

"The old ticker has been making quite a racket lately." She steadied herself.

"Does anything hurt?" I bit my lower lip and held on to her arm.

"No, no. We oldsters just take longer to get the motor running." she plunked a big kiss on my forehead. "I love you, Emily." She moseyed toward the kitchen, her rosebud-print flannel nightgown hung almost to the ground under a seersucker spring duster straight out of the J C Penney catalog. After shuffling over the threshold, she grabbed the door jam and turned, "You okay?"

"I'm good."

"There's nothing to fret about. The good Lord's seen me through this far. He's not about to abandon me now." She smiled sweetly, like a bouquet of fresh, hand-picked wildflowers being released into the alpine air.

"He'd better not," I murmured, whisking away the threat of a tear after she was out of earshot.

"I'll head up to the market and pick up a dozen eggs and some vegetables while you shower and dress." I nabbed my purse and headed for the front door.

"Could you get a bottle of milk too?" Nana poked her head out of her bedroom.

"Half a gallon in the glass bottle. It tastes better, like it really came from a dairy cow on a country farm."

"Sure. I know the organic brand you like." I closed the door.

"Hi, George." I pushed my shopping cart behind his and started loading my purchases on the conveyor belt. "Any prospective buyers for your bookstore yet?"

"Not a single one in the past three months. I may have to abandon my plan to sell the place as a business." The clerk rang up the last of his groceries. George was stout and short, shorter than me. His intense, hazel-green eyes were hidden behind sandwich-loaf-size, gold, wire-rimmed, bi-focal lenses. I tried to make eye contact. but he seemed to be in a hurry. Little beads of sweat glistened on the back of his neck, and the florescent lights reflected off his bald head.

"Oh, that would be such a loss. It's a wonderland for readers, and you have the best children's corner on the entire lake."

George pushed his glasses back on the indented ridge of his nose and ever-so-slowly turned to face me. "You're one of my best customers and you send business my way all the time. You always read to the kids when you stop by and they absolutely love your interactive storytelling." He paid in cash, then pulled his fully loaded cart forward and off to the side.

"I'm here for the summer, on a sabbatical. I'll go back to my full-time job in Sacramento in September." I slipped my checkbook and pen out of my purse.

"Have you considered staying? Becoming a year-round local?" My face must have betrayed me because a big, toothy smile spread long and wide, practically connecting his hyper-extended ears.

The next thing I knew, I was walking my cart alongside him in front of Lake Cottage Book Haven.

I climbed the rickety ladder to the top deck of the pier, laid my beach towel over the web-woven folding lounge chair, and dropped my tote bag next to it. With my back to the sun, I fitted Nana's floppy straw hat on my head and settled in for a good long read. Nana was taking her afternoon nap, so I had at least two hours to veg. There were a few teenagers down below, but all the boats were out except the speeders.

George had sent me home last week with a bagful of free paperbacks. I delved into, *Beaches*. The movie is one of my favorites, but I'd heard the book was much better, as is usually true. I had high expectations for the novel. Smart business move letting me handpick my summer reading. Mild-mannered George Smithers could be quite persuasive when it came to preserving Book Haven for future generations. Funny how our passions drive us far beyond that comfort zone we grow accustomed to settling for.

The chair's aluminum framework burned against my fleshy underarm as I fumbled around in my bag for a bottled water to rehydrate. I flipped the page to the beginning of chapter six and chugged down several big gulps of cold water.

Infectious laughter bounced off the lake and resounded around the cove. I raised my head just enough to see the Lambert siblings rowing in their skiff under an endless blue canopy of sky.

Our neighbors, ten-year-old Sasha, and twelve-year-old Stephen, were sharing a brother-and-sister moment no one else would probably find as hilarious as they did. Silliness spilled over the sides of the boat as they pretended to be pirates. Spying on us unsuspecting landlubbers, charting out a future raid. Using a spyglass telescope, they haphazardly took turns peering through the magnifying lens, each with their one good eye. A swarthy black patch covered the other.

They exchanged exaggerated boasts of their dastardly deeds and swashbuckling battles. Stealing treasure chests so full of gold doubloons that coins fell to the depths of the ocean as their schooner sailed off to plunder another galleon.

Stephen raised their skull-and-crossbones flag on a makeshift mast. He pulled out and popped Sasha's eye patch. In spite of her screams of protest, he sat on the bench rattling off orders to his second mate. "Steer toward the tavern, you sassy wench, and fetch yer captain a pint of rum."

When Stephen wouldn't share the spyglass, Sasha whipped out a pair of modern-day binoculars and reported a look-out sentinel in the crow's nest of a Spanish galleon. She stood, her curly red mane capped under a blue bandana, and raised her sword high in my direction.

"Aye, matey, return your cutlass to its scabbard an' draw no attention our way. Set sail fer the Spanish fleet! Avast ye, 'off to pillage the king's coffers!'"

I squinted watching the buccaneers row out of our cove, so engrossed in their voyage I don't think they saw this scallywag wave. I listened until the last fragments of their frivolity fell silent on the rippling waters.

Flipping over on my belly, I lowered the back of the chair to even out with the foot-rest and grabbed my tote bag to use as a pillow. The sun shone down with a relentless intensity, but I cast my hat aside and closed my eyes falling asleep, wondering if Beddie and I would have had summers like Sasha and Stephen—lazy, crazy nothing days full of wonderment. I felt cheated.

I sat playing with my brother in a shaded corner on the front deck of the cabin.

Nana emerged from the kitchen in a delicate, cotton print sundress with Papa on her arm. With sudden clarity, I knew this was the day Beddie would disappear forever.

"Mama, that dress is worthy of a Southern ladies social," my mother gushed and offered Nana one of the fancy handheld fans she'd brought out from the desk drawer.

"It's as humid as a Louisiana bayou." Mama fussed with my hair, but the sticky strands stuck to my head like glue. She waved her fan back and forth over me, and I stopped playing with Beddie briefly to enjoy the momentary relief.

"Must we continue languishing as if we were Southerners living in the heart of Dixie?" Mama asked, sprawled out on the chaise lounge, fanning herself and sipping ice cold lemonade from a tall glass filled to the top with a mixture of crushed ice, freshly squeezed lemons, sugar, and water. I'd helped Nana squeeze the lemons and add the sugar. When Mama bent forward, sweat dripped down her back and dribbled past the waistband of her form-fitted, starched white sailor dress.

Daddy and Papa sat opposite her in matching chairs. Nana rested on the deck's wood paneling, giving Beddie and me long sips of the refreshing nectar from two straws bobbing around in her glass. We sucked up the sweet and sour mixture without stopping to take a breath, our cheeks puckered.

"This is the oddest weather for Tahoe." Papa appeared downright perplexed by the muggy afternoon air that seemed to weigh us down in our steps.

"Does seem a bit odd," Daddy agreed, trading in his lemonade for a bottle of beer.

Papa followed suit.

"You boys shouldn't be drinking alcohol in front of the children," Nana scolded.

"Hannah, my dear, normally I would accommodate your wishes. But if ever there was a day for gentlemen to indulge, today is that day." Papa lit his pipe and puffed away. Soon the pleasing aroma of cherry tobacco floated through the air. Daddy pulled the round-pedestal metal ashtray between them, opened his pack of cigarettes, and flicked his lighter. He offered one to my mother but she refused, stating she'd actually quit for good this time.

"Good for you, Abigail," Nana encouraged. "Where did you find the matching sailor outfits for the three of you?"

"On our last winter trip to New York City, at Sak's. I had to guess the sizes for this summer. Eddie's is a bit loose, but the boy doesn't have a smidge of fat on his bones." Mama tugged at my brother's trousers to see if he wanted to cool off in just training pants, but he fought her to keep his outfit on. Blond curls partially covered his eyes, as he looked up at her with an insistent gaze, making his preference clear. She let go with a sigh. "My son is as stubborn as his sister is compliant."

Nana laughed heartily. "They are as different as night and day. I absolutely love that about them. You'll have your hands full with these two."

Beddie was busily sailing his boat between the cracks of the deck while I taught my dolly how to dance like a ballerina across my lap. Our cheeks and shoulders were slightly burnt from the boat ride out on the lake earlier that morning. My brother had slipped away from his seat long enough to get close to the stern, and if I didn't know better I would have thought he wanted to jump in for a swim. Daddy snatched Beddie up by his shirt and plopped him right back in his seat with a tender whack on the bottom.

Mama told us to be good while she and Nana went in to fix lunch. Papa reached out for a hug, and both Mama and Nana obliged him before they went inside. I heard my mother whisper, "I love you, Daddy," as she drifted by her father. He called her his baby girl. I thought I was the baby girl, so I pouted the rest of the afternoon, all through supper and right up to naptime.

"Emily." A deep voice echoed in my mind. "You're as red as a cherry."

"Daddy? Is that you?" A dark figure stood over me, blocking the sunlight.

"Daddy?" Jack chuckled. "Well that's a first!" He took a few steps back. "You fell asleep."

Straining to focus through the glaring sun, I noticed a look of shock on his face. "I'm confused."

"You do seem disoriented." He knelt beside me. "You may have a mild case of heat stress."

"No, I remembered something I'd forgotten. We were ghosts."

"Okay, now I am mystified." Jack placed his hand in the center of my back.

"Ouch!" I flinched in mid-turn.

"Em, the heat radiating off your skin could fry an egg."

"Let's go over to the office and get some aloe vera gel slathered on." Jack offered his hand to help me up.

"I need to sit for a minute."

"That's probably a good idea. Your face is ashen. Do you think you might throw up?" Jack's voice transitioned into the medical tone of his profession.

"No."

I did feel dizzy, and started swaying right where I sat. "I saw a scene in my mind. I watched it like an observer. I tell you we were all there, even Beddie. Nana and Papa were young and she was wearing that sundress she has on in the photograph with Papa. The one sitting on the nightstand next to her bed."

Jack started to take my pulse. "Were you one of the ghosts?"

"Yes. We all were. It was earlier in the day that Beddie died."
I tried to focus.

"A dream?" Jack looked into my eyes and moved a finger in front of my face.

"No, a memory. Something I'd forgotten. I'm not crazy. Don't treat me like David did, like I'm half-witted." I was getting sea sick trying to follow his movement and struggled to get on my feet, but my body hurt whatever way I turned. "It was so real."

"Don't compare me to David." He frowned. "Let me help you to the office."

Jack, careful not to touch my skin, let me support myself on his arm until I could stand, and take baby-steps the length of the pier. I had to stop before we walked across the beach, and up the slope to his office.

Doc popped in, and Jack murmured his diagnosis, then left the room.

"You were dreaming about ghosts?" Doc applied the soothing gel across my shoulders and back. He rubbed some into my scalp too. He took his little pocket light pen and moved it back and forth.

I followed his instructions, my mind still a bit foggy.

"How long were you out there?"

"I don't know. I feel asleep listening to the Lambert twins play." I closed my eyes. Tiny dots of light swam all around the room.

"They're not twins, Emily." Doc stopped for a second, then began checking for blisters.

"Did I say twins? I meant to say siblings." My head was fuzzy, and nausea swept through my stomach like a violent wave. I made a dash for the bathroom. Jack was holding the door open for me, the toilet lid was already up.

Part Three

Winter White Snows of Silence

Pure, white, crystalline flakes silently settled upon the lake and blanketed its shores in a virgin shroud of soft powder. Flutters of angel's wings hovered above, spreading an immeasurable expanse of downy feathers from the heavens, over the spellbound earth below. The full orb of the guardian moon anchored in the midnight sky, bore solitary witness to the ushering in of winter. Wisps of wind whirling above the placid waters whispered tales, reminders of a century past when the snow fell with such intensity, the footprints of man and beast disappeared under a weight and burden that few survived. Now momentary flurries bluster a storm forewarning. The inaudible message falls utterly still, hushed by the gentle first dusting.

Chapter Fifteen

David

Our bodies speak a language in movement and expression, or the lack of it. Some speak in prayers, utterances spoken from the heart when there are no words to be found nor ability to bring them forth. There is One ever attentive to the sweet incense of this eternal language.
— Note found in Nana's Bible, 1960

This was our last chance. I'd carefully charted out every detail of the weekend.

The monstrous blizzard that presently held us captive in our sub-zero cabin hideaway was not on the agenda. Every ski resort on the mountain was battened down.

The champagne bottle that had popped with promise hours ago, now sat in a pool of melted ice in the sterling silver bucket. Ornate seventeenth century, I digressed, scrutinizing the baroque trim. Exquisite workmanship.

A disheveled stranger with a full day's stubble stared back at me from my Aunt Henrietta's polished wedding gift. Twenty-something years later, it still looked brand new. *How deceiving.*

Emily stirred restlessly, pulling covers up to her neck while clutching sheet, blanket, and quilt together as one. She turned her exposed back as the smoldering embers in the fireplace burned out, reduced to a heap of gray ash.

From my dark corner of the window seat, I watched her every move. The woolen covers I'd wrapped myself in offered little protection from the bitter wind blowing in through the frozen panes of glass. I briefly contemplated crossing the room and getting into bed with her.

Sleep continued to elude me. I closed my eyes and tried to organize my thoughts. I took another swig of whiskey from a leather-bound flask, swallowing hard. The last gulp burned going down my throat, thawing me from the inside-out.

White flashes whipped across the murky sky, blurring all landscape through the circular patch I'd rubbed clear on the frosted glass. I hovered close and my breath fogged over the last remaining link to the outside world.

"Why did you rent this god-forsaken pit?" Emily demanded, hands on her hips.

"Look, I know you would have rather stayed at your Nana's cabin, but I wanted to do something different this time. I thought it would be a nice change." I shoved our luggage she'd never bothered to unpack out of the way.

"A ski lodge at Squaw Valley would have been better than this. At least we wouldn't be isolated in this blizzard in the middle of nowhere." Emily threw herself headlong across the bed, her waist-length blonde hair cascading over the edge, down to the floor.

I stared at her a long time before speaking. "Give me a break, sweetheart. I planned this months ago. Even the weatherman didn't know the storm was going to be this fierce."

"You've always resented taking our vacations at Nana and Papa's cabin. Every five years we've gone to other places—Hawaii,

Mexico and Canada. I wanted to spend our twentieth anniversary at the lake where we met, fell in love, and married."

Tears brimmed over her intense blue eyes.

"And I didn't want to ask your grandmother to leave her home for the weekend so we could have sex in her bedroom." I offered her a box of tissues. "We are at the lake."

"I grew up here and I don't have the slightest clue where we're holed up."

"A cozy little cabin in Homewood—for a romantic weekend of wedded bliss."

"No, David. We're snowbound in a dilapidated shack on top of a mountain," she smeared her make-up with a swipe of her hand.

I flung my hands up in the air in complete frustration, shot off the side of the bed, and headed for the kitchen.

"Nana never minds giving us the cabin. She goes next door to Doc's and sleeps in the guestroom." She rose, crouching knee deep in rumpled sheets.

"Yes, and isn't that romantic. Doc and Nana next door. Oh, and let's not forget Jack. He always manages to show up for breakfast on any happy little weekend getaway we have." A twitch started below my eye and spread to the eyelid. I ran my hand over it twice to try to make it stop.

"I can't do anything about Jack. He'll never go away. He's like a piece of furniture." Her footsteps padded in my direction.

"People buy new furniture all the time, Emily," I grumbled, and grabbed a couple of coffee mugs from the kitchen cupboard. Every single cup was coated in layers of grime. "Disgusting!" I slammed the door shut, and flipped on the water faucet. A resounding thud confirmed my suspicions. The pipes were frozen.

"Well, if that isn't perfect." Emily stood rigid in the doorway. "No coffee, no shower, no toilets."

"Mankind survived without the three essentials of modern society for a long time." I forced a smiled, hoping to lighten the conversation. "It'll be fine. We're seasoned campers. We can rough it. Remember our fifteenth anniversary at Lake Louise?"

"I do. Even Canada's campgrounds had flush toilets, piped hot and cold water, showers—just like the brochures promised." Emily folded her arms, sounding triumphant.

"At least nobody showed up there unannounced at our tent at six am for breakfast. Your friend Jack has a two-decade-long, unbroken record of that annoying chirp. "Are the pancakes ready yet? How does he find out when we're coming?"

"Certainly not from me. I think Nana slips because she's so excited to have visitors. Jack usually heads home for the weekends unless he parties somewhere in town all night and crashes at Doc's." She added. "At least he doesn't drink and drive."

"Someone needs to teach that boy a lesson."

"Are you volunteering?" She clutched her nightgown to her chest.

"Em, there is something about that jerk that still gets to you. He can finish any sentence you start, he knows things about you I don't, and you're a wide-open book."

"Jack is an irritating pest from my childhood, a bloodsucking leech you waste too much time and energy complaining about. Besides we're alone now. Is there something you want to tell me?" Her defiant stance weakened as she braced herself against a wall.

"What do you mean?" I immediately regretted my question.

"Your car phone rang incessantly on the drive up here. You never picked up a single call after checking out the first number."

"It was just the college calling."

She swallowed. "Who, from the college, David?"

"Probably the front office."

"I think you knew exactly who it was."

"I didn't take the calls, Emily." My shoulders slouched forward as I flopped in a kitchen chair. I strummed my fingers on the wooden arm like a distress signal. If I didn't get her to back off here, we were headed for trouble.

"That doesn't make it okay."

"Don't do this now. Let's not ruin the weekend." I lifted the side flaps of the picnic basket and rummaged through, avoiding direct eye contact. "There's a feast in here: smoked gouda, crackers, olive tapenade, kippers, lox, cream cheese, bagels, and about half a dozen fresh fruits." The wicker creaked when I lifted out a wine bottle and corkscrew from the bottom. "Great selection. I love a smooth merlot."

"I know we have food. Do we still have a marriage?" Her hands were trembling.

"I don't know." There, I finally said it out loud. My words bounced off the four walls of the cabin, echoing as if an avalanche had plummeted down the mountainside right in our path. She stood motionless, not even breathing. I felt the impact bury us alive.

"Is she really worth losing me, and the girls?" Barely a whisper escaped her lips.

"I'm not leaving. It's over with her."

"It's not that easy." Emily swayed and stumbled in the opposite direction.

"We still make a good team. I brought the champagne and caviar, you packed the basket, luggage, and case of bottled waters. We can work our way through this. That's why I wanted this place, away from all interruptions, even Nana."

"She has nothing to do with our troubles. Nana isn't the one having an affair. You are always good for the champagne and fish eggs. There never has been a balance in our relationship. The scales are always off kilter. Actually, David, you're a lot like Jack. A perennial teenager, flirt, and flatterer. At least he never hid behind a family. He knows his deficiencies and is honest about them."

"That's not fair and you know it." I thundered back.

"You want to talk about what's fair?" Emily spun around on her heels.

"You know what I mean. This is a no-win situation for me."

"The girls and I are the big losers here."

"You're not going to tell them are you?" A queasy uneasiness rolled in my gut. "Olivia."

"No. I won't say a word to them. But not for the reasons you think."

"What are your reasons?"

"Nothing I want to share with you." She screamed. "What were you thinking?"

"I don't know? This thing got way out of hand. I never intended for it to carry on this long." I yanked the chair next to me closer, scratching the hard-wood floor. "Come on. Let's talk."

She rounded the edge of the table and stood perfectly still, locking her gaze upon mine, penetrating deep in search for any hint of a lie.

"Just tell me why." She collapsed in the chair opposite me.

"I don't know myself." I could have told her Caroline pursued me. It was the truth. I put her off for almost a year. But, I liked the attention, her compliments, and our lunches when she made me laugh. I started going to Caroline's classroom, anticipating the scent of her perfume when I walked in the door. She was always there, available, smiling. And I was lonely. Locked inside myself by choice. Caroline was the easy way out. I didn't even have to try.

"Do I know her?" Emily shimmied in the chair, legs away from me, poised for a quick exit.

"No."

"Would you even tell me if I did?" Doubt clouded her face.

"She's the new professor from back east. You've never seen or met her."

My stomach lurched. Lying wasn't as easy as I thought it would be. My head buzzed, ears rang. I'd hoped to avoid this. I didn't think she suspected a thing. We lead such separate lives, working in different towns, our daily routines rarely connected. Home ground should not have been compromised.

"How long?"

"The past six months."

"I thought so. You've been more distant than usual." She ran her fingernails against the loose weave of the brown tablecloth, repeatedly poking a finger in and out.

Pale and delicate, her hands moved smoothly over the rough surface. I was struck by how fragile she seemed, vulnerable in ways she'd rather conceal under a veil of camouflage.

"You've been just as unavailable." I risked reaching out for her hand.

She cringed. I rested mine on top of hers anyway. The complete absence of warmth was chilling.

Silence occupied the space between us, hurling accusations of betrayal in my direction. I knew she was waiting for me to say something, anything. It was unusual for her to keep quiet this long. I shot a somber glance her way.

Pity swelled her eyes. Pity, not sorrow or grief. She saw the emptiness I no longer wanted to have to try and hide. Why should I? This double life was taking a toll on me, not her. Covering my tracks had become real work. Like this miserable weekend.

"Em, why didn't you tell me you knew?" I laced my fingers through hers and lightly squeezed.

"I loved you." Em's words tumbled out, dry and raspy.

"I've never been the man you choose to see."

"What do you mean?"

"You see who you want to see."

Her shoulders stiffened as she sat up, released my hand, and walked over to the front door. "There's a break in the storm. You probably should get out there and shovel the walkway while you can. We can make our way to the car and get the case of water. It may already be frozen from last night." She grabbed my parka and tossed it half-heatedly, not quite far enough for me to reach.

"Okay." I collected my gloves, hat, and scarf off the chair as I yanked my coat off the floor. After zipping up, I grabbed a shovel from the front doorway. "You want to help?"

"I'll get a fire going and start lunch." She pulled a sweatshirt over her head and loaded her arms with logs from the fireplace hearth.

I slammed the door behind me, jarring loose mounds of packed snow and icicles from the gutter. Wielding the spade wildly, I tried to deflect the icy onslaught from entombing me. I speared the shovel deep and pitched snow, trudging my way the twelve feet to the car trunk. Fumbling to get the car keys from my jeans pocket, I tore off a glove with my teeth and struggled to straighten my raw, numb fingers to grasp the clicker.

Emily peered out the door. "It'll be dark soon. Grab the case of water and come inside." She pointed to the snowplow forging a way down the street.

I did as I was told. Fat lot of good it did me. While I was in the bedroom changing into dry clothes, she took the keys, got in the car, and followed that blasted vehicle right out of town. Just left me there. I couldn't believe it.

I sat in front of the fire, opened the wine, poured it into a coffee mug, and snagged my cell phone off the lamp table. I started to punch in Emily's number, but stopped before the last digit. After taking a sip of wine, I direct-dialed Caroline. She picked up right away.

"Why haven't you been answering my calls? Are you alright? You didn't even leave me a message."

"Emily knows. She knows everything."

"I'm glad you told her. Now we don't have to sneak around anymore."

I slid back into the stiff vinyl sofa. "I'm stuck in a cabin at Tahoe. Why don't you drive up once they clear the roads and we can spend the rest of the three-day weekend together. Better bring your four-wheel drive, it snowed hard. Who knows? Maybe by Monday we'll be able to hit the ski slopes."

"Sure babe. I'll throw some clothes together and check the weather reports. I can't wait to see you."

The eagerness in her voice warmed me. She was always so willing to please. "Look, could you grab a change of clothes for me? The pipes are frozen here so I can't wash anything. I think I have jeans and a couple of sweaters in your closet."

"Yeah, they're still here from that Northern California Science Conference weekend in Napa." She giggled.

"Thanks. You might want to bring a couple of steaks. I have a picnic basket of snack type foods, but we'll want to eat a real meal after skiing." I chugged the last of the wine in my cup, and poured more.

"Anything you want. I'll swing by the market and pick up some champagne. I know how much you like it. Thanks for telling Emily. It was the right thing to do. Now we can move forward." Caroline sounded almost too serious.

"Hey. When we get back, I should probably stay at your place. We can drive to work together Tuesday. You going to let me drive that little red Porsche? I'm kind of tired of sitting on the passenger side."

"I thought you liked me chauffeuring you around," she teased. "Dave, if you want to get behind the drivers wheel, go ahead."

"Call me when you get up the mountain. I've missed you."

Chapter Sixteen

You offered a hand, with an open-end plan. The earth
stood still and let go a reluctant sigh. Upper crust crumbled away, exposing cracks in the land. I managed a smile,
lugging all my baggage, while preparing to mourn. Where
to run and where to hide? He left me empty and crossed
to the other side. The day he fooled me, laid down, and
died. I waited for the waves to take me out with the tide.

—Emily's journal entry 1995

The doorbell rang a second time. I sat in the chair with my cup of
coffee and stared at the front porch. A uniformed officer peeked
through the side window. *What have the girls gotten themselves into now?*
Quickly pulling my robe tight, I slugged my reluctant body to the
cold tile entryway, and cracked open the heavy oak door.

"Yes, deputies?"

"Are you Mrs. Emily Taylor?" The older of two sheriffs
glanced behind me.

"Yes." I tried not to let my mind go looking for trouble. Olivia
had broken curfew several times these past months. With their dad
and me gone for the holiday weekend, I thought maybe Sarah and
Olivia didn't actually stay at the Callahan's home.

"Ma'am, I'm Deputy Barnett. This is Deputy Rutland. May
we please come in?"

I glanced at the name tags and badges pinned on chest pockets of their long sleeve shirts. After mentally verifying what I saw, I nodded, and let them in.

I walked in to the living room. "Is there a problem?"

Both men made direct eye contact with me before the older one spoke.

"We regret to inform you that there's has been a car accident."

"Oh, no" My heart pounded hard and fast. "Are my daughters okay?"

"I'm sorry, Mrs. Taylor?"

"Are they at the hospital?"

"Ma'am, there isn't any easy way to tell you. Your husband David was killed in an accident this morning on Capitol Freeway. We understand he was on his way to work at the University of California in Davis. We are so sorry for your loss."

I grabbed the back of the recliner for support. "David is dead?"

"Yes. Mrs. Taylor, is anyone here with you? We can stay while you call a friend or family member." The deputy asked, "do you understand?"

"What happened?" My knees weakened. "I need to sit down."

"Certainly, Roger, help her to the sofa. The daughters you mentioned were not in the vehicle with him. So they are probably fine."

"One is a senior at Del Campo High School, around the corner." I sat in the middle of the sofa and rambled. "My other daughter came home from college to spend the holiday weekend with her sister. She leaves to go back tonight." My nervous chatter made no sense. "I didn't go in to work this morning. I called in sick."

"Take a deep breath, Mrs. Taylor. Do you have a neighbor my partner can ask to come over?" He spoke in a patient and calm voice.

"No, we all work. I'm usually at work. Was David drunk?" I started shaking.

"No Ma'am, he was driving the car hit by a suspected drunk driver someone had reported. It was a hit-and-run. The other driver plowed into a tree after he got off the freeway exit. He was the second fatality."

"What car?" I remembered David's was still in the garage. I'd driven it home from the Homewood cabin. At least it was the last time I checked.

"The car was totaled. We were able to get the license number off the plates." He unbuttoned a flap on the pocket with his name tag, and took out a notebook. "It's registered in the passenger's name, a Ms. Caroline Whitefield. She's been admitted to the hospital with a concussion and can't answer questions at this time. Do you know her?"

"Yes, I know her." I tried to breathe and tightened my grip on the arm of the sofa.

"We are trying to locate her ex-husband, a Mr. Steven Whitefield. The car was actually registered in both their names. We've tried his work and home numbers. Do you know of another way to reach him?"

"Yes. We were close friends with them when they were married. Steven moved back to Colorado after she left him a couple of years ago. His new phone number and address should be on our rolodex." A wave of nausea swept through me draining any strength I had.

"Can you get the rolodex card for us?"

"Sure. It's in the den." I made a quick dash to the desk and turned the big, black knob on the side to Steven's name. The Sacramento address was scratched out and the Colorado condo one was written over it in red ink. Same with the landline phone numbers. On a hunch, I flipped one card after, and there was Caroline's outdated information, nothing new was listed. "You wicked people." I took Steven's card with me to the living room and handed to the sheriff.

"Thank you, Mrs. Taylor. This will help in our investigation."

"What else do you know?" I brushed my overgrown bangs back and hugged the edge of the sofa trying to appear more mentally stable than I was at the moment.

"Preliminary investigation by the C.H.P. officers who responded to the 911 call states that both professors were on their way to Davis. Your husband was driving the 1991 Porsche 928 GTS registered to the Whitefield couple. Ms. Caroline Whitefield was the passenger in the car at the time of the accident. About six-thirty this morning."

"What time is it now?' I asked.

He checked his wrist watch. "Nine o'clock sharp."

"Was David drunk?"

"No forensic toxicology reports are available yet. Ma'am, your husband's body was taken to the Sacramento County Morgue."

"Of course." My heart fluttered. The cup of coffee in my empty stomach churned.

"Do you know where the morgue is located?" Deputy Barrett asked.

"No, I don't." I started to cry, and I couldn't stop. "I'm sorry." I tried to say something intelligible, but blubbered while trying to stave off increasing nausea.

"Mrs. Taylor, is there anyone we can call to come be with you?"

"No, not really. Wait, could you call my grandmother? Doc will drive her down to be with me." I rattled off Nana's number between sobs.

"May I use your telephone?" The younger deputy had already whipped out his note pad and written it down.

"Yes. Please, do. There's a wall phone in the kitchen." I grabbed a box of tissues from the end table next to me, pulled a few out, and blew my nose.

"I can give you a card to contact the coroner's chaplain. He can help with grief counseling. Usually someone from their office

accompanies us, but there several accidents early this morning."
He motioned to the chair across from me, "may I sit here?"

"Certainly." It was David's chair. I could care less, but I
didn't want him to know. I realized he probably thought me to
be a new grieving widow. His compassion was well intended.
I was grateful he could not see through to the black heart that
beat screaming accusations of betrayal and unforgiveness within
my chest.

"I have a pamphlet from the MacArthur Mortuary that may
help with information you are going to need."

He gave me the glossy tri-fold informational paper that had
all the necessary steps I needed to put what was left of my husband
in a coffin and bury him six feet under. I thought he was a kind
man. I glanced at his ring finger. A solid, wide, plain gold band
encircled it. He probably had a faithful, loving wife waiting for
him to come home safe every night.

Deputy Rutland rejoined us. "Someone named Walters is on
the way with your grandmother. He says they should be here in
about an hour and a half." He sat next to his superior, or captain, I
wasn't sure of the proper rank and file for a sheriff.

"Thank you." I whispered in a raw, hoarse voice. I sat dazed,
hoping they would stay a few more minutes, and needing them to
leave so I could yell out loud.

"I have jotted down the case number for you, Mrs. Taylor. If
you have any questions, you will need this as a reference."

"These will be helpful." I added the piece of paper to the
pamphlet and chaplaincy business card in my hand. Not sure what
to do or say next, I strained to think of questions I knew would
pop in my head the minute they walked out the door. All I could
do was stare at their shiny black boots. Four lace-up boots in a row
on my beige loop carpet.

"Is there anything we can do before we leave, ma'am?"
Barnette asked.

"How can I tell my daughters?" I bolted upright with a terror and dread neither of these men could possibly understand. A second wave of nausea swept through me more vengeful and violent than the first.

"Would you like us to help you make the phone call to your daughters?"

"They're at the Callahan's, a few blocks away. Probably getting ready to take off for the day." I answered. "Yes, I would appreciate it. The number is on the fridge, under a Tahoe magnet." I stammered. "I'm so sorry, I get chatty when I'm nervous, and I don't make much sense."

"That's okay. This is distressful for you." He turned to his partner. "Roger, can you get that number and call? Don't mention anything other than their mother needs them to come home immediately, there's a family emergency. That's all you tell them."

"Yes, sir."

"Do you need us to stay when they get here, Mrs. Taylor?" Barnett offered. "We will need you or another family member to come and identify the body." He spoke softly.

"No, I'll tell the girls by myself." I made that decision as the words left my lips.

"Can I wait to go to the morgue until my Nana and Doc get here?"

"Yes. It's better to take someone with you. Does Ms. Whitefield have someone who lives locally to check on her at the hospital?"

"I have no idea." I murmured, and squeezed the sofa cushion I was sitting on tight, until my fingers cramped.

"Your daughters will be here in a few minutes. They asked a lot of questions. I didn't tell them anything other than what I was told to say." The rookie looked nervously at his senior partner for approval. He didn't appear to be much older than Sarah.

"We're going to head out now." Officer Barnett stood and handed me his card.

"Thank you for all your help. "I rose and reached out to shake his hand. "What is your name?"

"My name is David, Ma'am." He shook my hand respectfully. He and his partner walked to the door. I followed them more out of habit than hospitality.

"Thank you, Officer Barnett. I appreciate you trying to make this easier for me."

He seemed appreciative for the acknowledgement. Or maybe he didn't. I couldn't tell. They left in their green and white marked car that had drawn a small crowd in front of my house. I slipped all the papers in my open purse, closed it, and set it on the carpet between the sofa and end table.

Barely a minute after they drove off I heard Sarah's car pull into the driveway. I hoped they hadn't seen the sheriff car driving away and tried to prepare myself for when they burst through the door.

You can do this.

Sarah and Olivia rushed into my arms all at once. "It Nana okay?"

I pulled back a little, biting my lip and tried not to lose it. They looked at me with puzzled expressions and pleading eyes.

"There's been a car accident. A hit-and-run by a drunk driver. Your father was on his way into work this morning. He ... he died." I finished the sentence in a hushed whisper.

Sarah gasped, but oddly, showed no emotion.

Olivia crumbled to her knees at my feet. She shrieked in anguished, almost animal sounds. She seized my robe and clung, unable to do anything but hold on.

My mind went blank.

Darkness encircled us. An unforeseen power, without pity, fell like a shroud shutting out sense and reason, and any hope that the life we had known would ever be restored. Under the intensity of this harsh weight, this unyielding burden, I found myself alone, buried in the knowledge of my husband's betrayal, left to face the consequences yet to unfold.

Chapter Seventeen

Once I thought I knew you. Believed what you said was
true. But in time, I came to find, Your circle of lies began
to unwind. I had no clue. And didn't know what to do.
You left me behind in a terrible bind. How could you be
so deliberately unkind? You betrayed all trust with your
wandering lust. In the end, will it be the death of all of us?
                                    -Emily, journal entry February 1995

The last of a continual crowd of relatives, neighbors, professors, and childhood friends dissipated into the dusky fog as I
secured the heavy door behind them.

They came sincerely desiring to bring comfort, along with
enough covered casseroles to feed a Third World country for a day.
Fragrant flowers filled every room of the house: roses in elegant
vases, orchids, beautiful and exotic floral arrangements from all
the local florists' shops, and a variety of potted plants—ferns, ivy,
succulents, all for me to nurture and grow. Therapy to help me
through the grieving process, so I was repeatedly told. All accom-
panied with intense sympathetic hugs and well-intended albeit
unwanted advice for the reluctant, recently widowed wife of
Professor David Talbot Taylor.

"I'm sick of hearing what a great guy Dad was." Sarah
tossed her raincoat over the arm of the chintz sofa and flopped

to the middle of the cushions. "I know he was having an affair." At my alarmed expression, she added, "Don't worry. Olivia doesn't have a clue her perfect daddy, was such a jerk!" She neatly folded her angora sweater in her lap, and pounded out the winkles.

"How did you know?" I asked, sitting across from her.

"I saw them together, here. The week Dad sent us off on that 'girls only' cruise to the Caribbean. You know, the one we all thought he was such a gem for arranging every detail. What a guy." She grumbled.

"You saw them?"

"Remember? The night before we left, we stayed at the Hilton in San Francisco. I drove back home to get my favorite swimsuit? That Abercrombie & Fitch number I used to reel in Nick. He so wasn't worth all the extra trouble. I was still moving some of my stuff back from the dorms for winter break. So I checked in after you and Liv later that night, after coming here first.

"Dad didn't waste a second bringing her over through his revolving door." Sarah trembled. "The music was so loud they didn't hear me come in the house. I saw them in your bedroom drinking champagne, sitting in robes like this was their home. She was wearing your robe, Mom, the one Dad gave you for your birthday. There they sat, casually nibbling on caviar."

"In our bedroom?" The invasion of my home in my absence, made my skin electrify. What else of mine has she touched, worn?

"I knew something was up, but never thought he would be so—open." Kicking off my heels I slumped in the oversized chair across from Sarah and pulled an afghan around me in a vain attempt to disappear. The funeral had been hard enough to get through, but this.

"I can still hear their laughter echoing through the house. I've tried to drown out her insidious cackle for months. 'Heh, heh, heh, heh, heh.'" My daughter's imitation was jarring.

"I'm so sorry you've had to deal with this by yourself. Why didn't you come to me?"

"I didn't think you knew. You were having such a wonderful time on the cruise. It was the happiest I'd seen you in a long time." Tears welled up in her big brown eyes. Anger distorted her pretty facial features pulling her jaw tight and narrowing her eyes to mere slits.

"I was happy being with my girls. And I didn't know for sure then. I suspected something was up with you, the way you were sneak drinking and flaunting yourself at that zero personality supposed Athens entrepreneur."

"Why couldn't he at least go over to her place? He didn't have to bring her here." Sarah's voice trailed off. She stopped rolling her sweater like a pie crust.

"We'll never know the answer to that question." Hostility edged my reply.

"What question?" Olivia came into the room and slid onto the wooden rocking chair, her eyes still puffy after washing the remnants of her make-up off. She blew her nose into a tissue whipped out of the box she'd been carrying around.

"Wasn't it wonderful how many people came today? All those professors from the college, which would have pleased Daddy. I still can't believe he's gone." She buried her face in a wad of tissues.

I shot a warning glance in Sarah's direction. "Why don't we tidy-up? There's food everywhere. I'm exhausted but I know I won't be able to sleep." I turned away from my daughters and tried to wipe my blearing vision with my sleeve.

Sarah tied her hair up in a knot on top of her head. "I'll throw away all the perishable stuff. She snagged an apron off the hook on the hallway door and strode into the kitchen in a black velour dress I now realized had nothing to do with mourning.

"Can we do the dishes tomorrow?" Olivia sobbed.

"I need to try to keep busy." The hollow part of me told her the truth.

"All day people have been telling me things I never knew about Daddy. I didn't want them to stop. It made me feel ... I don't know, closer. Like he was still here with us. I want to keep talking about him. Can we, please?" My youngest pleaded, something she never does.

I motioned for Sarah to come back to the living room with us. I sat on the arm of the rocker, beside my daughter, my mind fighting every muscle in my mouth for control. "What stories did you hear today?"

"All kinds of things. How he was always there for them. Willing to help out in a pinch." Olivia sniffled. "Several of the women said they could always count on him for a ride. And Patrick Henderson said Dad was the most faithful of his golf buddies. She laid her head against my shoulder and wept as I combed my fingers through thick clusters of her straight brown hair. "What will we do with his gold clubs?"

"We'll leave them right where they are for now. Let's concentrate on getting by one day at a time, okay?"

"One of the woman professors asked about the golf clubs for Caroline. For when she gets out of the hospital."

"Why on earth would she ask for Dad's clubs?" Sarah's cheeks burned and her nostrils flared as she expelled a mouthful of air. "I don't remember them ever golfing together." She flipped the basket of sympathy cards off the library table, scattering them across the room.

"What's wrong with you?" Olivia knelt down and began picking up the cards and dropping them into the basket. "I was hoping we could sit down and read these together."

"Yes, what healing that will bring!" Sarah snapped.

"Sarah, please." I fiddled aimlessly with the buttons on my sweater sleeves.

Olivia sat back in the rocker, balancing the basket on her lap. She ran her finger under the triangular flap of a pastel blue envelope and pulled out a card with a beautiful ocean scene. A vast sea of white-capped waves rolled under a breathtaking sunset. Olivia read the caption. "Those we love are never really gone."

Well, I wanted David to stay gone. Forever. I couldn't imagine he made it to heaven, and an eternity in hell suited me fine.

"Olivia, would you like to take those to your room and pick out the ones you'd like to keep?" My voice cracked as I wrung my shaky, useless hands together.

"I'd love that." She scampered off, almost happy for the first time today.

I took her place in the rocker. Sarah came over and knelt at my feet.

"Your sister isn't ready to hear the truth right now. She needs time to grieve for the father she believed he was."

"You're right. But don't wait too long to tell her. It will only get harder every day. Then she'll never be ready. Neither will you."

"I'll tell her when the time is right."

My daughter, with nary a tear in her eyes or on her cheeks, wrapped her arms around the entire mess of me and held on tight. "We'll get through this, the three of us, together. Dad made his choices and he didn't chose us."

"No. He didn't." I stroked her arm, then her cheek. "That was his loss."

"Mom, you do realize Caroline probably wasn't the first." She delivered her words with care, trying to gauge my ability to handle the depth and severity of the full context of her statement.

"I know." I couldn't bear to say more. In the past week, pieces had started falling into place, snippets of my life that never made any sense before. Arguments David initiated out of the blue. I never had the slightest clue what they were about. He'd storm out of the house and didn't return until the next day, when I'd still be trying to figure out what I'd said or done to set him off. If I asked where he'd been, he'd say it was none of my business. Hang-up phone calls were common when I answered. He'd take the phone outside to talk, even in the rain.

"I was such a fool."

My daughter tipped my chin in her hands and lifted until she was looking deep into my eyes.

"Mom, you loved and trusted Dad. He had the whole world, and it was never going to be enough for him." She kissed me on my forehead. A tear escaped and traveled down her cheek. She didn't brush it away. It dried, leaving a noticeable track, like a scar to mark her for life.

She rose and offered me a hand. "Let's go do the dishes."

Olivia's sobs carried past the walls and filtered through the air vents above us.

"I'll go sit with her for a while." I took Sarah's hand and let her pull me up.

"Do you want to go with me?" I asked, though I knew the answer.

"No, I'll start the dishes." She melted in my arms when I hugged her.

I walked down the hall and stood in the open doorway. Cards and envelopes were strewn all over Olivia's bed. She sat in the middle, her pajamas piled nearby, seeking any form of comfort from the words of sympathy conveyed in the verses and handwritten messages.

"Why doesn't it help, Mommy?" She wept.

"It takes time to heal from a broken heart." At least I could be honest with her about that much.

"Can I sleep with you tonight?" She rushed over, abandoning the pile of papers on her bed.

"Of course." I couldn't hold her close enough.

She pulled back. "You don't mind I'll be taking Daddy's place?"

"No." If she only knew, that place had been vacant for years. I was struck by her thoughtfulness. While in the throes of her own tormenting grief, she put my feelings and needs before hers. My heart ached even more for her. How could I ever compound her suffering by being the bearer of a devastating revelation that would cause more anguish? *She's better off never knowing.*

"You go ahead and crawl in bed. I'll change into my pajamas and see if your sister wants to join us in my room."

"Is Sarah mad at me?" Her black knit dress swallowed every bit of her petite frame in solemn despair.

"No." I reassured her with another hug. I squeezed my eyes shut, obliterating David's face from my mind, furious at his intrusion in our grief. I wanted to scream. *She's mad at you, you cheating, lying, conniving excuse of a father!* Instead I held Olivia, kept silent, and let her cry out her pain.

Sarah wandered in. "I finished the dishes. It was relaxing somehow."

"Do you want to sleep with us in my room tonight?" I hoped she would say yes.

"I think I'd like to be alone," she answered with a quick, sharp delivery.

"Please, Sarah, stay with us," Olivia begged her sister.

Turning so Olivia wouldn't see, I mouthed my own silent plea. "Your sister needs you."

"Okay. Let me change."

I slept sandwiched in the middle of my daughters that night I thought would never end. I continually glanced at the brightly lit digits on the alarm clock as I tossed and turned, seeking elusive slumber that would offer temporary escape. About four in the morning I awakened to the sound of muffled crying. I turned to Olivia, who had succumbed to an exhausted, emotionally drained slumber. When I realized it was Sarah, I did not want to intrude in her private grief, but I could not bear to let her suffer in isolated misery. I turned to face her.

"Sarah," I whispered and wrapped my arms around her back.

"I hate him." She uttered bitterly. "He didn't love us, he only loved himself."

"He did love you." My words seemed empty, even to me.

"No, Mom. He never was a part of us. He was always off in his own world. Don't make excuses for him now."

"I'm sorry, baby." I hesitated, fearing I was letting her down even more.

"I'm glad he's gone," she whispered. "What kind of person does that make me?"

Her stark honestly made me shiver. I felt the same way and wondered if I'd somehow subconsciously projected my own condemning judgment to influence her.

"You are not a bad person, Sarah. Just deeply wounded." I curved in closer.

"Why weren't we enough?"

Even with her back to me, I could feel Sarah's heart pounding in her chest. I needed to choose my words carefully. "I don't know. Maybe he never really knew either."

"This will kill Livie. She'll never be the same."

Sarah's anger at the impending loss of her sister's innocence pierced my heart. A hardening had already cemented in the once-soft center I had naively exposed without reserve to a man I never truly knew. Soon concrete would solidify and weigh me down.

I held her. That was all I could do at the moment. This was ugly and hard. I couldn't save Olivia or Sarah from the onslaught that was coming their way.

Sarah cried inconsolably. "I hate him, I hate him, I hate him." She sucked in air between outbursts. "I'm not crying for him. He doesn't deserve any of our tears."

Fully spent, sleep overcame, and spared her.

I drifted off with the first glimmer of hope that we would make it through. Despite the harshness of our uninvited reality. Maybe in time, we could eventually heal.

Chapter Eighteen

Swimming underwater—I might find you, somewhere in the crystal clear blue. Deeper, wider—a little farther each time. Hold my breath and watch for a sign. Listen, the mountains are calling. See how gently snow is falling. Waves roll out from you and back to me. Seasons pass reluctantly. You vanished and left me behind. I waited, hoping you'd find, a place in my dreams. I'm so alone. Will your travels never lead you back home?

> - Emily, journal entry 1977, anniversary
> of when Beddie left me.

Beddie shook me awake from a deep slumber. We sat on the comforter playing making his teddy bear dance with my dolly. A peculiar quiet resonated within the cabin, the sun shining through windows cast shadowy images against welcoming walls. Beddie stared out past the girded panes of glass toward the vast ocean of blue.

We crawled to the side of the bed ready to help each other over the edge. Our legs dangled as we stretched our toes to touch the floor. Beddie donned his cap and went first like always, and I followed close behind. We toddled barefoot to our parents' room where they slept nestled in each other's arms. I headed through the doorway, but Beddie pulled me back. I longed to be held by my mother, or even better, to climb up right in the middle of the bed with them. My brother led me to the kitchen door and out on the deck.

Glancing back toward Nana and Papa's bedroom, I noticed the door was closed.

Sunlight kissed our cheeks as we scooted on our bottoms down the few steps to the beach. Dolly was tucked safely under my arm, but Beddie left his bear on the last step. We marched in unison under giant pine trees that were lined up like toy soldiers, dressed in the matching sailor outfits Mama had dressed us in that morning.

Rays from the midday sun tap-danced across the lake, sparkling in vibrant hues of sapphire and aqua. Black-capped birds flew overhead and sang their warbling songs, winsome lullabies without lyrics.

Beddie strode across the glistening sands along the shoreline. He frolicked about, waving his arms like an airplane, dipping from side to side. Swooping down, he ran humming and sputtering until he crash-landed onto the pebbly beach. He clapped his hands, pleased with my laughter and obvious delight. He rose and began filling his pockets with pebbles, one by one. He examined and approved each stone before storing it in his bulging pockets. I watched his little toes struggle to anchor the weight of his body in the sand.

The navy sailor suit and cap made him look older than almost four, perhaps a distinguished five-years-old. An observant eye though would notice the difference. His long, skinny legs tottered, camouflaged under flared trousers.

My brother showed me another handful of the rocks before adding his treasures into the side-pockets of his shirt. I wasn't interested. Tender blades of grass grew in abundant patches closer to the cabin fence line where I settled on the sandy part of the beach. Twirling strands of hair around a finger as I sucked my thumb, I'd contentedly stop and stick my hand in the oversized pocket of my dress, making sure my baby doll was still there, sound asleep.

The sun bore down through a cloudless sky, hotter every minute. My cheeks reddened and perspiration trickled to my chin. Water rippled in, washing over the gleaming mixture of sand and stone, before ebbing away—a hypnotizing, rhythmic ballet.

Yawning, I lay against a pillow of tufts of green, facing my brother. He called for me to join him. "Me-lee, Me-lee." My eyes fluttered while watching him try to climb in the skiff. The boat shifted in the sand as he shoved it away from the shoreline. One leg in, one flopping above the waters lapping against the boat's aluminum hull. Beddie waved, beckoning.

An unnatural drowsiness fell upon me, one I could not fight off despite my curiosity. Darkness flickered between bright flashes of blinding sunlight as images of my brother drifted gradually into the distance.

"Me-lee, Me-lee!" Excitement tinged the air with his fading laughter.

A rush of wind swept over me, forcing my eyelids open. I caught a glimpse of my toe-headed brother bending over, reaching for something floating just beyond his fingertips. The boat rocked forward.

Streaks of sunlight streamed through my line of vision as a heaviness weighed down, enveloping me in a silent cocoon.

Eddie visited my dreams as a grown-up sailor boarding a ship ready to set out to sea. His muscular frame filled in a crisply, starched white uniform. A canvas hat topped his shaven head. Once aboard, he stood at attention, and with immaculate white gloves, saluted an officer.

I knew Eddie wasn't supposed to, but he turned to smile at me as soon as his superior started climbing the ladder to an upper deck. My brother mouthed the words, "Goodbye." But I didn't answer. He waited for me to respond, risking a reprimand. I stood transfixed, fully aware that if I waved, he would follow the officer up the stairs, and disappear from my life.

There was a commotion on the top deck. Shouts erupted and shipmates scurried as the clamor increased. My brother stowed his duffle bag against the metal compartment wall and raced up the steps. Men's voices pierced the air with an urgency that could not be ignored. Eddie turned, one last time. He didn't smile. He didn't wave. He just stared straight at me with those big blue eyes.

Anguished sobs of women weeping hysterically drowned out all other voices.

The heavy clanging of a bell rang over and over, the cold steel pounding hard against the quiet of the day.

In the rush of the next moments, chaos ruled. Someone scooped me up in strong arms, compressing all of me into the darkness of layered fabrics.

It was my mother, holding me with a death grip I could not escape. Water splashed, drenching our clothes, as she rushed along the shoreline screaming my brother's name. I shielded my ears and struggled to see beyond her head, out toward the center of the lake where the skiff rested on the water ... empty.

Nana grabbed my mother, calling out to Papa and my father as they repeatedly dove and swam around the boat. I tried pushing myself free of my mother's grasp. She tightened her arms, kissed the top of my head, and pressed me closer and closer to her heaving chest, suffocating my every breath. I drew my head upward, gasping, and beat my fists wildly in the air, striking her shoulders and neck. Sweating, crying, I continued struggling against her arms of steel.

The deafening alarm echoed across the lake as the iron clapper hammered against the bell at a quickening pace. The minute my father burst through the surface with something in his arms, Doc abandoned the bell, dove off the pier, and swam out toward the boat.

My mother collapsed to her knees and let go a wail, a shrill, shattering reverberation, that pierced my eardrums, caused momentary deafness. Neither Nana nor Annie could comfort her. My father emerged with what appeared to be a bundle of wood, and a pile of clothing. My mother moved in and I saw, it was Eddie on the shore. Doc ran up and pushed on my brother's chest, breathed into his mouth, pushed on his chest, breathed into his mouth, over and over and over. But it didn't help.

My mother released her hold on me to gather my brother close. Nana picked me up. The water continued to roll in and back out without ever whispering a word of what had come to pass. A hush settled over us as a devouring cloud cover shut out all elements of light, every syllable of joy, and the last remnants of innocence.

The rocks in the pockets of the soaked clothing that hung on Eddie's lifeless body had weighed him down to the sandy bottom of our beloved lake, and claimed him forever. The icy waters drank my mother's grief, and carried her cries to the depths of Tahoe's unseen graves.

Hollow echoes entered my heart and memory that afternoon. They have owned me ever since. Taken the other half of me without any discussion, explanation or bartering. I would have sold my soul for my brother's life. For a long time, I assumed any of us would.

I awoke in a cold sweat and heard myself moaning. Nana was sitting beside me.

"I killed Beddie! It was all my fault." I thrashed wildly to get out from under my bedding, kicking the covers that trapped my feet in the tangle of the sheets.

"Emily, it was not your fault!" Nana grabbed my shoulders, her grip forceful.

"Listen to me. It was an accident."

I buried my head in her lap, whimpering, "I killed him, I saw him get into the boat, and I didn't stop him. How could I just watch like that?"

"You were asleep. We had to wake you." She struggled against the raw power and might of my delirium. "There, there, child."

"Why didn't I stop him?" I begged her for answers.

"You were just turning four years old. How could you realize he was in danger, or understand drowning?" Her calm tone offered refuge.

"But I saw him. He was waving, calling me to join him." Tears warmed my cheeks. "Is that why Mama always blamed me? She knew I watched?"

"Oh, Emily, all those years, your mama blamed herself, saying she was the one who put you two down to nap. You wanted to sleep with your parents, but your brother didn't." Nana's words bore years of sorrow.

"I don't remember that." I pulled away. How could it be true?

"We all remember that day differently. For decades each of us tried to piece together exactly what happened. Why, I don't know. It didn't change a thing." She spoke in such anguish of heart. It cut to my soul.

"Mama never wanted me after that. She mourned for Beddie. I was still there. All the decades of my mother's melancholy separation from our family resurfaced.

"Emily." She stared into my desolate eyes. "Your mother loved you. She was consumed with guilt that haunted her until cancer ravaged her insides." Nana lowered her head. "No mother wants to outlive her child."

"When she'd look into my eyes, she was always searching for him, as if he was somewhere to be found if she kept looking." My shoulders slumped forward. "He was so happy that day, Nana, pretending he was an airplane and picking up rocks, all shapes and sizes, his treasures." I fumbled for the sheet to dry my eyes.

"That's why all his pockets were full of rocks? We never understood." Her face reflected a realization that brought both pain and illumination.

"I wanted to go with him, but I was so sleepy."

"It was the first time in your young life you didn't follow your brother. If you had, we would have lost both of you that day." She cried and she held me in her arms. "I am so grateful, you stayed."

I raised my head. "Nana, how did Beddie get out to the middle of the lake?"

"It must have appeared that far to you, but he was only a short distance out, in about ten feet of water. That's how your dad and Papa were able to bring him up so fast. He had been under a couple of hours by the time we noticed you two were missing."

"I saw him reaching for something, on top of the water."

"You never actually saw him fall in, or jump?" She seemed surprised.

"No. He was still in the skiff, the sun shimmering on his hair."
She gasped, "It must have been his sailor cap. Doc found it
floating when he went to bring in the boat."

"Beddie put it on when we climbed out of bed and he was
wearing it on the beach." I began putting it all together. It seemed
so simple, so clear. "His hat must have fallen into the lake when I
saw him reaching over the edge of the boat. The sun was shining
on his hair the last time I looked before I fell asleep."

"Bless his little heart." She clutched her dress to her chest. "All
these years later, to know the truth. You had the missing piece to
the puzzle." Her hand trembled in mine. "All those pebbles he'd
collected. He never had a chance."

"I thought the adults knew everything that was why no one
ever talked to me." I stammered, realizing so much had been
assumed, unsaid.

"Emily, the Anderson's blamed themselves. Do you remember
the lovely family that moved away when you were six? They had
borrowed the skiff, and when they returned it that day, they forgot
to turn it up-side-down."

"That's right. You never left it facing up." My mouth was dry.

"Your dad thought it was his fault for talking your Mama
into staying with him instead of checking on you two. Papa and I
closed our door so we didn't hear you when you got up. Doc and
Annie were grieved because they chose the front porch that afternoon for their picnic lunch. If they'd gone out back, they would
have seen you for sure. There was no shortage of people blaming
themselves." She motioned for me to draw closer.

I melted into her embrace. She resumed stroking my hair,
running her fingers slowly from the top of my head to the ends; a
soothing ritual from my childhood.

Peace flowed out from her like a river of life.

"You lost a child that day too, didn't you?" I already knew the answer, but needed to speak the words out loud. I sucked in air and tried to breathe.

"Your mother never recovered. She closed out the world and chose to live in the past. All I could do was love her. And you." The sweet breath of Nana's kiss brushed tenderly upon my face.

My lower lip quivered. "For years I didn't know why he vanished and left me behind. I was waiting for him to come back for me."

"We all cringed the next summer when you demanded to learn how to swim. You sat on that beach watching all the adults and mimicked their every move. Your parents hired a private lifeguard. By the end of the season, I started calling you, *Little Fish*." Nana tugged on my nightshirt.

"Nana, it feels like there's a gaping hole inside me. When I swim, it's partially filled." I whispered in her ear. "I saw Beddie in a dream last night. He was all grown up, a soldier going on a voyage. He was happy, like that day on the beach. He said good-bye to me."

"Let him go, Emily." She held me sway.

"Forgive yourself, Emily." She whispered. "Then you'll be set free."

The shelter of Nana's arms was secure, like a strong refuge. I yearned for the inner glow of tranquility she emitted. Her heartache was no less than mine, and the extent of loss was even greater. Loneliness never seemed to overwhelm her as it did me. She was my rock. I certainly gave her no foundation to rely upon.

We talked about Beddie, and she told me things I'd never heard about my mother before. What she was like as a young woman, before my father. Nana brought a small box of photos to my bed. There were many pictures I had never seen before of my mother, from infancy to about the age my brother and I were when he left us.

"Life has many mysteries, and not all is told from the beginning, or ever understood." Emotion flooded her speech. "Loss will either expend you or strengthen your spirit." She held a picture that was taken the day my mother was born.

"I ran my fingertips over the photo. "I have always loved her name, Abigail."

It means 'father of exultation.'" Nana placed the picture in my hand. "She loved you so much, Emily. May you find it in your heart to forgive her."

Chapter Nineteen

I asked my nana once if she prayed underwater. I meant if she got down on her knees like I had grown up seeing her do at her bedside. Her door was always open enough to catch a glimpse of her bowed head. I was seven then. Now, as an adult, I know the answer. Yes, she does. She prays everywhere, all the time. She never isn't praying.

-Emily, journal entry, the summer of 1989

I couldn't sleep trying to process everything Nana had told me about my mother. The ceiling loomed overhead like an eternal sea of white. I studied every indentation of the spackle pattern, then got up and switched off the light. Lying in pitch dark, or closing my eyes and counting sheep didn't help either.

My insomnia prevailed, so I wandered downstairs. Nana's door was open. I stood in the doorway, watching her. Jack's words rang in my ears. The rise and fall of her breathing was shallow, her chest barely moving. Nana sighed in her sleep. The hall light shone on her pallid face. She looked peaceful. The faintest hint of a smile spread as if she were enjoying a lovely dream.

I couldn't take my eyes off her. Twice she seemed to stop breathing. I drew closer and closer until I was at her bedside, stroking the side of her cheek. I hovered over, then bent down to kiss her.

Her eyelids flickered. "Emily? Is something wrong, child?"

"I can't sleep," I murmured. "Didn't mean to wake you."

"Do you want to get under the covers with me?" She pulled back the quilts.

I wanted to crawl in with her, but hesitated. I don't know why. "That's okay. I'm sorry I disturbed you."

She rubbed her eyes. "You want me to hold you for a while?"

"I'll be all right." I turned to leave, stopped, looked back, and knew I wanted to cuddle beside her more than anything. "You sure you don't mind?"

"This is what grandmothers are all about."

I crawled in close and nestled under her arm as she lowered the cozy, warm quilts.

So many times, as a little girl. I ran in here and waited for her to come to bed. We'd talk until sleep fell upon us under these same toasty covers.

"I said a prayer for you tonight." Nana gave me a quick hug. "I say one every night."

"I know you do." Somehow that comforted me tonight more than it ever had before. Remembering my brother's death had drawn out such raw emotion. This was the first night since he'd left us that I no longer felt part of me was missing. Maybe I could be whole again.

"What's troubling your heart?"

"What isn't?" I answered in a deep sigh.

"It takes time to process everything. Let it sink in and settle a while." Nana's confidence gave me pause. Maybe this once I should heed her counsel without an argument.

I lay quietly beside her, content for the moment to be the sole focus of her attention. Often I resented sharing her with anyone but Doc. People were drawn to her, even perfect strangers. Rarely did I have her all to myself as I now did. Thoughts flooded my brain, whirling and swirling about at high speed. I closed my eyes tight to keep them from gushing out.

Nana seemed to sense my struggle and began massaging the tension out of my upper back. Slowly she followed the muscle from my neck out along my shoulder, a result of whiplash from a car accident. I'd never told her David was driving drunk that night when we crashed just a mile away from home. He'd totaled our brand new car just months after he drove it off the car lot. A purchase he'd neither discussed nor agreed upon with me. I flinched as she kneaded out a knot.

"Is this helping or hurting?" she asked, halting at once.

"Helping and necessary."

"You just say when." She resumed with a balanced mixture of pressure, relieving pain I didn't even know existed. Mounting stress and frustration that was tied up in tight knots loosened, dissipated, and left my body relaxed.

Nana always says we store the truths we hide from ourselves and others in our bodies. If left to fester, it cripples and decays from deep within until ultimately, it destroys and kills. I used to think she was a bit extreme in her thinking. Not anymore.

"Thanks, Nana." I took hold of her hand and kissed it twice. Where did the strength in those wrinkled, bony hands come from?

I rolled over and faced her. "David was drunk every time he wrecked our cars."

"He and I had a little chat after the third accident, when you ended up with a broken leg that took you out from skiing all winter. I left it up to him whether or not to tell you about our discussion."

"That's why he switched to the passenger side?" I had wondered. "There were never any other cars involved, so he didn't report the accidents to the insurance company. I quit riding in the same car with him. I took the girls in my car with me whenever we went out. David always met us in his own vehicle, usually coming to or from work."

"Emily, after a broken leg in the first accident and fractured ribs in the second, Doc and I were fit to be tied, and Jack was right along there with us. Working alcoholics are pretty good about hiding their drinking, but it shows through in ways they can't cover up. Oh, he made all the usual excuses. The only one who believed what he had to say, was him. I'm sure he probably went to his grave in denial."

"Unfortunately, others are still suffering the long-term consequences." I lay on my back, gazing at the ceiling. Nana followed suit and pulled the quilts up to our chins.

"Slightly different perspective from this angle," she mused.

I tightened both hands on the edges of the blankets and clamped down. "It looks like a big empty page waiting for words to be written."

"That's an interesting point of view." Nana responded in a delighted tone. "Maybe that's something you can work on." She nudged my shoulder, staring at an angle similar to mine. "What would you write?"

"I have no idea. But an empty page is certainly appealing to me right now. I feel changed somehow. Does that make sense?"

"Yes, it does. The nice thing about a blank page is the lack of limitations."

She grabbed a spare pillow off the rocking chair next to the bed, propped herself up a little higher, and turned onto her side.

"Will you hold me for a little while?" I scooched closer.

She opened her arms and wrapped them around me like a hen gathering her chick under the cover of her wings. I snuggled, trusting in the safety of that refuge.

"You smell good, Nana, like lilacs."

So many nights I'd wanted David to hold me like this. I hated the stench of whiskey on his breath, his clothes, and in his mustache. But I held my breath for a few seconds, and let it go. My chest squeezed, momentarily constricting airflow. I exhaled slow breaths. The muscles in my heart, back, and neck relaxing letting the fragrance of lilacs float above, encouraging a balmy slumber.

"Hush, hush, Little Fish." Nana's calming voice transported me to a gentler day.

Carefree and irrepressible. My brother's laughter lightened the skies and his big blue eyes danced across the lake, deepening the shades of the sparkling waters.

"Beddie," I whispered his name at first, then spoke it out loud. The familiar sound dressed my old wounds like a restorative ointment.

I must have dreamt that night, but I remembered nothing the next morning. It didn't matter. I had no need for anything as fleeting as twilight dreams. Even when pleasant, they drift away in the waking hours of the day and they leave nothing solid to hold on to, pin down, or build on.

There was more of a tranquil calm—like what I see in Nana all the time. Even the usual reoccurring thoughts of David's obnoxious antics didn't dampen my spirits. I determined my day would start without rehashing those old hurts that hang around. Like stinky fish in the back of the fridge.

I gave Nana a peck on the cheek as she slept, got dressed in my room, then headed out the door.

A light mist hovered over the lake creating an eerie fog that floated in wavering layers inches above the water. A cool breeze blew, a gentle zephyr filtering through the parts of me I rarely left vulnerable to the elements.

I snapped off a couple of bright orange and pink Gerber daisies at the base of the stem when I stopped along the driveway. It took time to single out the key to my car from my jeans pocket. I hopped up into the driver's seat. After tossing the flowers on the passenger side, and started the engine, then backed out. The early sunlight guided me beyond the Jeffery pines lining the dirt road entrance to a tiny patch of land. Fifteen minutes. That's how far away my brother was from the cabin.

Stepping out into the airy sticky-sweet scent of honeysuckle, waxy white-headed gardenia hedges, and trumpeting morning glories, I gathered the small scentless daisy bouquet. Pressing it to the heart thumping against my ribcage. My zories crunched heavy on dry needles, and spent cones, until I stood before a graduating row of marble headstones.

Red-breasted robins chirped in the nearby trees-tops, and a unique three-note whistle chimed in as a little black-capped mountain chickadee chimed in, flew by and perched on the cross crowning my brother's grave. I knelt on the hardened ground where sparse tufts of green grass grew on the outer fringes of Beddie's final resting place. The woods beyond appeared endless. Tall trunks of puzzle-shaped brown bark stood with outstretched evergreen branch fingers reaching skyward, as the unseen roots beneath, tangled and intermingled deep into the earth. The birds sang their harmonious lullaby in the quiet commencement of the day.

With gradual and deliberate intent, I inched over on my knees to the white headstone. "I have called thee by thy name; thou art mine." Isaiah 43:1 Born July 29th 1955 - died June 1st 1959. Nana had picked out the verse.

Beddie was not written anywhere on the thick slab. I ran my fingers in and out of the smooth craved grooves of my brother's name, Edward Prescott Maxwell, and the words 'Our little angel' that my mother had had etched below 'Beloved son, brother, and grandson'.

I'd never thought of Beddie as an angel and I'd told my mother so. It drove her to a torrent of tears and two entire days and nights secluded in her bedroom. It was the truth.

He was the furthest thing from an angel he could be. Actually he was more like a little devil—not evil, just curious, getting in and out of predicaments every moment of his life. His eyes widened with excitement when new discoveries garnered his interest, captivating his mind and enticing him into immediate action.

A joyful laugh escaped my lips and lingered. The chickadee cocked his head and kept his dark, pin-dot eyes on me, following my slightest movement. As I scattered the colorful flowers on top of the gravesite, the bird didn't take flight but remained perched, talons tightly clamped on the cold marble.

A glint of light alongside the bordering fence line caught my attention. I wandered over to inspect. I picked up broken pieces of granite, beautiful, sparkly, nuggets of white with ripples of a black river running through. The rock had recently been smashed. The cuts were fresh, not weathered at all. Beddie would have gathered every last piece and put them in his pockets. Returning to his plot, I sprinkled the bits of the rock over the flowers, blades of grass, and the headstone.

Standing back, it struck me that his was the sole tiny plot in the surrounding radius of Maxwells, Harrisons, and other non-relatives. A babe, an innocent lost to a family that knew not how to grieve his untimely death. Neither did we know how to celebrate the joy and zest he lived out during his fleeting mortality. My mother died with my brother as surely as if we had shoveled dirt over her in his coffin.

Only Nana had faith that death had no permanent grip. She believed something the rest of us refused as we chose to live in silence that robbed the living of life.

This resting place for the dead had never appealed to me. I always thought of my brother and the lake as though they were one. Water meant life. The depths of the earth where we entomb bodies offers no light, no hope of return, no redemption.

Nana never comes here either. Yet when she leaves this world, this is where I am to lay her to rest. She has ordered a simple pine box, not even lined. At the time I read her funeral paperwork I was shocked. But now I understood.

I glanced at my parents' and Papa's tombstones and said my quiet good-byes, murmuring words I could never utter before.

I lingered at the foot of Beddie's grave, stretching my toes over the edge of my zories so they touched the earth above him. "I miss you, baby brother." I strained to choke out the words. "What adventures we would have had together." My voice trailed off but I was determined to say the things I'd locked up in my heart. A requiem for the one with whom I shared a mother's womb. The protective world where our lives began and were nourished, buffered safely in life-sustaining amniotic fluid.

The first lake, the first swim, the first miracle.

The chickadee took to flight in a circular loop above me before landing back on Beddie's marker, then stared straight at me and whistled it's melody. Such a small fellow in the midst of the massive ornate marble slabs and the surrounding conifer forest. I listened to each musical note, grateful for the impromptu performance of the tiny creature's serenade.

"Good-bye, Beddie." I whispered and blew my farewell kiss up to the sky. Past the clouds, into the atmosphere, to drift weightlessly among the stars that would light up the universe. I returned to my car. Once behind the wheel, I glanced back. The bird was gone and the forest stood, it seemed to me in a reverent watch over the long dead. Their bones were all that remained of the heart and soul, love and laughter, of those we cherished.

I drove all the way around the lake. Past Kings Beach, Incline Village and Sand Harbor. In and out of Cave Rock tunnel, which had delighted my brother so much, he hung half-way out the car window every time, completely unnerving our mother as our father grinned ear to ear. On past Zephyr Cove to the south shore state line row of towering, multi-colored, blinking light-bulb-lit casinos, rivaled solely by the Las Vegas strip that Nana had no passion for at all.

Heading up to Historic Camp Richardson and Taylor Creek my grandmother claims are the south shore's redeeming graces. I cautiously inched along that harrowing stretch by Emerald Bay. Maneuvering several hair-pin turns carved out of the forested mountain landscape, and over the narrow ridge two-lane highway with a sheer six thousand-foot drop down both sides. As a child I used to close my eyes and prayed every time my father drove that pass. I steered my car within an arm's reach of the jagged formations jutting out of the mountainside that define Rubicon Bay's stark beauty and incongruous danger. Osprey soared overhead.

Then I headed for home, past familiar landmarks I could map out blindfolded. Vibrant purple columbine, yellow buttercups, and sunset-red Indian paintbrush wildflowers swayed lazily in the alpine breeze. Diligent ants labored in columns along the roadside where I sat stuck in stagnant afternoon tourist traffic, ingesting toxic carbon dioxide fumes. It didn't even faze me when vacationers honked their horns, their drivers apparently thinking that if they continued tooting incessantly, RV's, boats, trailers, and buses would magically move on at 55 miles an hour. I knew better. We were all in for a snail's pace, bumper-to-bumper ride into Tahoe City. I slipped in a cassette of classical music, tapped the button to roll down my window, and settled in the comfortable glove of my seat.

The piano concerto filled my Explorer with a far more desirous sound than the unpleasant bleating outside. We crawled at five miles an hour from Homewood to Tahoe City. At the triangle Y where the lanes narrow from two to one, motorists not willing to yield to other cars nearly caused a fender bender in front of the fire station at Commons Beach.

My speedometer hit fifteen miles an hour when I passed the former location of the pine that stood most of my life in the center of the highway across from Rosie's Café. I loved that old tree and thought it would grow old with me. By the time they chopped it down, it had suffered the ravages of drought and drunk drivers, bearing the numerous scars inflicted by both. Every time I drive by, I still see that tree.

Blazing past the Dollar Hill and Dollar Point developments, I finally hit 25 MPH.

I turned on my blinker in ample time to indicate my intention of a turn right, into the cabin driveway. I had come full circle. Home.

The amber brilliance of the high-noon sun spooned overhead in a cerulean sky, warming up the day and the lake. I knew I could convince Nana to take a jaunt in the *Martha* with me. Just the two of us girls. Maybe a picnic lunch stop on the west shore. The Tahoe Gal paddle-wheeler would be on her way to Emerald Bay. Nana loves to wave to that boat when I drive by. I might surprise her today and wave along with her.

Chapter Twenty

For every time I listened, there were ten times I didn't. I'd sit on the beach bursting to blab. When underwater, if I opened my mouth, the water rushed in, so I had to keep my mouth closed. And that was a good thing. I heard so much in the below-the-surface world that I was completely deaf to in the world above.

-Emily, after listening to the Lake, journal entry, 1990

J slept through the night without interruption and woke revived the next day. Nana begged off the trip into town to pick up what few groceries we were out of and set herself up out on the back deck for her morning read. All she asked for was a small package of 9-volt batteries for her transistor radio.

"The Giants are playing tonight," she shouted through the glass, sputtering a persistent hacking cough until she caught her breath and gave me a thumbs-up with a big smile.

"Should I pick up some hot dogs and buns?" I asked, half-jokingly.

"That sounds like a great idea. We can sit out here and listen to the game. I have a hankering for a cola too, but be sure you get the glass bottles."

"Nana, I'm surprised."

"I am too but it sounds like the perfect way to wash down a hot dog." She sounded serious enough. "Be sure you get enough for Jack and Doc. They eat more than we do."

"Okay." I smiled as I tried to picture the four of us sitting around Nana's little transistor radio out on the back deck. The television at Doc's would remain unused this evening, there will be no adjusting the rabbit ears tonight. *I'm turning into an old fogy before my time.*

I parked in town so I could run into the Tahoe Trails Motel and leave a recommendation for Rosa's application to work there as a maid. She'd approached me at Doc's the day before, after I'd complimented her immaculate job at the office and house. She was desperate for steady full-time employment to support her three little children since her husband's sudden departure in the middle of the night with a casino Keno runner.

I'd known Rosa since before the kids were born. Jess had never been the most committed husband or father, but running off like that surprised everyone who knew the family. Doc would keep her on so she could earn extra income and work around the children's school schedules. Frank over at the TTM would do the same. He'd be an honest and fair boss.

As I dashed back to my car, I saw Jack in front of The Station. I thought it odd he would be there for breakfast this close to time for his first appointments of the day. But I headed over to say 'hello' anyway.

Janie came rushing out of the restaurant arguing with him. I hung back. Her voice raised to a squeaky high pitch that was impossible to ignore.

"Jack, you promised. No more lies!"

His back to me, he spoke to her civilly at first, so low I couldn't make out what he was saying. She faced me dead on and her head almost snapped full-swivel when we locked eyes.

"You'll never change. You're always cheating on the woman you're fooling around with." Her voice carried across the parking lot like an electric charge. "I've wasted too many years letting you keep coming back." She raised her hand high and waited a few seconds, then slapped his face. She swung her hips around and stomped back inside the restaurant, coffee swirling around in the glass pot clenched in her fist, steam spewing in the cold morning air.

Jack went up the steps after her and disappeared. Numb, I got in my car and drove to the market and sat. "I am not going to cry. I am not going to cry over you again!" I slammed my hand against the dashboard, and sobbed, my head bumping against the wheel every time I sucked in air. Cars drove by, parked, and left before I regained even the remotest measure of composure.

"Why did I think he had changed? He's just like David. I'm repeating the same mistake. You stupid, stupid, woman." My voice hoarse and raspy, I placed sunglasses over my eyes and begged God not to let anyone I knew run into me. After blowing my nose into the last tissue from the packet in my purse, I managed to enter the store unnoticed and hit the aisles that had the items Nana had requested, and tossed in a few selections of my own.

I didn't see Selma Sue round the corner of the lunchmeat aisle until I practically ran into her with the cart. She turned her nose up at the packages of hot dogs I had in my hands.

"How can you eat those disgusting, processed, intestine-lined capsules loaded with fillers, preservatives, and nitrates? You should at the very least buy beef instead of the franks."

"I must have grabbed the frankfurters by mistake." I mumbled and switched packages. "I have to hurry and get back for the barbeque. Have a good day."

A hand flew to her chest. "You aren't going to be serving Doc those for a meal are you? Why, I just dropped off a healthy home-made casserole those boys can eat for the next couple of days."

I fumbled to lower the sunglasses on top of my head to cover my puffy eyelids and the swollen bags under my eyeballs. Selma shot a look at the mascara-smeared tissues overflowing out of my open purse. I zipped it shut, but not fast enough.

"You don't look so good, Emily. Is something wrong? You can tell me. I won't repeat a word."

Yeah right. "Thank you for your concern, but I'm fine. The hot dogs are for Nana." I offered the extra information hoping it would sidetrack her long enough for me to make my escape.

"You can't feed an old woman those sodium-riddled wieners of death. Her system can't handle the garbage pressed and packaged for the ignorant masses."

I rushed to an open front register while Selma rattled off a political statement about elder abuse. If I didn't check out fast. she'd catch up to me. I grabbed the hot dogs, buns, cokes, and batteries from the top basket, and dropped them on the conveyor belt. "That's it for now. I don't need the rest of what's in the cart." I handed the cashier a ten dollar bill, and took a brown paper bag as Selma forged her way in my direction. "Keep the change." I grabbed my purchases and threw them in the bag, then exited through the automatic door that didn't open fast enough for me.

What planet did that woman come from? Someone needs to buckle her in and send her back to the mother ship. I swiped a multitude of wadded up tissues off the passenger seat to the floor, then tossed the grocery bag over until it bounced off the passenger door.

"I grew up eating hot dogs and they haven't killed me yet. Considering the extra pounds on your petite frame, Miss Selma Sue Crumbly, I'd say you've consumed your weight in juicy frankfurters in big fluffy buns, topped with canned chili and plenty of cheese." I muttered several choice obscenities under my breath that I truly wouldn't have minded for her to hear.

With trepidation, I shoved my sunglasses back and checked the rear-view mirror to examine the hideous puffy bags hanging most unattractively on my face. Not even a quick patch-up job with my make-up pouch was going to remedy this swollen mess. I sat there, wondering what the all-fired hurry I was in to get back. Jack was sure to be at the office by now. I was scheduled to work in the file room for half the day. I would not be showing up for my part time job this morning.

Debating with myself like a crazy woman, I sat in my car for over two hours. I need to deal with this latest infraction head-on. No, arguing, justifying, and rationalizing. I'm done with him, the old snake charmer.

I punched the automatic button and my window rolled down. Fresh air flooded in instead of the gas carbons I was expecting to invade and take over. I reclined my seat level with the one behind me. I didn't care. Well I wanted to not care. The vinyl seat sweated beneath me, I squirmed sideways, out of the line of direct sunlight. I propped my feet up on the dash, straddling the steering wheel, adjusted the side mirrors, and turned on my hazard lights.

There I sat in my little corner of obscurity, lights flashing intermittently, alerting all around me to the imminent danger Jack Conner was to those he selfishly exposed to incessant lies and charismatic hogwash.

Tires rolled in and halted with a squeal beside me. Flashes of red light swirled as the whine of a siren interrupted any opportunity to plot vengeance. Within seconds, a tall, muscular, uniformed male sheriff stood peering into the open space where thick tinted glass normally deters intruders.

He looked down at me and held my reluctant gaze. "Ma'am, are you alright? Do you need some help?"

"Yes. Could you do me a favor and arrest Jack Conner? I can give you a litany of criminal charges of which he is absolutely guilty." I pressed my chin on my criss-crossed forearms stretched across the open window, attempting to appear sincere while adjusting my seat forward electronically.

"Ma'am, have you been drinking?"

"No, sir, I've been believing. You can charge me with being stupid and disillusioned." I hung my head out the window, gazing up at the young man.

He removed his sunglasses. "Emily Taylor?" He looked straight in my bleary, reddened eyes.

"Yes." pulling back into the car, I sat straight and rigid.

"Could you please step out of the vehicle?" He backed away, leaving plenty of space.

Great. He'll probably do one of those Breathalyzer tests, and give me a ticket for loitering. I stepped outside, watching to see if his hand went for his service revolver.

"Having a bad day?" he asked grinning.

A distinct change softened his tone of voice. And there was a hint of amusement, maybe even laughter when he turned sideways.

Recognition hit with relief. "Derrick Thomas?" I backed up to the metal door.

"So you want me to arrest Jack Conner. What is the formal charge?" He reached into his shirt pocket and whipped out a notepad with a pen clipped in the spiral binding.

"Are you going to give me a ticket?" I asked, somewhat stunned.

"No, but if you want to press charges, I can take your report." His smile spread wider and he reclined next to me against the car.

"No formal charges, just informal complaints and regrets." My shoulders sagged with embarrassment. At least he didn't think I was drunk.

He wrote on the paper, then flipped the tablet shut. "You don't look so good. Are you feeling okay?"

My make-up was smeared, mascara smudged, and eyeliner streaked. I could have passed for the sorry loser in a wee-hours-of-the-morning barroom brawl. "It hasn't been the best of mornings." I angled to get a glimpse in the side mirror, then realized, maybe I didn't want to.

"Well, off the record, I can't say I'm disappointed to hear you say that Jack should be reprimanded. I've never understood what you saw in that bad boy. He, uh, gets around, if you know what I mean." He stood taller than I remembered Devon Thomas's little brother being.

Everyone in town must know my personal life story with the infamous playboy candidate for the Rat Pack.

He didn't look like my high school summer swim teammate's kid brother at the moment. In fact, the man standing before me filled out his uniform with the muscular build of a dedicated regular at the gym.

"Also, off the record ..." He scribbled a couple of lines on a page he tore out from the notebook. "This is my home phone number, in case you need to talk. My address is on there too. I'm free for a lap swim if you need to work things out. You do still swim, don't you?" He gave me the slip of paper.

I palmed it without reading what he'd written. "Yes, I still swim open water laps, daily."

"Good to hear. Do you need an escort home?"

"No. But thank you for the offer. Nana's waiting on me, so I'd better get going." Phantom strands of hair fell across my face. My hand rose almost involuntarily and I waved good-bye.

He got into his patrol car and slowly drove out of the parking lot. I watched him adjust his rear-view mirror.

Belting myself in, I took a long look in my visor mirror. It wasn't pretty.

Did that young man just ask me out? Is that how men ask women to go on a date these days? I tucked the paper in my wallet, under my driver's license.

Chapter Twenty-One

Hail hammers down, pounding, pounding. Heavy laden
gray skies darken. The lake changes, the forest rages. Futile
efforts are undone. Freezing, stinging, dodging, the bitter
cold is crippling. Blinded by directional force, destiny has
set its course. Deluged by unrelenting fire. Battered, seeking cover from a merciless assault. The mountain branches
offer shelter, sanctuary without default. Rock-hard balls
of icy anger, pierce the pitch-black sky. No end in sight
for birds of flight. Their cries tarry throughout the night.
Frenzied fury, accusatory words, two worlds collide, shat-
ter and divide.

-Emily's journal entry 1995

"Sorry for being so late." I told Nana when I found her
on the back deck watering the flower boxes. She followed me in and rummaged through the paper bag I dumped on
the kitchen counter. "We can still have hot dogs and listen to the
game. But I need to take a shower first." I hurried up the stairs.

Standing under the pulsating downpour, I scrubbed my face
with make-up remover, attempting to take off the grimy film of
smeared mascara that wouldn't wash away.

Clouds blocked out the light streaming through the opaque
sheers, darkening the bedroom to match my mood. Flipping a

panel back, I scowled at the unstable sky. The brewing storm was moving in earlier than predicted on the radio station I'd tuned into on the way home. I wondered if the ball game would be rained out.

I joined Nana downstairs on the sofa trying to appear revitalized. "Looks like this one's going to be wicked."

"I think the ballgame may be in jeopardy." She sighed. "It would have to be a merciless downpour before there'd be a cancellation."

I stretched to warm my hands in front of the glowing flames that flickered in the fireplace, making an unearthly whining, and hissing noise. Thick, sooty smoke rose steadily up the chimney to mingle with the menacing formations brooding above.

"Doc stockpiled wood inside the door. Said a big one is rolling in." Nana seemed to resign herself to the inevitable: the Giants game was done for.

"Maybe we could spend the day alone, just the two of us. Some quality time." I yanked a loose strand of thread hanging from my cut-offs.

"Too late. The men will be here soon. I called to invite them before the phone lines get knocked out."

"Wow. Is it going to get that severe?"

My attempt to avoid any contact whatsoever with Jack had innocently enough, been thwarted by my diminutive grandmother, determined to hitch our wagons together and send them out on the dusty trail.

Hands on her hips, Nana shot me a discerning glance. I was beyond caring if she caught on. I was done with Jack. No more lies, no more chances, no more Jack. I'd rather not have it out with him tonight, knowing Doc and Nana would be within earshot. That was now unavoidable. I got up and opened a bottle of wine.

"Is something wrong?"

"I'm just going to sip some of this zin for a while in front of the fire. Would you like a glass?" *If only this once she would say yes.*

"You know I don't drink alcohol." Nana's eyes glanced at me in a quizzical sweep, a sort of deep-penetration.

"What happened in town this morning?"

"I ran errands." I avoided further discussions by disappearing into the kitchen for a wine glass and corkscrew. "Where's that bottle of zinfandel I brought up from Napa Valley?" This had all the makings of a great inquisition. Nana had a way of peeling through the layers until she focused in on the precise subcutaneous wart threatening to erupt to the surface.

"In the liquor cabinet, next to Papa's Irish whiskey."

I opened the door and pulled out the zinfandel, one of a few bottles not caked in decades of dust and ropey spider webs. "Geez, these bottles must date back to Prohibition."

"Just since your Papa passed." Maneuvering herself off the sofa with one momentous shove, she struggled to regulate her breathing by doing what appeared to be some kind of exercise. "It's time for this napster to rest her noggin," Nana said and sauntered off in her favorite orange and cream polyester pantsuit.

I took the bottle and my wine glass sat to the chaise and sat cross-legged facing the storm blowing in from the west. I poured and toasted. "To courage and confrontation." Swishing and swirling the fruity burgundy bouquet in the glass, I sniffed, then sipped. "Who needs self-control?"

Biting cold swept in under the back door like a snow-making machine stuck on automatic, blasting unrelenting gusts of frigid air. I stuffed a bath towel from the laundry room into the crack and hurried back to the fire. Flames roared and sap sizzled, shooting out sticky red-hot specks of ammunition. I instinctively covered my head and ducked.

With one tug, I scraped the sagging, blackened hearth screen across the stone, scritch-scratching the river rock, and closed off the intermediate gateway to Hades.

A pocket of pitch crackled and popped, like a couple of rapid gun shots. The hailstorm opened fire outside, pounding the cabin and deck in unrelenting continual sheets. The battering increased by the minute, hammering in with such fierce directional force, the glass sounded like it was cracking and breaking. Deafening thunder claps rocked the murky sky, followed in succession by jagged, lightning flashes fiercely cracking a whip across the lake. It was frightening and mesmerizing at the same time.

The deck doorknob jerked back and forth. I jumped, startled A bright yellow slicker appeared in the glass window of the door. "Unlock the door!" A blurry face pressed against the glass. The yellow hood blew back in a sudden gust of wind, revealing Jack's face.

"For heaven sakes, let me in!" He bellowed, twisting and turning the knob. He banged on the wooden frame in swift repetitive thrusts.

I got up, unlocked it, and stood back. The door rushed open and a bloodied hand reached in, followed by a muddy boot that shoved the towel and rug back. Hail peppered the floor, bouncing and rolling all the way into the kitchen.

"What is wrong with you?" Jack growled. His drenched clothes adhered to his skin. He slammed the door shut behind him. Rivulets of water dripped from hair soaked to his scalp. The raincoat hadn't offered much protection for the walk between the cabins.

"Do you have a towel?" he asked with a tone of bewilderment.

"Where's Doc?" My lack of any polite offer was intentional.

"He stayed home to work on some files."

Jack dragged the towel with his boot to soak up water. "Where's Nana?"

"She's sleeping." Before he could remove his coat, I got down to business. "I saw you in town this morning. With Janie. You lied to me."

"I haven't lied about anything."

"I saw her slap your face."

"You were there?"

"That's the last lie you're going to tell me. Get out!" I flung open the door.

"Let me explain." He grabbed my arm, gripping tight.

"It doesn't matter what you say. Go!"

The angry sky hurled a barrage of ice balls in our direction. The deck was layered so thick it looked like a blanket of snow had fallen. The earth howled and the wind carried mercenary threats across a dark moonless sky lit solely by lightning strikes.

"Em," Jack pleaded.

"Leave. Now."

He stood there for a moment, opened his mouth, and then closed it. His steely eyes pierced through me. A bulging vein running up his neck flared out in a vibrant shade of purple as he clenched his teeth. He pulled up his hood and turned away before slamming the door so hard it rumbled like thunder inside the cabin. He stood on the deck a few seconds longer, then he left, walking head-on into the full fury of the storm.

Stumbling over the hail-littered floor, I flipped the lock, then dropped to my knees and shoved the soggy rag back underneath. It took another half dozen towels to mop up the mess. Before tossing it all in the laundry room, I peeked in on Nana. She slept, blissfully unaware.

Dragging a wool blanket off the quilt rack, I wrapped myself up and sat in the rocker. Anger and adrenaline pumped up the more I thought of Jack's incredulousness. He acted so innocent, like he didn't have a clue. My insides churned, my eyeballs ached, heavy and burdensome. My head pulsated at the temples, straining to burst constricted blood vessels. My heart skipped beats, slowed to almost a dead stop, then palpitated wildly, jolting into an irregular rhythm. Soon the rush plummeted, leaving me drained.

I crawled to the fire place and tossed a few more logs on the grate, grabbed the poker, and shifted the wood around until I knew it would catch. Only then did I realize I'd been crying. I laid the poker on the hearth and curled up on the rug, longing even for my old life with David, preferably pre-adultery, though I wasn't entirely certain what time frame that involved.

I lay awake until an peculiar stillness settled over both worlds. The insulated inside, warm like the woolen quilt covering me, remained a sanctuary. The dark, cold mountains outside would be much altered. Tree branches broken, cabins damaged, and forest animals forced to rebuild or relocate their dwellings.

I drifted to sleep wondering how different things would have been if all those years ago I had gone to the University at Reno. I wouldn't have met David, I wouldn't have my daughters, I wouldn't be the woman I was this frozen night.

Jack opened the door to his room at the boarding house on North Virginia Street, to welcome me in. I was surprised how bachelor bare it was other than a twin-size bed and a dresser. A few psychedelic posters of rock groups were thumb-tacked into peeling plaster walls. An electric hot plate with the remnants of fried to a crisp potatoes and onions stuck to the bottom of a small cast-iron skillet, sat on top of a wooden crate.

"You're just in time for dinner," he said, brushing back hair as long as mine, he'd pulled back into a ponytail. This was a different look, for Jack. He unplugged the burner.

"This is what I gave up Sac State for?" I stood in disbelief, reluctant to cross over the threshold where mottled paint and a distinct odd, unidentifiable odor pervaded.

"Come in, I'll give you the tour." He clasped my hand in his, ferrying me over to the other side, into his world. "Over to the left, we have a private bathroom. Well, semiprivate. I share it with the guy in the next room. To the right, a closet. And there's enough room here for both you and me." Jack let my hand go and spread his arms out wide.

I stared at the lumpy mattress, suspended inches above the floor on a rickety steel spring with a metal headboard. Candles lined both windowsills and an empty wine bottle with tubes coming out of it sat on the dresser next to a stereo.

"What's this?" I asked, moving in to investigate.

"A water pipe. I'll explain later." He slid his hands in his back jeans pockets.

I noticed his Simon and Garfunkel concert tour tee-shirt was wrinkled, like he'd been living and sleeping in it for days. It hung lose on a much leaner frame. His jeans dragged on the floor, almost covering his bare feet. Other than his guitar case in a corner by the window, I didn't recognize a single thing.

"Are you all checked in? Did you already go to the administration building?"

"Yes. It's a beautiful campus with a great English department. I walked the grounds earlier. Older buildings, but love the architecture." I tugged down on my hot pink mini-skirt. "I have my own room in the dorm across the street, third floor." *In the newer, better smelling building.*

"I knew you'd come. For a while I thought you were still mad at me." Jack flashed that charismatic, foxy smile, then kissed me.

I caught my breath when he pulled back and grabbed his suede jacket off a chair. "What are you majoring in?"

"Right now I'm in the process of making some changes. My guidance counselor recommended some phycology courses." He slipped into moccasins, and grabbed his wallet and keys off the dresser.

"You aren't interested in a medical career anymore?" I shifted the braided strap of my purse on my shoulder. "Do Doc and Annie know?"

"Haven't told them yet." He locked arms with me. "Let's head out. There's a few places on campus I want to show you before dark."

"Okay, but I need to go finalize my class selections first."

Jack walked me out into the hallway.

"You left your door open."

"Yeah, I know."

Part Four

Spring ~ Sapphire Revelation

Time rolls in and out again,
Endlessly cresting waves.
The rise and fall of many men
Began in deep and darkened caves.

Light broke through and followed you,
Granite stone gave way,
An angel proclaimed, what all heaven knew,
The dawning of a brand-new day.

Not all believe and let the Spirit lead.
It's easier to stray,
Yet faith small as a mustard seed
Touches hearts to begin to pray.

Crystal clear, no longer fear,
Washed in the living Word.
Freedom for those who draw near.
Eternal whispers of hope are heard.

Chapter Twenty-Two

There is a beauty and melody to human speech, and our ears are finely tuned receivers.

~ One of Nana's favorite sayings.

*T*ugging at the window shade, I fumbled to snag the bobbing string by its crocheted loop but it eluded my every attempt. I lacked the special touch needed for that silly contraption, and it snapped all the way up and spun around in its tightly wound spring.

"Sorry, Nana. I didn't mean to blind you with the bright morning light." I carefully raised the second shade with a slow, steady pull.

"Looks like I slept through the big one," Nana commented, dropping her ear plugs on the nightstand. "How long was I out?"

"After twelve hours I thought you needed a nudge. I can't believe you still use those things."

"Old people are creatures of habit. Your Papa's snoring used to keep me up all hours of the night. I just kept using them. These little nubbins of foam could block out a roller derby." A croaky exhaustion hung in her voice. "So I missed the men last night?"

"No. Doc stayed in and Jack went back after the hail nailed him walking the path between the cabins."

"He didn't stay and eat?"

"No. I sent him home. For good." I didn't wait for her inquiries. "I saw him with Janie yesterday. He's lied to me for the last time."

"Did you ask him about her?"

"No. And don't start defending him."

"Emily, don't assume the worst," Nana said, an irritated edge hinging her words.

"Please back me up on this." I sat on her bed, pleading with my eyes for her support.

"Life is so short. Don't waste your opportunities." She fell back into her pillows, propped herself upright and rigid, then folded her hands saying nothing more.

That was fine with me. I wasn't up for a row. Jack didn't deserve her loyalty. She'd see the light—maybe not now, but she'd come around. He'd be quick to move on. Jack was good at improvising. It surprised me he was still partners with Doc. He could have been in a much more lucrative practice by now. He'd had many offers over the years, even out of state. Men like Jack are always in demand.

Nana uttered not a word while I brewed her tea and delivered it to her bedside.

"Emily, if you have time, could you check up in the attic for me?"

It almost sounded like a punishment.

"There's a box I tried to get myself before you came up for the summer." She clinked her spoon against the bone china tea cup.

"Don't you dare climb on a ladder by yourself," I warned her. "I have an appointment in town in about an hour. I'll go up first thing when I get home."

"Okay. I'll read a little in bed this morning while you're gone."

I knew what she meant. She'd be reading her Bible, praying I'd see the light.

I could swear it was already there in bed with her, under the covers. I noticed it had disappeared from the night stand when I set the teacup down.

I grabbed a bagel, got a file from my bedroom, and headed into town. Book Haven was already open. I handed the file to George just before a couple of men dressed in expensive, tailored Italian suits stepped in behind me. The jangle of the door bell announced their arrival. They greeted "Giorgio" with a profusion of "Buon giornos," ignoring me, before switching to near-perfect English.

"We will wait for you in the office," the younger gentleman declared while sauntering to the rear of the building. His partner followed, his Zelli shoes clicking on the worn tile squares. It was clear they were not in town to buy any books.

"Do you mind, Emily?" George asked.

"Not at all. I'll shop until you get back."

"Thanks." He rushed over and joined the Armani attired foreigners, easing the office door closed. The lock clicked.

Checking out the classics section, I browsed for a book to buy for Nana. I almost passed over the Hemingway shelf, but got distracted by a first edition of *A Farewell to Arms*. It was in mint condition. I gingerly picked it up and carefully turned the pages, checking for creases and tears. George must have made a recent acquisition, or I would have noticed it before.

The little bell chimed again when the door opened. I recognized the customer, quickly turned away, buried my face in the book, and shuffled farther back in the store.

He headed toward me, waving. "Hey, I know you. You're Jack's lady."

"My name is Emily." I snapped back.

"I'm Daryl, the lead singer in the band. You were dancing with Jack at The Station the other night. So you're the one."

"The one what?" My jaw tightened at my failed attempt to force a greeting.

"The one he gave up everyone else for."

"I think you're mistaken."

"No, no mistake. The minute he found out you were widowed, he cut off all the ladies and waited for you to come home."

"I saw him with Janie yesterday." The words rumbled accusingly off my lips.

"Yeah, she's been hard on him. Yesterday was bad. She caused a big scene at work when he came by to ask her to lay off once and for all."

He was telling the truth? "You mean they aren't seeing each other?" My heart sank.

"Oh, no. She's been out of the picture for a couple of years." He shook his head. "She's relentless. Basically stalks him around town."

I clutched the first edition in my hands tight.

"I see you know his favorite author." He tapped the book. "Say, is George around? He has a special order for me."

"He's in the office with a couple of men discussing business."

"I'm taking off for Reno on a gig for a couple of weeks. Could you tell him I'll pick it up when I get back?" He tossed back a thick wave of gray-streaked, sandy blonde hair revealing a gold stud pierced earring.

"Sure."

"Great to officially meet you, Emily. That Jack, he talks about you non-stop. Daryl gave me a big brother-like hug. "Guess I'll be seeing you around."

The bell jingled again. I flopped into the little ladybug kiddie chair next to me. The table and chairs, dwarfed by my presence, might as well have been a jury box of my peers. I was wrong in my assessment of Jack's character. I'd shut him out of my life based on—eavesdropping. Janie had looked right at me, the wretched bottom dweller. She put on quite the show. Maybe I could blame her instead of Jack this this time. Nana, was right, I was being foolish with what life brought my way.

The walls of knowledge surrounding me closed in until I was—small.

The Hemingway book almost burned in my hand. Indistinct voices carried through the office door, and it didn't sound like the conversation was winding down. I debated waiting it out and sat for another fifteen minutes doing absolutely nothing. The gaily painted red ladybug chairs encircled a garden table, with daffodils, heather, and roses blooming up the legs and across the surface. I traced my fingertips over all the butterflies, dragonflies, and hummingbirds flitting and flying about until nothing was left to discover. Finally I decided to leave George a note with Daryl's message. I'd pick up my folder later.

By the time I got to Doc's office, Jack was gone. He'd asked Doc for some time off. Personal reasons. Jack never asked for time off.

I arrived home empty-handed. Nana asked questions until I broke down.

"I was wrong." I choked. "I accused him of sleeping with that waitress."

She scurried behind me into the living room.

"And today he's taken time off." I stood at the window. I could hardly breathe.

She sat beside me with a stunned look that addled me to the core.

"He'll be back." She didn't sound so certain.

"Things will be different between us." I couldn't steer my gaze from the lake.

"Give him some time to work it through." Nana said. "No fretting. It won't change anything."

"How could I be such a brat? He tried to talk with me." A dull throb pounded in the back of my head. "Last night after he left, I had a dream. I went to the University in Reno, like we had planned all those years ago, before I got mad at him and never even applied. He waited on me then too. All I could think of when I woke up was that he had a water pipe on his dresser." I wandered out on the deck.

Nana shadowed me. "What's a water pipe?"

"It doesn't matter. Don't you see? I was still judging Jack in my sleep. His room was old and smelly, the furnishings were sparse and below my standards. He was just happy I showed up."

"That young man has always been easy to please. You take some work. People are meant to be different. We add balance and flavor to each other's lives by complimenting, not competing."

She shepherded me to the patio table. I went under protest.

Nana pulled out a chair. "Sit. I'm going to bathe, and get gussied up a little. Do some baking in my prettiest sundress and favorite apron. I'm inviting Doc to have supper here this evening. You come on in and join me whenever it tugs at your heart to have some company."

Hours later Doc stopped by. The shade had shifted and overtaken my sunny spot.

Doc sat beside me, positioning himself within my line of vision without crowding me.

I struggled to look up at him. "When is he coming back?"

"He requested an indeterminate period of time off. We don't have a full schedule, so I can take over his patients for a while."

Doc moved the old webbed lawn chair to face me. "May I ask what happened?"

I lowered my gaze. "I jumped to conclusions. My facts were erroneous, my words harsh."

"At some point you have to make a decision to either trust Jack or not. He's been riding this see-saw for a long time."

And there it was. The truth doesn't so much set you free as strike the bulls-eye, piercing the heart of your being. "Direct hit, Doc, and it bleeds." I slumped deeper in the shadowy seclusion of my corner of the deck.

"Wounds can heal, Emily." Doc offered well-meaning encouragement.

Hard as I tried, my heart and head found no solace in those words.

"Did he tell you where he was going?"

"I didn't ask." Doc cast his glance aside. "He said he'll call to check on his patients."

I could see Nana through the kitchen window watching us while she worked at the sink. Doc stayed with me for a while. He spoke no words of condemnation nor did he offer trite, unsolicited advice. He simply remained available.

Wind rustled, swishing through the surrounding tree branches, swaying pine needles and knocking down cones that snapped, landing with a thump. Birds called out to one another in high pitched screeches and cautionary tweets, then swooped by, their wings spread wide as they glided in for a landing.

Nana called us in for supper. I declined and went up to my room, closed the door, and curled up in the bed under a mountain of blankets. My sun-burned skin scratched against the sheets. Still I burrowed in deep and covered my head, leaving only a passageway open for air to breathe through.

After my body warmed up, I reached for the phone on my nightstand and dragged the old blue princess handle and cradle between the sheets with me. Raising the covers for light, I hooked my finger in the cut-out circular dial and entered the eleven numbers to my home residence, hoping to catch Sarah.

Olivia picked up on the first ring. "Hello?"

"It's Mom. How are you and Sarah doing?"

"She's out on a date with the violinist. They're seeing each other every day."

"That happened fast."

"Todd wants to say hi before we leave. Wait a minute, Todd, I'm not done talking with her yet." Olivia's voice carried a tone of exasperation.

An apparent scuttle transpired.

"Emily, I had a great time up there. Any chance I can trip on up again?" He spoke with cool confidence, expecting his request to be fulfilled.

"I'm sure Nana will say yes."

"Way cool. Livie says you've got kayaks."

"Oh, you want to come back before the winter?" I knotted the phone cord around my hand and squeezed.

"I can take off work for a weekend. They won't miss me. Hey, does the old lady kayak?"

"Sorry, Mom." Olivia was back on the line "Todd hasn't stopped talking about our day up there."

Rotten timing. They're going somewhere. I twisted the phone cord tighter.

"Todd's taking me to Fannie Ann's in Old Sac tonight. We were heading out the door when you called. Can I get back to you back tomorrow?"

"That's fine." I lied. *Go away, Todd. I need to talk with my daughter.*

"Bye." Her voice became muffled. "No, Todd, I said good-bye for both of us." Click.

I slid the receiver on the cradle and put the phone on my chest. I lay there and realized I didn't have a single girlfriend to call. Jack was my best friend. My only friend. David had never been my friend. Caroline, the last girlfriend I'd had, bedded my husband right under my nose.

I bolted upright and screamed, "Why don't I trust anyone to be my friend?"

The phone tumbled off the bed. I left it there until it began bleeping the repetitive recording to hang up. A continual buzz followed.

Hanging over the side, I sobbed until my insides ached. I shook my fists at God, "How can you just watch all this muck from above at a safe distance?" I pulled myself back into the bed and screamed into the mattress until no sound issued forth but air hissing up from the deep caverns in my lungs. All energy spent, I lay there without moving, half in, and half out of the covers.

The chill in the room numbed my toes. Wind outside howled, rattling glass in the warped wooden molding like a pent-up animal shaking its cage. Goose bumps raised the hair on my arms, my extremities shuddering in a state of shock like pre-hypothermia.

Still dressed in my clothes, I forced myself to get up, and pulled thermals over my shorts and shirt, slipped into a pair of woolen knee-hi stockings, and tugged a knit hat over my head. Sufficiently bundled, I stumbled in the dark, tripping over the phone while trudging back into my cave.

Buried deep under the blankets, I closed my eyes, trying to imagine some kind of a future with purpose. I had no desire to return to my former job and had no idea what else I wanted, or could do for the rest of my meaningless life.

My daughters' lives were turning a bend, Sarah with her violinist and Livie and her Todd. Maybe I'd been too hard on him. Lots of people don't realize how cold the lake is and run in without thinking. Apparently Todd and I had more in common that I wanted to admit.

Chapter Twenty-Three

Photographs float like paper boats. Images gaze back at you. Unsigned notes, intentionally leave no clue. The years pass by and now I wonder why. You stayed when it was past time to say goodbye.

- Emily, unfinished journal poem. 1994

Two weeks passed before any word came from Jack. I busied myself helping Doc in the office, filing papers, updating charts, and answering calls. It was the least I could do. Luckily, there wasn't an overload of patients. But everyone wanted to know why PA Conner's leave was so sudden.

I fielded non-stop questions that ranged from normal interest and concern to the bizarre. Was he ill? Did he need chicken noodle soup? What made him take a vacation? Did he go to visit his mom in Paris? Did he elope? Who was she? Did he go follow his dream to help the poor children in Africa? And my personal favorite, did he get that mean woman pregnant—you know the one who's too old for him but wants to have his baby even if it's by artificial insemination?

Tongues were wagging, lips flapping, and the drooping jowls of jaded old women speculating, spreading juicy morsels of gossip faster than you could say, "Jack and his band of monkeys were swinging from the trees in Botswana." And all because of me.

Doc never helped me out by explaining anything to anyone. I repeated the same answer over and over: "PA Conner requested personal time off." It was the truth. But I quickly learned no one was interested in the truth.

I called to see if the girls could break away and come up for a weekend. Todd had asked, and that gave me an excuse. But lifeguards work weekends. I was on my own.

After updating all the charts, I mailed out the bills for Doc. He sent me to Jack's desk to gather more files and receipts. Sitting in his chair, I noticed stacks of old snapshots in a pile. They were out in plain sight, so I shuffled through them like a deck of playing cards. There we were, so young. And he *was* a fox, a stone-cold one. We were Todd and Olivia's age, just kids.

"Turn out the light when you leave, Emily," Doc's said. "I'm heading to Reno."

"Do you want me to lock up?"

"I do now for insurance purposes, but you know I trust my neighbors."

He closed the door behind him and went out the back deck. I never heard a click.

Photos still in my hands, I slid back into the oak chair and rolled over to the window from behind the desk. I looked at pictures of Jack and me on the beach, out in the lake, in boats, under a full moon at a bonfire, on Nana's deck. I'd never laid eyes on these before.

Most of the photographs were shot from Doc's cabin. Annie must have taken these. I couldn't remember Doc ever having a camera in hand, like my Papa always did. The majority of the pictures were from my junior and senior year in high school. All four seasons were chronicled in order—making snow angels on the beach, kayaking together, boarding the *Martha* on the deck, swimming in cut-off jeans, fire-pit roasts, and swinging side-by-side on

Doc's deck in the old hammock with the weathered fringe swaying in the autumn breeze, like we didn't have a care in the world.

"Jack has his own personal stash," I said out loud. "Why hasn't he ever shared these with me?" I pulled out a picture with a bent corner and realized there were several in sequential order with the same folded-over tip. About a dozen or so of what must be fifty snapshots, half close-ups of me, all with the same ridiculous smile on my face.

What a nerd. I looked like a … a happy person. I stared at the teenager looking back at me. She had something I sure didn't.

All the other pictures were of Jack with me—laughing, seriously working on some kind of a project together, eating watermelon that was dripping down our arms onto our legs, eating marshmallows off sticks—I remembered those sticks. He cut, whittled, and carved them. He made sets for Doc and Annie, Nana and Papa, Mom and Dad, and the two of us.

The two of us. He saw us as pair. "How could I have been so blind for so long?" The chair groaned, hinges stressed and in need of oil. My body slumped back, limp like a rag doll with only paper stuffing for brains. I sat confronted by Kodachrome-color proof of my foolish ignorance. Sharp, clear images, preserved over time in square frames of my past, bordered with a band of white trim, stamped and dated in the middle of the bottom border. I ran my finger over the date. July 1973. Any further denial was futile.

I hadn't just led him on. I willingly participated in every aspect of his life, imprinting myself on every page in vivid, everlasting color. I held the photographic proof, evidence that could not be disputed. Jack must have looked at them a lot over the years. The edges and once high-glossy finish had worn with age and handling.

"We were real once. The genuine article." I glanced around his office.

No one was there to bear witness to my words. But a hundred faces looked out at me from the photo cork-board in front of Jack's desk—Christmas card pictures, family portraits, hospital baby announcements, school and graduation wallets. I moved in closer.

Who took these? Annie? Baby Brianna and her brother Bobby were pinned in the lower-left corner, overlapping stuffy old Mable Parker in her spiffy peach Sunday polyester pantsuit. Annie couldn't have taken these.

I opened the top drawer of the file cabinet, the brass key nestled snuggly in the lock. A Canon camera box sat in the front of the drawer, batteries and a faux-leather case lined up beside it. When I opened the box I found a pristine, well-cared-for camera from the 1980s. I discovered a flash attachment box underneath.

After replacing everything exactly where I'd found it, I gazed up at the board more intently taking notice of the angle and distance from which the photographer shot. Each subject was photographed with a keen, artistic eye, portraying the person in a complimentary fashion, accentuating their features to enhance them at their best or better. Mable's triple neck was well-hidden because of a downward angle shot from a higher height. Her sparkly blue eyes and wavy silver hair drew me in. That and the fact that her mouth was closed.

"So Jack is a shutter bug." I wondered what else I didn't know about him.

Shuffling aside some paperwork, I came across two envelopes from Long's drugstore. Making myself at home in his chair, I sifted through some of the most breathtaking photography I'd ever seen of the Tahoe area. Sprinkled here and there were random shots of people who must have caught his eye. Babies with cherub faces, ruddy cheeked with wonder and awe; toddlers teetering to one side, spellbound at the foot of a mighty mountain; elderly folks, winkled and weathered, bundled eccentrically in multi-colored woolen layers of sweaters and scarves with snowballs cupped in their mitten-clad and gloved hands. The mischievous look of childish pranksters was written in exquisite delight across the maps of their faces.

Jackson Luke Conner, who are you?

I rifled through the Yosemite pictures he'd recently shot of Mirror Lake and El Capitan. So this was how he saw the world around him. The entire roll was of the highest professional quality and could have filled a calendar that I would have purchased.

After replacing the pictures, I sat mystified. I'd put Jack in a box decades ago, stuffed him in and clamped the lid down tight, shutting out light, air, and the slightest measure of compassion. I barely let the man breathe around me.

I rummaged through scattered notes about his patients on the desk-top. Danny is afraid of the dark and not getting enough sleep. Tommy is biting his nails until they bleed, being bullied at school. Sara Eldridge's son is the bully, drinking all the time and behaving strangely. Remember to test Sheila Oldham for juvenile diabetes, it runs in her family. Joey Fischer is still wetting the bed. Recheck the kidneys. Minnie Alderman isn't long for this earth. Stop by on my way home now and then to chat with her.

Perhaps there was more to Mr. Conner than I chose to see. He couldn't fake caring about his patients. Other than his SCUBA gear and a guitar tucked away in one corner, everything in the room reflected how his patients came first. Stacks of research and reference books weighed down bowed bookcase shelves, and an entire lower shelf was filled with *Raggedy-Ann and Andy's Grow and Learn Library.* I pulled *Volume 4, Raggedy Dog to the Rescue.* The pink book was definitely not Jack material. Teddy bears, dolls, Tonka trucks, an Etch-a-Sketch, crayons and coloring books over-loaded a cane basket near the door.

Maybe I was giving him too much credit. Annie probably shopped for and bought all these things years ago. But she didn't take the scenic photographs and write the patient notes. I couldn't have missed all this.

Jack had positioned his desk sideways so he could look out the window.

Ordinarily it would be facing the door so he could greet patients when they walked in. But he had arranged it so when they sat across from him, he could clearly see the lake behind them, the board of photos to the right and an original Madeline Bohanon Tahoe watercolor to the left. It was one of her early paintings, before she switched to more abstract oils.

Bookshelves lined the opposite wall. Ernest Hemingway's work was prominently encased between gray-clay-sculpted, *The Thinker* bookends. Decades of medical journals and magazines were neatly organized and separated with colored tabs. The entire bottom row was filled with binders, each spine labeled, dated, and alphabetized from conferences and classes attended up to the present date.

This was not your average mundane medical room arrangement. A defined design and personal flair bespoke of the dweller's presence. There was a distinct sense of order and efficiency highlighted by Jack's own style, with art, literary books, his old guitar, and the coolest Surveyor's Spotlight that was converted into a floor lamp.

I hadn't even given him credit for not being a slob. How wrong I'd been.

Chapter Twenty-Four

Life fades away, our bodies fail us, and frailties replace
strength. Disinterest overrides lust, we are destined to
return to dust. Rust to dust. The mind and knowledge
no longer rule. Memories diminish, control is no longer a
sharpened tool. Rust to dust. Dust to dust.

-Post-It note in Jack's handwriting on his desk

"Now, don't be getting yourself all worked up into a tizzy,"
Nana told me.

"It's been three weeks. Is he ever coming back?" I paced, digging my heels into the warm sand of the gritty beach. My noon
swim had been briefly therapeutic, distracting my disparaging
thoughts and fears.

"Doc heard from Jack yesterday." Nana disclosed. "He'll
resume taking his patients on Monday."

I halted in place. "That sounds—so formal."

"He's been scouting out other places to practice."

"What?" I said, trying to keep my voice from cracking. "I
thought he was being groomed to take over for Doc."

"He was."

"This is my fault, isn't it?" I fell to my knees and sank.

Nana laid her hand on my shoulder. "I think Jack needs to
move on."

"What have I done? Doc needs Jack. How can he leave after all these years?"

"Doc understands," she said with conviction. "I think you do too."

"I found pictures in his office. Old snapshots of us growing up together." I bit my tongue, but it was no use. "I never realized before how Jack saw us."

"Well, you were the only one around who didn't get it. Even David knew."

"Why bring him into this?"

"Because he's always been a part of the whole picture." Nana knelt beside me and lifted my chin into the palm of her hand. "He always felt Jack's presence between the two of you because he was always there." Her calm eyes met mine.

"No. No, that isn't true." My body shuddered and quaked. "I was a good wife."

"Yes, you were. You gave it your all. But David never got your whole heart. Part of it has always belonged to Jack." Nana gently tipped my head to her chest.

The sand was forgiving as the full weight of my body sank deeper with each sob.

Nana swayed with my movements in a rhythmic motion, bearing the physical burden of my spasmodic outbursts. Hard as I tried to stop, there was no holding back. The dam had broken. It was useless to try to regain control.

"I didn't know." I moaned. "I swear I didn't know."

"We're always the last to know things about ourselves." She sat beside me and pulled a handkerchief from her jeans pocket and wiped sandy grit away from my eyes. "It's easier to look from the outside in."

"I've been mad at Jack for so long." I drew my legs up to my chest.

"What have you been so angry with him about?"

"I don't know exactly. For letting his head swell too big. For stopping being my friend."

"For growing up and forgetting you were the center of his world and noticing other women?" Nana brushed hair behind my ear. "For trying to find himself?"

"Yeah, I guess." I sniffled. "Sounds pretty lame."

"No, just part of growing up."

"I think I was afraid he'd go away—like Beddie."

"So you pushed him away first." Her words hit like a sledge hammer, though she spoke them with quiet affirmation.

"I did. That way he couldn't disappear."

"He's waited a long time, Emily."

"Well, I blew it." I raked my toes through the sand.

I sat on the thick carpet in the hotel room, scratching my dog behind his floppy ears. I thought a weekend here in The Biggest Little City in the World would take the edge off. I'd catch Daryl's band, sit at the bar and have a drink. I had two possibilities to consider for moving my practice: one in Truckee, not far away enough, and the other from my friend Gil on the East Coast, too far away. I slipped a cookie out of my shirt pocket and lowered the treat to Hemingway. Tail wagging and banging into the black lacquer coffee table, he devoured the biscuit in one bite.

"Slow down, boy." I looked into his brown eyes. "You're a faithful friend, He licked my cheek, slobbering, drool dripping. "Oh, yeah, that's love." I wiped my shirt across my cheek.

Hemingway circled three times before curling up and laying back in the same spot. A sigh exited his open mouth as he yawned.

"Hem, this offer from Colorado is more what I was looking for, and it still involves ski slopes. I hate to abandon Doc like this.

He says he understands and I know he does. But I also know he was counting on me."

Hemmingway barked a retort.

"Yeah, I know, old boy. I'm letting Doc down. He deserves better than being abandoned this close to retirement." I petted Hemingway's shiny chocolate coat and rubbed his underbelly. He responded by placing a paw next to my hand. I shook it and stroked the top of his head. "Thanks, boy." He rested his head on my lap and whined before burrowing into the plush carpet.

"Don't worry. I'm okay."

I lay on my back and tried not to think about Emily. But it was useless. She invaded my every thought. That was the problem to begin with. She's always there no matter what's up. I remember things from our past or wonder how she can fit in, and if she doesn't, what I can change to make it work.

Having her back at the cabin had made me start to believe we could plow through our past differences and make a go of it. Maybe I'd even ask her to marry me. I'd already done it a hundred times in my head. I know now that I want to settle down. No more partying. No more scary stalkers.

"Hey, Jack, you in there?" Daryl knocked on the door.

"Coming." I rose and stepped over my slumbering Lab to get to the door.

"What's up, bud? You've been hunkered down in here for two weeks. I only play one more night." Daryl grabbed a beer out of the fridge and sat next to Hemingway.

"I'll be there tonight. I check out tomorrow morning."

Daryl twisted off the bottle cap and swallowed a long sip.

"I'm moving out of town."

"What?" He gulped down hard. "Why?"

"Let's just say, personal reasons." I sat next to him.

"I'm blown away." Daryl set the bottle on the end table.

"Yeah, so am I." I took a sip of his beer and put it back.

"Wow, and I just met your lady at Book Haven a few weeks ago. We talked for a short while. She's beautiful. Oh, I get it. You two taking off together."

"No. Actually, she told me to leave, for good." Saying the words out loud to someone other than Hemingway didn't make it any more real."

"That doesn't make any sense. She never let on that anything was wrong. Except." He scratched his head.

"What?"

"She thought you were still with Janie. I told her you hadn't been with her for years. But that it didn't stop her from trying to get you back."

"And she believed you?"

"Yeah. I could see it in her face." Daryl polished off his beer. "I don't think she knows you're leaving, Jack."

"She probably didn't then, but she does by now." A flicker of hope sparked. Maybe this got through to her. Yeah, until the next time.

"Listen, buddy, I think you're making a mistake. You've always planned on taking over for Doc. Why such a big change? You said she's only here for the summer." He got up and went to get another beer.

"I've given it a lot of thought. She'll always be at the cabin. I'll be next door twiddling my thumbs. I don't think she's ever cared for me the way I have for her."

"You in love with her?"

"Yeah. I'm tired of trying to find someone to replace her. Maybe if I move on, I can meet someone who will love me too. Settle down. Have a family, if it's not too late."

I said the words, but I didn't believe them.

"If you love her, why don't you fight for her?" Daryl didn't open his beer.

"Don't you see? I've been doing that most of my life." I hung my head in my hands. My elbows wobbled on my knees.

"If it was me, I'd give it one last shot. I'm asking Heather to marry me. Don't know why I waited this long."

"Where did this come from?" I sat stunned.

"We're both in our forties, Jack. Fifty is next, then sixty, seventy. I love the music but not the road trips anymore. Sleeping in fleabag motels with aging groupies, two-bit hookers, or some chick I pick up at the bar that might very well be a run-away minor. I'm done with that part of it man. The thrill is gone. My voice will go next."

"But music is your life."

"You said it yourself 'If it's not too late.' Heather and I can still make music together. I'll play guitar until my fingers don't work anymore. The passion for the music is different than the stinking grind of the business."

He got up and put the beer back in the fridge, let the door hang open for a while, then shut it and came back and sat on the sofa. "You sound certain."

"It isn't all glitz and glamour. I used to think I was all about the music, but the truth be told, I fed off the applause, the adoration, the whole rock star image. Not any more and I'm not just having a bad day. I've been mulling over this for a while." Daryl said, lit up a cigarette, sat back and inhaled. "I want off these too." He dumped it in the empty beer bottle to fizzle out.

"I had no idea."

"I'm forty-eight, a couple of years older than you. There isn't a single stable thing in my life, except Heather." He got up. "The Station hired a younger band and didn't mention having me back. Look at the crowd next time you're there. I'm an old man compared to those young studs, and they play just as good as I do. Some even better." He looked the room over. "This black vinyl and lacquer isn't you. Go home my friend, before you do anything permanent you may later regret."

I followed him to the door. Daryl pulled me in and hugged me hard.

"I love you, bro. Do what's right for you," he said and let go.

I looked into his red-rimmed eyes and suntan-creased face. He looked tired.

"Thanks for stopping by. I'll be there tonight." I patted his shoulder and he went out in the hallway. I stood watching him walk to the elevator, his gait slowed by a slight hitch in his left leg from when he tripped off a stage. That was how I'd met him. I sewed him up and he invited me to come hear him play that night at the Biltmore on the Nevada side. Over twenty years ago, back in his wild days. I'd miss jamming with him.

I dialed the Colorado number I had for after hours and left a message that I was still considering their offer. Asked them to let me know how long I had to make up my mind. I'd deal with the other two responses tomorrow. I knew I wasn't going to go with either of them, but I needed to reply.

"Hemingway, what do we want for dinner tonight? More Hotel food? Fast food? No, that's not good for either of us." I glanced around the room at the stark white walls, black lacquer furniture, and framed blasé art, and decided that Daryl was right. This wasn't me at all. "What do you say we check out early and go home after the show?"

Hem barked in agreement and wagged his tail, toppling over a plastic vase.

"Yeah, I think so too. Come on, let's go pack and get out for some fresh air.

I knelt and gave Hemingway a good old-fashioned petting fest. When I stood, I patted my chest for one of his famous knock-you-to-the-ground, Labrador hugs. He sprinted over to me with a look of glee in his eyes, jumped up, and flung his massive, paws over my shoulders, balancing on his lanky hind legs. His tail was thumping against the vinyl sofa a mile a minute. "You know boy, there's got to be some Great Dane mixed in you somewhere. The sheer power of all one hundred pounds of you when you get a running start is a formidable force."

I went down like a receiver on the ten-yard line, overpowered and straddled by a determined, furry lab linebacker. His gigantic tongue covered my face with drippy-drooling kisses until I rolled him over and made a dash for the bedroom. I dragged out the suitcase from under the bed. Hemingway came in with my wallet in his mouth.

"Yeah, you're ready to go home too, aren't ya? Why didn't you say so earlier? I'll load up the car now and check out. We'll hit the market and get some decent dog food and people food, and we're out of here after I listen to Daryl play a few sets." I slipped my wallet in my back pocket, grabbed my shaving kit from the bathroom, finished packing, and we left the land of lacquer and one-arm bandit slot machines in the dust.

Chapter Twenty-Five

Jack

My Nana treated everyone the same. You were family. If
you visited the cabin when you came to the lake, she
welcomed you with open arms, set a place at the table
for supper, and offered shelter. I never once saw her turn
anyone away. The door was always open.

-Emily, journal entry, August 24, 1989

"Glad to have you back." Doc bear-hugged me. He petted
Hem, who then raced out the king-size doggie door in
the kitchen for his evening run on the beach.

"I thought you had to go to Truckee hospital after the office
closed today?" I set my backpack on the floor.

"Wanted to welcome you home, Jack. I have news for you.
Your test results came back while you were gone. Can we sit down
and go over them?"

I froze in place. "We need to sit down?"

"Relax. The biggies were all negative. No STD or AIDS. So
you're in the clear. I would retest in six months to a year." Doc led
me into my office.

I sighed with relief. "Okay. No problem."

"But something else showed up."

I sank into my desk chair.

"I packed your lab slip with all the tests and panels for an annual physical. Your Hemoglobin AIC was 132. You did remember to fast didn't you?"

"I fasted. That's a pre-diabetic number, actually it's over."

"Do you remember if diabetes ran in your family? Did either of your parents ever mention any relatives having type 1 or 2?"

"No."

"Is there any way you can get a medical history from Zack or Helen? It would be helpful as you get older."

"I don't think they'd provide it if I asked."

"You're so athletic and you eat healthy. This has to be a heredity issue.

And you've never been a big drinker like them," he paused.

"I'm not even sure the last addresses I have for them are current, especially France. They seldom let me know when they move. I've always had to track them down." Acid lurched in pit of my stomach.

"We should have pressed for this information before. Annie and I tried several times to get it for you. We sent forms to the house when you were little and offered free medical services to all three of you." He clicked his tongue.

"They never went to doctors, not that I ever saw before. I don't know about in their older age."

"I put a meter kit in your file drawer, next to the camera. I want you to start testing first thing every morning." His request wasn't urgent, but insistent. "This could be a fluke, a miss-test, but we need to be sure."

"I don't need this in my life right now." I gave a deep sigh and shrugged my shoulders. The thought of contacting my parents brought only grief.

"I know. But you need the information. How old are they now?"

"I'm forty-four, so my dad is turning seventy this December and my mom will be sixty-six in November." I rolled my eyes. "They were very big about celebrating their birthdays, always a big party that sometimes went on for days."

"Can you remember ever being sick as a child?"

"You know, I do remember having something that made me burn up with a fever when I was in kindergarten. My grandmother took care of me." I struggled to bring the vague memory back. It was boxed, shelved and stored in the suppressed recesses of my mind where I shoved all my life with my parents. "I recall being at her home, sleeping in her bed while she slept in a nearby cot. She kept putting cool cloths on my forehead and chest."

"Could have been scarlet or rheumatic fever. Those can weaken the heart."

Doc was working away on a possible diagnosis.

"Do you remember having a rash?"

"Yeah, on my chest. I kept telling her I was cold inside."

"You had the chills."

"It comforted me that she stayed so close. I was scared."

"Was your family living at your grandmother's then? Where your parents there too? Or did they come to visit?" Doc pursued.

"I only remember the two of us. She sat and read to me from a big book that didn't have pictures."

Doc took a step back, "Was she reading the Bible?"

"Could be. Sometimes she didn't look at the pages because she knew it by heart."

"Do you remember any of the stories?"

"One was about a nice man who said children could go to him and he wouldn't let the other people stop them. I think his name was Luke, my middle name."

"You had a praying grandmother, Jack." Doc sat in a chair across from me, hand over his chin.

"I did? How do you know?"

"I'm guessing. Who gave you your name?"

"My parents named me Jackson, after Jackson Hole, Wyoming. Where they met skiing the slopes on a college holiday break. My grandmother picked my middle name, she said the Luke she knew was a physician." I chuckled. "I thought she'd said magician, but she corrected me just before she passed away. "I don't even know if she was my mom or dad's mother." I took a pad and pen out of my desk drawer to jot down what we were talking about.

Doc pulled a notepad out of his shirt pocket.

"I wanted to be called Luke after she was gone. My parents would have none of it. I clicked the top of my pen repeatedly. "I've always liked how Emily calls me by my full name, Jackson Luke. Of course, she's usually mad at me." I handed him a pen.

Doc laughed. "She does draw it out when exasperated. He wrote a couple of sentences in his note pad. "Why did your family move to Tahoe?"

"Not sure. I was with grandma in, I don't know what state, but it wasn't California or Nevada because we traveled here in a day and a night, in a brand new car. Maybe the mid-west?"

"Your parents must have sold her home, bought the car and gone somewhere new and exciting. They loved the casinos."

"Could be." It hit a raw nerve. "That's where the money initially must have come from. I thought we were rich, then the money was gone, and only trickled in when they won big at the casinos.

"I'm sorry, Jack."

"It's okay, Doc.

"I thought we could track down the information without having to go through your parents. You need to think seriously about approaching your parents for your medical history. In case you have children one day." He smiled.

"I'd never thought about how my lack of background might affect a future family. A young girl did used to come to the house for visits. She was about my age. She may have been a neighbor." I shrugged. "Don't remember her name, but I can still picture her face. She came to tell me good-bye the night before we left."

"Well, let's work on getting your blood sugar levels normal. He handed me my labs to go over myself. "Always give a copy to the patient."

"Thank you." I looked up into his eyes. "I appreciate you help."

" Anytime. You okay? I'm going to head on over to Truckee."

"Yeah, I'm good."

"You want to come with me?"

"No. I think I'll settle back in and catch up here at my desk. Flip through the files and see what I missed." I pulled about a dozen folders off the top of stack number one.

"I'll be home after visiting hours, about nine or ten." He waved and walked out.

"Drive safe." I sat in my chair mulling over this new diagnosis, and these recollections from my past. It perturbed me that my parents never talked about my grandmother, as if to nullify her existence.

Emily's Nana reminded me of my grandmother. Just being around Hannah evoked the distant remembrance of love and security I once knew. I couldn't see how either of my parents were born from that same bloodline.

After reading Doc's patient notations, I slid the files under the bottom of the remaining folders and scooped up my snapshots. It didn't take long to detect they were out of order. Even the dog-eared ones were categorized incorrectly. This hadn't ever happened before. Maybe Doc knocked the pile over going back and forth with the files on my desk while I was gone. One of the kids could have wandered in unsupervised. Doc never locked the door during or after office hours. I'd ask him about it later. I put them back in order, with Emily and me kayaking over at Cave Rock on the top.

Giving the room a quick look-over, I didn't notice anything else out of place.

Chapter Twenty-Six

A home is many things. Losing your home changes your focus and hurts your heart. I know. I'll be packing up soon, selling the home where I had my daughters to a stranger. Maybe they can make it work for their family where I failed.

-Emily's last journal entry

Our house seemed smaller. I sat in my rocking chair in the quiet of the living room. The girls were life guarding today. I'd told them I was driving down to pick up a few things and that I wanted to see them if possible. All the note on the fridge said was "Had to work. Sorry, Mom."

I moved the rocking to the middle of the room to be able to get a full view of my once happy home. The wooden rungs underneath me needed dusting, like everything else. The girls were not into housekeeping. Although Sarah's room was immaculate, Livie's was the polar opposite, as usual. At least they'd left their doors open. I wandered down the hallway and peeked in their doorways. The rooms seemed so empty.

I'd fought David to have this dark cherry furniture, the massive entertainment center, dining room set, and antique hall tree. What a senseless battle. He wanted the claw-foot, Amish traditional light-oak that was the trendy wood of the day. I desired the liberty to mix antiques with a richer, deeper grain. I'd be selling all of it now. Since he borrowed against the life insurance, I didn't have a choice.

I definitely didn't mind getting rid of our sleigh bed. I'd spent a lot of nights sleeping in Sarah's room when she went back to college. He'd bedded Caroline in our room. I didn't care if I ever stepped foot in there again.

I'd loved antiquing with him. Indulging in long, luxurious lunches at quaint bistro sidewalk cafes, conveniently shaded by silver maple, California ash, and red liquid amber trees lining the downtown main streets. We relished the distinct regional flavor of each postcard town, dotted with unique gift boutiques, gourmet patisseries, and Dean and Deluca's brewing strong, caffeinated espresso.

He'd order ridiculously expensive bottles of Napa Valley zinfandels and mellow merlots, pouring endless glasses that carried us into the magenta sunset glow of the dinner hour. Carmel, Monterey, Mendocino, all up and down the coastline; we'd stroll, wandering leisurely through chic galleries, critiquing the art and artists.

How he had fooled me. He always went out of town on week-long seminars and conferences after he'd intoxicated me with our little weekend escapes. I was all doped up and satiated. He could have done just about anything. And he did. No wonder there wasn't any money. David was supporting two lives, and I was the cheap two-day affair.

I'd already packed my selections in brown paper grocery bags; more clothes, books, pre-David photo albums, a couple more swimsuits, and a Scattergories board game. I had to teach Nana something new or I was going to lose my mind. I told her, "it starts with an 'S' like Scrabble, and you play with words." The twenty-sided letter die may be too heavy, but I'll roll for her. She'll love the extra points you get for alliteration.

Rummaging through the kitchen cupboards still awaited me, but for now I just sat and rocked. Our family portrait hanging in the hallway kept staring back at me, making me want to scream, "It's a fake!" I'd insisted we sit for it before Sarah flew from the nest to go away to college. I was the only one who wanted our wonderful family captured for posterity on sixteen-by-twenty inch canvas and stretched over wooden bars. I'd shelled out an exorbitant fee to have it textured to look like an oil painting. The backyard was in full bloom, bursting forth with an abundance of color, creating an almost magical backdrop. When the proofs came in, I was ecstatic and could scarcely narrow down my selection to that one perfect picture.

I mentally made a process-of-elimination assessment of what I'd keep and what had to go. The girls would need a sofa for their apartment. Hopefully, they wouldn't ask for any of the furniture I intended to sell. The entertainment unit was so oversized, I didn't think there was any danger of that being a problem. I now had to finance their college education. Thank you very much, David Taylor.

Where was the college fund we paid into for almost twenty years? The savings account had a measly $154.98, and the 401k's were gone. If I hadn't opened that separate savings account with the early inheritance Nana gave me on my fortieth birthday, I'd have nothing. David didn't even take out a home loan that paid off the house if he died. There was enough equity in the house for me to help the girls out a bit, but it would have been nice for them to be able to come to their childhood home for visits. Maybe bring their families later. But David didn't think ahead for us. He only lived in the moment for himself. This house was nothing but a place of habitation. He occupied space, ate, slept, and watched TV here.

Stop it, Emily. Getting into a dither about it won't change a thing.

I got up and headed into the newly remodeled kitchen. When one is involved in a long-term affair, one should not send the spouse out to box DIY store to pick out new appliances and countertops. The Realtor said it will be a big help for the resale value. And, we're in a highly desirable area so the house should move fast.

Opening cupboards was a real treat. Chaos reigned. I searched for the three things on my list, but the girls rearranged all my cabinets. I took out boxes and boxes of store bought cookies, prepared meals, and cold cereal that were up front, and pulled out my herbal teas and organic canned foods. I found my vitamins in with the spices. But it looked like I was going to have to leave without Nana's only request since her favorite troop of girls doesn't go knocking on her door anymore. No mint cookies.

Someone came in the back door as I was leaving out the front.

"Sarah?" I called out. No answer.

I put my bags down and waited. "Sarah."

"Mom. You still here?" she answered, rounding the corner.

"Have to get out of here before rush hour traffic."

"Livie and I worked all day. We left you a note."

She sat across the room, on the arm of the sofa in her red Speedo, which appeared to still be damp. I held my tongue trying not to complain about breaking the house furniture rules. Her tan was Caribbean-dark, her hair, sun bleached and loose down her back, and her attitude was not friendly. I thought it better to get on my way rather than get into anything.

"Do you know where the mint cookies are? Nana asked me to bring some back for her." I shifted my body weight over to the right, standing against the entry wall for support.

"Geez, Todd ate all of those weeks ago." She fluffed her hair and pulled it up into a scrunchie on top of her head.

"All? There were half a dozen boxes." The disbelief came through loud and clear.

"Yes, all. He's a teenage boy, Mom. If I recall correctly, he consumed the last box of thin mints in ten minutes while he and Livie watched some movie." She straddled the chair arm, revealing a wet ring under her swimsuit.

"Those were for the entire summer. You can't buy more until next year." Frustration edged my retort. *Pick up your bags and leave, Emily.*

"Since you're here, I wanted to ask you about the package Nana gave me when I was up there. She left, came right back, and handed me the box. "Mom, there's neat vintage jewelry. More your taste, but nice. Some pictures. And a check for twenty thousand dollars with a notation that it's for college. What's going on?"

"I don't know. She didn't say anything about this to me." I looked through the pictures. One was of Beddie and me, in our sailor outfits taken a week before he died. "Papa took this the day we arrived."

"I've never seen that one before. You two looked a lot alike. He has that same mischievous glint in those baby blues."

It was color, so you could clearly read our expressions. "I'd never considered our similarities, more what I perceived as our differences.

The slightest hint of a smile formed her lips. "Cute cap."

"He died trying to retrieve that out of the water."

"I'm so sorry. I didn't know." She retreated to the sofa.

"Neither did I, until a few weeks ago." My eyes locked on the square frame. Was there anything there to tell me more? I could see my dolly peeking out from the front pocket of my dress. Beddie's teddy bear was dangling from his tightly clasped fist. It looked like we were posed, but someone's legs had walked into the picture. The shoes resembled one of Papa's old pairs but he always took the pictures. So who snapped this?

"You can have it if you want it. I don't know why she gave it to me."

"No, Nana gave it to you." I slid it in her box and put the lid back on.

"Why the big college check? I can't cash that."

"Yes, you can. It's a gift, Sarah."

"There was a smaller manila envelope for me to give to Livie. She got a check too, some different pictures, and Papa's pocket watch."

"I hope she didn't mention the money to Todd." The moment the words slipped out I regretted the accusatory tone and delivery.

"Mom, you're so negative." She grunted in disgust. "Liv deposited it directly in the bank for college. Todd never laid eyes on it."

Sarah was done with me right then and there. I could see it in her expression.

"Your college funds have disappeared. I came down to see what I can sell."

"Did he have no shame?" She fumed. "What else are we going to find out?"

"I don't know. I hope this is it."

"Well, that witch Caroline keeps calling the house. She only asks for Olivia. If I pick up, it instantly clicks." Sarah's eyes narrowed and her cheeks flamed. "It's time to tell her, Mom."

"Not yet. Soon."

"You're right soon, because if you don't tell her, I will." She stormed out of the room, down the hall, and slammed her door, hard.

I stood there for a few minutes even though I knew she wasn't coming back.

I didn't want to leave like this. My eyes fixed on the circular wet spot on the arm of the sofa where she'd been sitting. *At least there isn't any chlorine. It's a lake, not a swimming pool. Besides, you're giving that sofa to the girls.* I picked up my bags. It would have been nice if she had offered to help me carry them out. It would have been nice if she'd given me a kiss and told me she loved me, like she used to. It would've been nice to be taking a box of Nana's favorite cookies back for her. She asked for so little and gave so much.

I left my once happy little home in suburbia on a cul-de-sac with concrete sidewalks, blacktop paved streets, and the sprinklers automatically watering the weed-infested front lawn in desperate need of mowing. I had one last stop before heading back. Debilitating dread strangled what courage I had left to face the appointment and possible test results awaiting me. Backing out of the driveway past the mailbox lettered with "The Taylor Family Established 1977."

Chapter Twenty-Seven

Holding onto grievances, holding onto fear, drains life slowly, subtly, and completely from the very depths of our souls.

—Emily, ournal entry, 1994

Approaching the massive log, I held my breath. Jack had every right to refuse to speak to me, and he just might. He sat in the midst of an idyllic watercolor, like the ones on his office walls. Turquoise waters washed ashore at his feet, licking his toes and sipping the denim cotton hem of his jeans. A bulky ball of chocolate fur was curled up beside him. Hemingway slept, his enormous head and floppy ears resting on Jack's lap.

They were nestled obscurely in an inlet cove. Surrounded by elder sentinels, the pine branches sheltering them from intrusion by the outside world. The vastness of Tahoe's majestic basin spread out before them. Crowned by the snow-capped peaks of the Sierra Nevada Mountains. Dare I intrude?

Held captive by fear to step any closer, I turned to leave, my bare feet heavy in the yielding sand. I could not move, to the right, or to the left. I stood immobile, my tongue mute, mind wiped blank, heart faltering. Jack's arm moved in steady strokes, petting Hemingway's shiny coat, massaging the drowsy but willing beneficiary of his complete attention.

"Jack." The word croaked out of my mouth, still half-stuck in my throat.

He didn't flinch. I remained where I stood. Sleepily, Hemingway raised up and gazed at me. He nudged his head under Jack's chin, pressing his brown nose into the flesh of his neck.

"What is it, boy?"

The dog stood on all four legs, turned, and poked Jack my way.

"Jack." I repeated, but it still caught.

Startled, he stumbled forward, then veered course toward me. The shock on his face said enough. He stopped. The silence that followed spoke louder than any words.

"Can we talk?" My stomach rolled. "I came to apologize."

He remained still. Hem made a dash for the beach and jumped in the water before Jack could call him back. I swear that dog knew what he was doing.

"There isn't anything more to say. You were quite clear."

"I was wrong," I stammered. "I'm sorry" It was too late. I could see it in his eyes.

He'd never looked at me like that before.

He turned away and ordered Hemingway back, snapping his fingers. The dog swam as if he hadn't heard.

"Please, Jack. Give me another chance." I spoke to the stiff ridge of his back.

He hung his head. "That's always been my line."

"I haven't been fair. Everything's been on my terms for too long." I drew back again when he started to turn. "But, I want to be your friend."

He threw his hands up high and wide. "Friends don't do this to each other. And it's all we ever do." He spoke so quiet, I could barely hear him.

"We can try again." A rush swept through me and I began to shake. "We always do."

"I can't anymore, Emily." He dug his hands in his back pant pockets and kept them there. He turned to face me.

Pain I had caused lined his face with a wash of sorrow. A tortured man stood hunched over before me, one who didn't want to be there. How could I blame him?

"Please don't give up on us." Terror flooded through me, froze my senses, numbing reality. A sick desperation weighed down to the bottom of my heart.

"You've never believed in me. I've been walking this one-way street for way too long." His chest heaved and jolted. "It's time to face it and, move on with my life."

"No, Jack." I lunged forward. "Please forgive me."

"Until the next time?" He stamped his foot into the sand. "No. We have to finish this. If you can't, I will."

"Hemingway! Get up here." He turned away.

I rushed the log between us, "I've been so wrong about everything. I saw the pictures on your desk."

"You're the one who rifled through those? You went through my things when I was out of town?" His nostrils flared. "Is there no end to what you'll do to a person?"

"I wasn't prying. They were sitting on your desk."

"What were you doing in my office?" he demanded, his face reddening, teeth clenched.

"Let me explain, I was working for Doc and had to pull some files."

"Those were private. Don't you have any respect for me at all?" His voice cracked, and his shoulders dipped forward.

"I have the utmost respect for you. I've taken you for granted for years and I'm so sorry." In my head all the things I wanted to say to him were swimming around in circles. Nothing was coming out right. "I've made a mess of everything. But we've gotten through everything in the past. We can make it through this too."

"How? The only difference right now is I'm not giving in."

He opened his mouth, again, but said nothing more to me.

Jack stormed past me. "Get yourself home, Hemingway."

"Jack, wait," He shoved me out of the way. I grabbed his arm and held on.

"Maybe, there is a future for us. Maybe, we can start over."

He spun around, full face. "What kind of a cruel trick is this?"

"It's not a trick. I mean it. I saw how we were in those pictures. I'd forgotten all the good and only remembered the bad." I inched closer until he tried to shake off my hold.

"I can't hope anymore. I'm drained. This will be the end of me." He shot forward, right in my face. "Can't you see what you do to me?"

I released his arm. "It's true, I haven't treated you right. All the gossip that's been milling around while you were gone. Everyone blames me." I doubled over at the waist. "Please don't leave the people you love—Doc, your patients—just because I'm a selfish woman." From the disorientated look on his face, I got through. "Doc needs you to take over like you two have been planning for years." I sat on the log, exhausted. "I need you to stay." My swollen eyes ached. I swiped my nose on my sleeve.

"I can't be your friend, Em. I've been in love with you my whole life." He sat a distance away from me.

"I didn't realize. I was too caught up in myself. But I'm trying to be honest with you now." My mind locked up. What else could I say? "I can't imagine my life without you, Jack."

"But you can't tell me you love me too." He shook his head sideways.

"I do. I always have."

"As a friend, a big brother, a substitute for Beddie."

"You are my best friend. But people in relationships need to be friends first, don't they?" I was afraid if I spoke the truth, I might lose him right there.

He looked up. "You've never used that word, relationship, about us before."

"I've been foolish, wasting my chances. There you've been all along, beside me all the way through life. I don't know how I missed you."

"I messed up too. Played around, slept around. Doc told me he thinks I would have cheated on you too. That hurt because, it's probably true." He took in a deep breath. "I had to get tested for STDs and AIDS, Em."

I could have helped you through that. I wish I had." I touched his hand.

"It's all negative. I got lucky. But it can lie dormant. I would never want to pass anything on." He reached down, picked up a rock, and skimmed it in the lake.

"I got tested right after David died. It was terrifying. They told me I'd need to go back if I thought he'd been cheating most of our marriage." Jack's fingers slipped though mine. "I was retested just before I came up, and went to Sacramento yesterday for the results. Still negative, so far."

"How did we get to this place, the both of us?" He gave my hand a gentle squeeze. He gazed into my eyes, put his arms around me and pulled me in.

Everything I was holding back surfaced. I needed to be in his arms, one of the few places I was safe enough to let go of the whole mess of me.

"I want to help you though this, Jack. Be there for you. Please let me be your friend again. Who knows where it may take us?" For the first time in my life, I hoped it would take us somewhere, together. That we could maybe be something special. In the middle of this muck, perhaps the grace Nana was talking about would find us. That was all I could pray for, grace.

"I'll stay awhile, see how things go. Doc would like that. That's all I can promise you." He kept holding me.

For now that was a beginning. We sat on that log, not talking much. Mostly watched the waves roll in and out, listened to the wash of water on the shoreline as it blended with the sand, leaving a glistening beach behind.

Hemingway ran up as if he'd just been called, licked our soggy faces, necks, and ears, then sat, head stretched across our feet. A few boats passed by, skiers waved, riding the wakes. Kayakers paddled in unison, strong and steady. Aspen trees quivered in the light breeze. I thought how fragile we were, the two of us. We let the lake do all the talking that long afternoon, listening attentively. I heard my name.

Part Five

The Lake's Anthem

Beginnings and ends.
Your heart either breaks, or it mends.
There is no way to prepare.
Or make someone else care.

Ask for wisdom.
Ask for truth.
To carry you through.
Receive grace.
Receive mercy.
Give love.

Ends and beginnings.
It is all part of living.
As for dying and death.
We all draw a last breath.
What will you take, when all is at stake?

Chapter Twenty-Eight

"Child, be content with what the moment brings you. Savor every second. No sooner will you turn your head, and that precise measure of time will pass, leaving you to what could have been, had you chosen to open yourself willingly."

-HMH

"Nana, what are you doing up so early?"

"Emily, the sunrise was glorious this morning. Golden streams of light danced across the blue basin. The water is calm, as if God reached down to still old Tahoe himself. Come on over, sit a spell with me." Nana's Southern drawl made her invitation almost irresistible as she pat-patted the chaise next to her.

My grandmother's glaucoma-ravaged eyes seemed to sparkle. Bundled in layers of handmade quilts, she reclined in a rattan chaise lounge that accommodated her with a clear view of the lake from our back deck.

She was truly a sight to behold. Her size five feet were buried deep inside furry brown-and-beige antlered-moose slippers peering out the end of her woolen covers.

Wind had whipped her stately white crown into a wild 1960's beehive-bouffant that poked out obtrusively from the top end of her comfy blankets.

"Careful, Nana, you're in grave danger of setting a new fashion trend certain to be the envy of all Tahoe's social elite." I twirled my finger around a rogue wisp of hair above her forehead and gently let it unwind in the brisk breeze.

"You know, these slippers were a Christmas gift from your girls and they happen to be the warmest pair I've ever worn." She maneuvered her feet to be sure I fully appreciated her coveted present from every possible angle. The antlers became tangled together in the process. I walked down to the bottom of the chaise to set the antlers free. "You won't ever have to visit Shirley at the beauty shop in town again if you can duplicate this hairstyle," I teased.

Nana wiggled her arms out, smoothed over her hair with both hands, and relaxed, quite satisfied with herself. She stared back towards the south shore.

I sat at her feet and relaxed the belt of my robe.

"I am grateful for this moment with you, these cozy blankets, and my fancy hairdo that didn't cost me a cent." She reclined, caught her breath, and smiled at me.

"Why, thank you, Nana. I'm grateful for you too." I took her hands and kissed them. "Your hands are freezing cold. Why don't you slip them back under the covers?"

I tugged the quilt over and tucked her in. I wanted to ask her to come inside where it was warmer. But knew she wouldn't. The deck was her second home these days.

"I talked with Jack yesterday. I apologized. He's agreed to stay a while longer and see how things go. We made some headway so I invited him over for breakfast this morning."

Nana sat straight in her chair, unwrapped her blankets and reached out to hug me. "I love you Emily—every stubborn bone in your body and imaginative thought in that whirlwind mind of yours.

I wrung my clammy hands together. "Guess I'd better start frying the bacon and eggs." I fished in my pocket for a scrunchie, but it was empty so I started toward the kitchen. "You and I can pick up our chat out here this afternoon."

"I'm glad you and Jack talked things out. It is a brave thing to face up to your mistakes. I'm proud of you."

A raw hoarseness grappled in her voice as I gave her shoulder a quick squeeze on my way inside. Through the kitchen window I watched her wiggle down into the chaise. That ancient cotton nightgown and those ridiculous slippers swallowed her up whole. I cracked eggs into a mixing bowl, added several tablespoons of milk, reached for the wire whisk, and then flicked the radio on. Art Garfunkel sang "All I Know."

Flannel pajamas warmed my sleepy body in the Tahoe morning chill. Ready for my morning cuppa, I stifled repetitive yawns, but no dark-brown liquid caffeine sat in the clear pot. *Nana must have forgotten to flip on the automatic timer last night.* I pushed the On button and the miracle machine began working its magic. Soon the intoxicating aroma of Columbian beans filtering through the kitchen zapped some of what Nana called "vim & vigor" into my step.

I placed thick strips of hickory-smoked bacon in neat rows on the broiler pan and drug out the cast-iron skillet. After pouring a thin coating of olive oil into the pan, I dumped in an entire bag of frozen shredded hash browns and turned on the gas burners.

With renewed zest, I began chopping onion and red peppers to toss in for added flavor, as the sizzling strips of pork browned. Jack was in for a surprise. I knew he was expecting my usual Scottish porridge with blueberries and a dribble of fresh cream.

I began singing along with Art, raising my voice in tempo to the music until the piano instrumental came, my favorite part of the song. I strummed my fingers across the tile countertop as if Nana's old upright piano were in front of me.

Todd flashed in my thoughts. His voice was tailor-made for this song. I was certain we would be entertaining him before the summer's end. But this time I would ask Jack to stick around. Take the kayaks out and show Todd what Tahoe was really all about. If he was going to take a weekend off, Olivia wouldn't be able to come up with him. Maybe she could take a day off, trade time, something.

After switching off the burners and broiler, I glimpsed out the window for Jack.

He was running late. I snagged a crispy piece of Jack's favorite breakfast meat off the cooling pan, filled my coffee cup to the brim, and leaned against the fridge. *Don't push too hard, Emily,* I chided myself. *Give Jack the time he needs.* I licked the grease off my fingertips and took a swallow of coffee, instantly burning my tongue and lower lip. *A heavy carb-loaded breakfast might be coming on too strong.* I took another sip and set my cup down. *At least we were talking.*

"Nana, do you want to eat inside or out on the deck?" No answer. She must not have heard me. I opened the cupboards, grabbed three of everything and headed for the dining room table where we could see the lake from the bay window. "Nana." I tapped on the window and motioned for her come in. With increasing agitation I folded the napkins and laid out the silverware. The roses Doc had brought over from his garden the day before were still fresh, spilling over the center of the table in vibrate pinks, reds, and bursts of oranges. Strong, sweet fragrance burst from each blooming bud. Too bad he had to drive to Reno for the weekend. He would have been good company this morning too.

"Nana." I rapped on the window a little harder.

I covered the potatoes and took out a loaf of sourdough bread for toast. I'd wait to sunny-side-up the eggs until the last minute or they'd get cold.

"Nana, come on and give me a hand before Jack shows up." I shook her shoulder, "Hey, sleepy-head, did you drift off again?" I moved around to the front of the lounge chair. Her eyes were open wide, fixed on the lake. She didn't blink or speak. Strands of her hair blew in the breeze. I drew my hand back and gasped.

"Wake up, Nana." Crumbling to my knees, tears flooded my eyes, clouding my vision. I threw my arms around her and clung tight, moaning, rocking. "Please wake up," I begged, demanded.

"We haven't finished our talk yet. There was more you wanted to tell me." I took her hand from under the quilt. No warmth. No reaction to my touch. Nothing.

"You're too cold. I need to cover you up. You shouldn't have taken the covers off this morning. I pulled the quilts up around her and squeezed in beside her. "Talk to me, Nana." With heartbreaking clarity I realized I'd never hear her voice again.

I curled around my grandmother and held her close, wrapped my arm under her and whispered, "How will I ever recognize truth without you?" Running my fingers through her hair, I tried to untangle windswept clusters.

I heard Jack walk up behind me. The back of his hand touched my cheek.

I didn't move.

He knelt beside us.

A reflection of my own pain glazed over his moist eyes when I turned to him.

"She was such a gentle woman," he murmured. "She deserved to die a quiet death like this, looking out on her beloved lake."

"How peaceful her expression is, Jack. There isn't any fear on her face. This morning it was almost like she knew and came to watch the sunrise, to say good-bye to the lake. She chose to spend her last hours alone with her God, in these old quilts, wearing those silly slippers the girls gave her." I buried my face in the worn fabric, sobbing.

Jack stayed until I couldn't cry anymore.

I stood, her hand still in mine, and kissed it one last time, then I laid it to rest upon her chest. I touched her eyelids one at a time until she couldn't see me anymore. Wisps of her hair still blew in the breeze. Jack closed her mouth.

Tears blurred the layers of blue in the lake and sky into one. My heart sank to the bottom of Tahoe, dark and cold, deeper than I'd ever been before. Where there wasn't any shade of blue.

"I should call the coroner."

"I'm not ready to let her go yet."

"You can stay here as long as you need. We don't have to rush." He wrapped trembling arms around me and held on. He cried quiet sobs on my shoulder, soaking my robe.

We sat at the table for a while and said nothing, just sat beside each other like two little lost children.

"I'd like to go inside and call Doc, if that's okay." His throaty words were barely audible.

"Of course. He needs to know."

Jack wandered inside and got as far as the sofa, and sat with his head down.

I pulled a chair beside Nana and looked out to the lake. She was right. The surface was the bluest blue. She saw so many things I missed. How would I find them without her to point me in the right direction?

I kissed her forehead. Somehow, I knew her God was watching.

Chapter Twenty-Nine

I longed to comfort her but I knew all too well the hurt that festered, infecting her flesh, like stingers the wasps inflict rampantly in late summer as they swarm the lake in the muggy heat. There is no escaping them. Mercilessly they pursue even the smallest child to the water's edge. For a season, they rule the lake.

—Emily's diary entry 1988

*D*oc came home in record time after Jack called him. The coroner had just taken Nana away when he peeled into our driveway. I had never seen him exceed the speed limit in all the years we'd been friends. Jack and I stood aimlessly amid manzanita bushes and the perfect row of purple and red petunias Nana had planted last week.

"Emily." He wrapped his arms tight around me. "I'm sorry I wasn't here."

"I can't believe she's gone."

Doc lips brushed against my forehead.

Beside us Jack was trying not to lose it. He'd hang his head, then swipe his sleeve across his face. I heard him suck in a big gulp of air, and cough trying to expel it.

I couldn't bear the thought of Nana in that cold steel drawer at the morgue.

Doc cupped my face in his hands and stated in a low, steady tone, "She loved you so much. You will always have a part of her in your heart."

I searched his eyes for answers, for clear direction. Doc knew better than to tell me everything would be all right. My life would never be the same. A huge part of me was now missing, and I had the agonizing responsibility of burying my grandmother. The thought of putting her in the ground was beyond painful.

"I know she made all her own funeral arrangements, but I don't think I can do this. It's too soon after David." My mind was wiped and my body was numb. Did I have anything left to give?

"We'll get through this together." Doc took Jack and me by the hands and walked us over to the porch swing. "Let's just sit here a spell."

"*Sit here a spell.*" I could hear the words in Nana's voice, her southern drawl laced with an air of authority and sweet hospitality. It was momentarily comforting, like she was sitting there next to us. I ran my hand over the space alongside me.

Jack kicked his foot against the ground and set us into a full swing. The creak and groan of the chain link as it wore into the bolts, sounded like a mournful metal symphony. The sway of motion was soothing, the rhythm seemed to offer continuity.

I tightened my grip on Doc's hand, closed my eyes, and remembered.

"Emily Grace, whatever are you up to child?" Nana had been calling my name as she searched the cabin for me. The dull brass knob to Papa's coat closet, lined in musty tweed jackets and dank woolen overcoats, turned slightly. The door squeaked as a slice of light filtered into the darkened cave.

I sat in the center, draped in my grandfather's favorite green plaid flannel shirt, His turquoise bolo tie loosely fastened around my neck, and his brown felt hat practically enveloping my entire head.

"Please don't bury Papa in his favorite clothes." I begged.

"Oh, honey, don't you worry yourself about that." Nana sat next to me on the cold hardwood floor.

"They still smell like him." I drew in a deep breath of the flannel fabric.

She inhaled his scent on the sleeve as she put her arm around my slumped shoulder. "Yes, it does. It smells exactly like your papa and nobody but him." She took off her house slippers and slipped into a pair of his suede moccasins, one of the two pairs he wore daily. Nana offered me the other pair. My white Keds fit nice inside the tan, fringe-trimmed shoes. Nana stood and lifted a gray sport coat off a wire hanger. She enclosed herself in its warmly lined layer of protection and snuggled up next to me again.

I moved Papa's hat to her head. It fit her better, but it was still too big. She adjusted it slightly sideways.

"I miss him too." She scooted so close there wasn't any space between us.

"He didn't say good-bye to me," I cried softly, wiping my tears with the cuff of the dangling shirt sleeve.

"He didn't know he was leaving," Nana reassured me. "Heart attacks come unannounced sometimes."

"I like it in here. Everything smells like Papa, looks like Papa, and reminds me of him." I twirled the bolo tie around my fingers. "If I wait long enough, he might walk through that door, like you just did."

"Papa's not coming back our way. He's gone on ahead of us to heaven now." Nana tilted the hat back on her head so I could see her face. Her eyes were red like mine.

"You can crawl into bed with me tonight if you want."

"Can I wear Papa's shirt instead of my nightgown?"

"Of course, you may. I think he would like that."

"I'm sorry you don't have Papa anymore."

She ran her fingers over the bolo tie and held me until sleep fell upon both of us..

Chapter Thirty

Hannah's Letters

We leave a piece of ourselves behind in our hand-written words. They travel across centuries to touch the hearts of those we leave longing for our presence.

–HMH

As I rummaged the cabin attic for photographs to display at Nana's memorial service, I accidentally knocked over a stack of rickety wooden crates. Several small bundles tumbled out of a Saks Fifth Avenue hat box—letters bound tightly with faded, dusty satin ribbons. Setting down the box of photographs I'd found, I picked them up and noticed the exquisite penmanship that meticulously wrote out "Hannah Mae Hartwick." Nana's maiden name.

Flipping through the stack, I saw that the same return address appeared in the upper left-hand corner of each one.

Mister Jonathan Forrester
20 Bickford Avenue
New York City, New York

Graceful cursive decorated the front of each yellowed envelope with Nana's name and an address I'd never heard before.

Hannah Mae Hartwick
70 Stratford Street
New York City, New York

I carefully ran my fingers over her name and quietly spoke the words out loud. 'Miss Hannah Mae Hartwick." My heart ached at the sound of my own voice. I clutched the letters to my heart. This was a part of Nana I never knew, something she had opted not to share with me, yet kept accessible in a remote region of the attic she regularly visited.

Dried rose petals fell from the musty stacks of mail. Vintage three-cent postage stamps barely remained adhered, the discolored glue stains, now brittle.

The ribbons were frayed as if they had been tied and untied several times. The bundles were arranged in order, covering two years from 1920 through 1922.

Nana was born in November of 1904, so she was seventeen and eighteen years old when these were written.

She knew I'd come up here. In fact, she'd invited me several times the past few years, even this past week. I was always too busy. She never pushed or pleaded—that wasn't her style. Maybe she'd wanted to share these letters with me? She told me she had a secret or two to take to her Maker. I thought she was trying to sound romantically mysterious. But Nana was perpetually dependable, as constant as the rising and setting of the sun.

I carefully slipped the top letter out of the bundle, dislodging the final speck of glue that held the curled-up stamp in place. It fluttered to the ground like a dainty snowflake dancing in worn-out ballet slippers at last curtain call.

The paper was worn thin. I lifted it out of the fragile envelope, and unfolded it gently.

My beloved Hannah Mae,
I am counting each day your papa has asked me to wait to make you my wife.
I gasped and stopped, my heart trying to pound its way out of my chest. I reread the sentence. The words stared up at me from the paper like lightning bolts from the grave. I read on.
God ordains patience to be considered a desirable virtue in both husband and wife. Please do not be disappointed if I appear to be lacking in such a necessary and commendable character quality. My love for you is deeper than any measurement man has created. Perhaps the good Lord Himself is the only one able to encapsulate the exact amount. He sent you to me, my beloved. Fear not, we shall not be apart for long. I am honoring all of your father's requests to make myself worthy of your hand in Holy Matrimony. I understand his concern for the number of years that separate us in age, but I will redeem myself in his good grace yet once more upon my return from Boston.
Sending my best wishes,
Forever,
Your love,
Jonathan

The letter fell at my feet. I let it lie there for a moment before I bent forward to pick it up. My hand trembled as I reread the words that were clearly written in indelible indigo ink that had only slightly faded with the passage of time.

Jonathan was not my grandfather's name. Nana was in love with someone before Papa?

Well, who wouldn't love Nana? Anyone could easily love a woman so full of life and joy. She was exceptionally beautiful, graceful, and yet remarkably independent for her day, an avid reader, highly educated and cultured.

"A rare jewel," Papa had fondly christened her.

Just who was this older man—Mister Jonathan Forrester? All the letters were mailed from New York City. Why did Nana's family live there and absolutely no one ever spoke about any of this to me? Our family came from North Carolina.

I opened and read a second letter.

Miss Hannah Mae Hartwick
70 Stratford Street
New York City, New York
November 20 of 1921
Mister Jonathan Forrester,
Dearest John,

I am pleased to accept your formal proposal of marriage. Our courtship has been a great blessing to me. My Papa has given his approval to set a date at Saint Patrick's Cathedral upon your return this spring.

My love for you has no bounds and my heart overflows with joy. The hours and days seem endless as my patience is tested while praying for your safe journey.

Though I hold you dear to me, my arms long
to embrace you as my beloved husband.

Faithfully, I remain yours, and yours only,
Hannah
You are forever written on the pages of my heart.

"What?" I scanned the outer perimeter of the attic for any other potentially life-shattering objects of a foreign nature. Finding nothing suspicious, I replaced the letters in the bundles, tucked them under my arm, and headed for the ladder.

During my descent, a photograph fell loose and floated aimlessly to the hardwood floor. I snatched it up for a closer look. It was a sepia-tone photograph of a remarkably handsome young man. There was a familiar look about every bit of him except his old-fashioned attire.

Caring, deep-set eyes seemed to reach out and soothingly touch me. The slight hint of a gentle smile put me immediately at ease. There was a noble look about him, but not the moneyed look of arrogance, though he was well dressed. He was likely from a prominent family of affluence. A "humbleness" emanated from his image, something Nana would definitely have been attracted to.

But those eyes.

Who was this stranger? I stared holding the picture up close, then far away. My brother Beddie had those same eyes. This sepia-tone blue.

I turned the picture over and read the artistic handwriting on the back:

To my beloved wife Hannah, on this glorious day of the birth of our first child Abigail Elizabeth Forrester
Yours only forever,
Jonathan.

So this was her secret. How could she not tell me? I looked though the stack of letters again. The third envelope was white, not yellowed, and my name was spelled out on it in Nana's handwriting.

Lifting the unsealed flap, I found a sheet of stationery I'd given my grandmother for her birthday last year. Unfolding the paper,

I expected to find another letter. Only two sentences filled the unlined paper.

Emily,
Your mother asked me to promise never to tell you about my past.
Though I did not agree with her, I have honored what she asked of me.
I pray in time you understand,
Nana

Chapter Thirty-One

What is unspoken, untold, impacts lives for a lifetime. If you don't believe me, just ask someone when they find out the truth.

—Emily's journal entry this morning

*D*avid and I had gotten married on my family's private beach, barefoot. It was a simple but elegant ceremony under an arbor intricately entwined with fresh cut Double Delight roses from Nana's garden. The deep rich fragrance of the flowers perfumed the late afternoon air with an unwavering scent that I mistook to be a sign signifying a sweet everlasting union.

The "To death do us part" vow was never taken seriously by either David or me. We were too young then to imagine one might outlive the other, especially in our early forties. Our marriage had ended long before David went for that fateful drive in his mistress's red convertible. An insidious virus had invaded and eaten away all that was good and healthy in our marriage, leaving precious little untouched.

My mother could barely walk up the aisle on my wedding day. Cancer had ravaged her internally and metastasized. Everyone in the family later agreed she'd hung on by sheer determination. Everyone but Nana. She said God gave Mama "grace time." I had to wonder, then why he gave her the cancer that caused her to suffer so much pain?

Abigail Maxwell sat propped up by half a dozen pillows in a freshly painted white Adirondack chaise after she and daddy had walked me down the "aisle" of beach lined with scarlet satin ribbons that separated David's and my families.

Delicate sprays of Tahoe wildflowers in vibrant shades of heather, brick red, maize yellow, and deep hues of blue, connected each row of chairs. David's family did not approve of the outdoor church I'd chosen. So we conceded with their choice of a fancy restaurant in Incline Village for the reception. In the lobby of the formal and exceedingly expensive restaurant, I felt most uncomfortable greeting our guests beside the ostentatious white marble fountain overflowing with imported champagne from Paris.

If I had looked closely that day, I would have noticed more than the great divide of lavish excess and artistic sensibility separating our friends and relatives to their chosen sides of the celebration. I was so caught up in my wedding day, all I saw was my new husband, dazzling handsome in his black tuxedo. I neglected to take note of Mama's near collapse when David danced her across the banquet room floor. She paled beside him in her ruby, tea-length dress, anorexic-thin and frail, barely able to remain in her too-high heels.

After we left for our month-long honeymoon in Europe, a gift from David's parents, my mother had to be hospitalized for weeks. She died soon after our return to the states.

No one told me how gravely ill she was, at her request. She didn't want to take away from my wedding and honeymoon. Coming home to her deathbed was a sad and devastating way to begin a marriage.

I had but days with her to say my good-byes. It was not near enough time for our strained relationship. I sat by her bedside, held her hand and kissed her forehead. David went to work after the second day. I didn't see him again until the funeral.

Daddy, Nana and I stayed with Mama right up until she drew her last breath, all life forcing its way out of the emaciated shell her body had shriveled and contorted into. The once stunning southern belle had long ago, curtsied and bid us all farewell when Beddie had died. With a slight bow of her head, and a blink of her haunting dark eyes, she took her final leave.

Watching her laying there so quiet, I expected some kind of a peace to come over me—or at least relief. Nothing calming manifested. Instead, sorrow and regret swept through me with vengeance. My new groom had neither sympathy nor empathy for my guilt.

Daddy missed Mama so much he died a year later when his heart simply quit beating. So, once again, I retreated within myself.

My first child, Sarah, was conceived and born in the midst of brokenhearted grief and my struggle to survive in a darkening cave of loneliness, hollowed out by caverns of despair. She brought light and hope within her newborn cries, embracing the world and all it had to offer with an insatiable zeal for life and an engaging attitude my mama would have found endearing. I truly believed that my infant daughter would have captivated the shattered remnants of what had once been a whole, vivacious woman, and brought life renewing healing.

That was then. Now Sarah and I were at odds. I wondered if she realized how much more distressing this unwavering opposition to my decision to withhold the fact of David's infidelity from her younger sister becomes with every passing day?

Do our children need to know the secret sins of past indiscretions? What could it possibly profit them to be privy to sinister misdeeds we can never undo? Whether committed in foolishness or selfish indulgence, the damage was done. Why compound it by continuing to give time and attention to such reckless transgressions.

And who can speak for the dead? David could rot in his grave. I had no concern for his reputation. My desire was to spare Olivia the sordid details of her father's cavorting around with a woman lacking the remotest shred of integrity, who stole time from his children that they were entitled to by birthright. His absence when they'd walk down the aisle to wed was an undeniable consequence for his egotistical actions.

My mother had struggled to hang on for me at the end, and suffered for it. Back then, I felt abandoned. Now I realized her intentions were only the best for me. I wanted that stylish wedding, the European honeymoon and the romantic send-off. How silly to desire silk, flowers, and iridescent taffeta more than a human being.

Chapter Thirty-Two

I often sit at the water's edge, letting the waves roll up
my legs, soak my skin, then recede. It's a form of therapy.
I can't control the intensity, timing, or temperature of the
flow. I can relax under the sun, recline with my hands
planted in the sand, and rest.

-Emily journal entry 1992

I turned into the lot and parked in front of the Lake Cottage
Book Haven. Glancing at my watch, I was relieved to see I
was exactly on time, ten o'clock sharp. George unlocked the door
and waved me on inside.

Grabbing an armful of paperwork, I peered through the windshield at the little store. Every painted timber and scroll in the trim
accent of the quaint stone architecture drew me into a beckoning
world of new possibilities.

"I have tea brewing and almond biscotti." He ushered me to
the back office, a tiny room overtaken by a massive oak roll-top
desk and flourishing asparagus ferns in clay pots nestled in macramé jute-beaded hangers suspended from brass ceiling hooks.

George's balding head and portly frame bent over a whistling
tea kettle. "Are you sure asked about buying the place?"

"Absolutely," I replied, certain for the first time as I heard myself speak. I plopped my folder beside his mountain of multi-colored Post-it-tagged pages. "I'm ready to sign."

"Mom." Olivia's voice carried nervously over the phone line.

"Give me a minute, I just walked in the door." I shoved the pile of paperwork across the kitchen table and collapsed in a chair. "Is something wrong?"

She sniffled and blew her nose. "I know about Dad and Caroline."

"What?" How dare Sarah tell her before I decided the time was right.

"She came by the house yesterday with a friend of hers. Sarah and I were gathering pictures and baking casseroles for Nana's memorial."

My irritation at Sarah morphed into rage at Caroline. "Where are you?" I croaked out.

"We're half-way to the cabin. I'm calling from the pay phone at the Nyack gas station in Emigrant Gap. Sarah pulled over so I could talk to you. She's standing beside me so she can hear you too."

"Why did Caroline come to the house?"

"She and her friend wanted Dad's golf clubs."

My mind reeled at the boldness of my once-trusted friend.

"She's called several times while Sarah and I have been staying at the house. I've been putting her off. I wasn't ready to give away the golf bag yet."

I heard a hiccup, something Olivia only did when she's been crying really hard.

Another one followed in quick succession.

"I caved in and told her they could come by before we left for Nana's funeral. I actually thought she'd back off when she realized we'd lost another family member." Several sniffles were followed by repeated hiccups.

"Did she tell you about ...?" Hairs raised on the back of my neck and spiked to razor-sharp dagger points.

"No. She bulldozed her way through the house to the garage, one step ahead of me. When I pushed the button to open the garage door, so she could wheel the bag out to her car." A jolting hiccup halted her speech. Olivia's voice faded in and out before she spoke again. "She started to cry. Her friend tried to shush her. I don't know why, but I lifted a cover off one of the clubs and Caroline started sobbing, uncontrollably."

Traffic barreled through the circuit, an endless convoy of big rigs.

"Olivia?" I raised my voice to pierce through the road racket.

"I figured she wanted the clubs because she'd been golfing with Daddy. That's where he said he went weekends for most of the past three years."

Olivia let out a scream through the mouthpiece, a shrill cry that scared me.

"All the clubs were brand new, every single one of them polished, brand spanking new." her voice trailed off, obliterated by the blaring honks of hurried motorists on the highway.

"They never went golfing, Mom."

Her whisper traveled clearly across the miles between us, through cedar and pine trees. The prickly tips of the needle clusters repeatedly stabbed my heart. Trickles of blood spilled from places I'd long guarded, leaving pinhole puncture wounds not visible to the naked eye, but excruciatingly perforated by undying betrayal.

Sarah took the phone. "We're having a cup of coffee before heading on up. It'll be an extra hour or so before we get there. Olivia's not ready for the funeral."

"Okay. I'll be waiting. Drive safe."

Click. Silence.

A knock at the door interrupted my confused thoughts. *Nobody told her? She figured it out for herself? Sarah never said a word?*

"Em," Jack called out. He came in with Doc right behind him. "Are your girls almost here?"

"They just called from Nyack. It'll be another hour, maybe longer." I rustled the papers into the folder facing away from them. I'd decided to wait to share my big news until after Nana's service.

"What you got there?" Jack strained to get a look.

"Lots of paperwork." I turned around toward them and changed my mind. "I bought a business this morning."

"What?" Jack did a double-take "Where?" He opened his mouth, then closed it.

"Here, in Tahoe City. That quaint little stone cottage near the Safeway. I quit my job in Sacramento. There's no reason for me to move back there with the girls leaving for college. They can come here for the summers now." I tried to sound resolute, brave. But I wondered if I was making yet another big mistake in my life.

"That's wonderful." Doc gave me one of his big bear hugs. "Your Nana would be pleased right into the next county."

"You're going to live here? In Nana's home?" Jack was catching on quick. "Next door?"

"I think that's why she left it to me."

"What kind of business?" He scratched his head and sat in the chair next to me.

"A bookstore with a tea room." I beamed. "Nothing even remotely executive."

"How long have you been looking into this?"

He appeared to be processing the information, which surprised me. Kind of like, was this going to be a good or a bad thing? I wondered if the damage I'd caused wasn't going to go away, not even with time.

"About a month ago I bumped in George at the market and we started chatting in the checkout line. He was looking for someone committed to keeping the bookstore open. I ran my ideas by him for the addition of a tea room, serving scones, fresh fruit and loose leaf teas." I offered Jack a peach from the bowl on the table. He passed.

"Wow, Em." Jack seemed somewhat stunned and unaccustomedly speechless.

"I made a day run to Sac the afternoon we talked about, and got a Realtor." A new confidence filled me as the words rolled off my tongue and landed in Jack's lap.

He fumbled with a placemat. "Do the girls know?"

"They know the house is up for sale. They've been living there."

"I wasn't sure myself about the bookstore until this morning, Can't explain it, I just knew deep inside me I could do this. Make it a successful business and save a bookstore at the same time."

Doc squeezed Jack's shoulder. "Isn't it wonderful. We have a new neighbor."

Oddly, I thought Jack would be the first one to jump for joy. A befuddled look clouded his expression and muted his conversation. I'd hoped he'd be pleased, maybe a little supportive. This wasn't the reaction I'd anticipated at all.

"I want to run into town and walk through the store before the girls get here. Want to join me?" I opened my offer to both men.

"You kids head on over," Doc said. "I've got a few thing to finish before Hannah's service tonight. I'm still working on her eulogy." He exited out the screen door.

"It's just seven miles down the road. I'd really like to show you." I continued to urge.

"I'll get the Jeep." He stood, avoiding eye contact.

I followed him out the front door.

"Aren't you going to lock it?" Jack's voice tweaked in surprise.

"No."

"Jack hardly spoke the entire drive." I refused to let his somber mood affect my exuberance.

I turned the key in the pewter lock and led the way inside. "I bought the full inventory. George has all the classics, an excellent variety of genres, and a fabulous children's section. Look at the adorable ladybug table and chairs. I can visualize little people sitting here with a parent reading to them. Don't you just love the smell of a bookstore?" Inhaling deeply, I ran my hand over a top row of books on the shelf closest to me and pulled Hemingway's *A Farewell to Arms*.

"Em, why didn't you say anything to me about this?" Jack almost sounded accusatory.

"What was there to say?" I quit flipping through the book, which a moment ago I had intended to give him.

"I thought we were becoming friends again."

"So do I."

"Friends trust each other, help each other out." His eyes locked on mine.

"Jack, we are learning to trust each other. And I'm grateful to be getting to know you again, as a grown-up." I smiled. "But I need to start making decisions on my own."

In the quiet, amid the aisles of volumes of words of knowledge, we stood, fellow fledglings. "I need to learn to spread my wings and fly." I held the book out to him.

He read the title. Timid, almost shy in a way I hadn't seen since the first days we'd met, he accepted my gift.

"Can you sit with me a spell? I can put on a kettle for tea. And there's fresh oranges I picked up this morning." I tried to muster up all the Southern charm in that request that my Nana came by ever-so-naturally.

"Tea and oranges in the kitchen with Emily. Sounds like that Leonard Cohen song."

"Tea and oranges down by the river with Suzanne." He sang a bit off key.

"No river in my teeny-tiny kitchen." I grinned.

"Is there a man-size scone or a bagel in there somewhere?" Jack joked. Food was an important issue for him though I still have no idea why. Perhaps it was time I bothered to learn.

"I saw a loaf of raisin bread next to the toaster."

In the kitchen I popped in two slices and sat at the table to listen instead of talk. I peeled an orange as Jack shared about his parents … or, the lack of parents in his life.

Tepid sunlight filtered through the lace curtain and across the tabletop. Behind him the lake stretched as far as the eye could see, blue water and sky blended onto one canvas, peaceably extending beyond the bordered edges in calming hues and soothing brush-strokes. Jack's image emerged as the next layer on the canvas, his sharp features in stark contrast to the flow of the rest of the painting. His voice wavered periodically, stimulating the rise and fall of waves below the mountain peaks in the background. The palette of colors, thick and rich, enhanced the evolving definition with each steady stroke. We took slow sips of hot tea, treading cautiously onto the fresh paint of the landscape, dipping our toes into the lapping waters.

Jack peeled back the outer rind and offered me a segment of his orange slice.

The familiar rumble of tires scrunching forest debris and gravel in the driveway announced the girls' arrival.

I ran to the front door and swung it wide. Olivia tumbled into my outstretched arms. I couldn't hold her tight enough.

"Mom." Her puffy eyes searched mine for comfort. Jack stepped out from behind me. "Oh." She stiffened and pulled back. Sarah followed behind and rolled both their luggage over the threshold.

"Girls, do you remember my friend Jack Conner?"

"Gentleman Jack, the boy wonder from your youth?" Sarah didn't waste any time. "We've heard a lot about you over the years, good sir. Is it true you were as charming as you were good looking?"

I could swear Jack actually blushed as he gave a slow shrug.

She shoved the suitcase aside. "Nana used to say you were a man to watch out for and love up, rolled into the same batch of cookie dough."

He chuckled. "Well, there's an oxymoron for you."

"I think it was meant as a compliment. That Nana loved you." Sarah winked and took Jack's hand, shaking it vigorously. "I remember you from when we were young. You look different now."

"I'll give you ladies a little privacy." With that Jack bowed out, fast.

I watched him make a dash for the kitchen door. He left oranges on the table he'd brought from the bookstore. But the Hemingway novel was niched under his armpit.

"Are we sleeping in Nana's room?" Sarah shifted gears.

"If you want. You can bunk together tonight and change rooms tomorrow. It's up to you."

Sarah hauled the suitcase to the back bedroom. Olivia made her way to the neighboring bathroom before I could say a word to her.

I shadowed Sarah to Nana's room, then I glanced over my shoulder to make sure Olivia couldn't hear. "I wanted to tell you, I'm sorry, for asking you to keep a secret from your sister."

"I honored my word to you Mom, even though I didn't agree with you at all. I wanted to tell Olivia, but I didn't." Her voice was unusually soft.

"I was wrong. Please forgive me." Fear seized my vocal chords.

"I forgave you a long time ago. I was just waiting for you to forgive yourself. Sarah wrapped her arms around my shoulders and hugged me. "I knew you were doing what you thought was best for her. My anger was really at my father. But I took a lot of it out on you." She stood closer.

"I love you." Brushing wayward curls, I asked, "new hairstyle?"

"Brice likes this instead of straight." She flushed. "I needed a change."

Olivia wandered in and sat on the edge of the bed. "Why didn't you tell me about Daddy?"

"I honestly thought I was protecting you." My legs wobbled, threatening to give. I plunked down beside my daughter.

"You didn't know, did you? At least not for a long time."

"I found out that holiday weekend of the car accident. But he still lied about who, and I had no idea for how long. We'd separated when I came home. I never had the chance to tell either of you before he died." My heart didn't hurt for myself anymore, but for my daughters it ached.

Livie's jaw tightened, her left eye twitched. "I can't explain why I took off those blasted club covers, but when I did, I knew. And I got angry."

"Olivia sort of unleashed on Caroline. Her friend Dee ran for cover, but that stupid woman refused to leave without the golf clubs."

"The neighbors called the sheriff." Liv squeezed the mattress with both hands.

"What?" I tried to envision this public display in our quiet cookie-cutter suburban court.

"When they came, Caroline told them the clubs were hers, that dad meant for his golf bag to go to her. What nerve. Livie used some pretty unsavory language explaining to the officers the nature of Caroline's illicit relationship with our father." Sarah whirled around. "And they knew you, Mom. They said they were the ones who came to notify you about the accident."

"Were the neighbors outside watching all this?" I cringed. Most of those people spent the past twenty years at our holiday block parties and backyard barbecues.

"The entire neighborhood came out for the show." Olivia chimed in.

"Does the humiliation never end?" I rolled my eyes and flipped my hand through a wave of my hair, high in the air.

"In a last ditched effort, Caroline pulled a club out of the bag and tried to make a run for it. When the older sheriff grabbed her, she struggled so much the club walloped his buttocks. So they arrested her for attempted theft and assault on an officer."

"We back and watched from that point on. Not pretty I tell you, not pretty at all." Sarah mimicked hitting a golf ball to the sky. "Yeah, it's a good thing the house is up for sale." She added nonchalantly, flounced on the bed and stretched out.

I didn't know whether to laugh or cry. I sat half in shock and half in well, devilish delight. No matter how hard I tried, I could not envision what they were describing. A while back this scene would have destroyed me.

"You know, I kind of feel sorry for Caroline." My words surprised me.

Olivia's puzzled expression mirrored the one I'd worn for decades.

Sarah bolted up. "Don't you go forgiving that witchy-woman. You're starting to sound like Nana."

"I'm with Sarah on this one, Mom. That woman got what she deserved."

"As Nana would say, 'let's get on with the living part.' She'd be so glad you came, not so much to her memorial, but to the cabin, the lake."

Sarah tugged on an earring. "This is one of the last things Nana gave me. I would have liked to seen her one more time."

"Me too." Livie strained to speak louder. "I will miss the sound of her voice."

"Do we have time to go for a walk to the pier?" Sarah asked.

"We can make the time. And along the way, I have news for you two."

I led the way out the kitchen screen door. The girls followed in step with me down the deck steps to the path to the lake.

"I quit my job in Sacramento." I drew in a deep breath, then let it go. "And bought a bookstore in Tahoe City. I'll be annexing a tea room."

"Good for you." Sarah hugged me. "You'll do great with your own business."

Olivia added. "A bookstore tea room is perfect. You know if Nana was still here, she'd put on her apron and bake the scones and shortbread to celebrate with you."

"Wouldn't that be lovely." Sarah sighed.

"You don't mind me living here year-round?" I kicked up sand.

"I think this has always been home to you, Mom." Sarah pulled her baby sister in close. "We have news too."

Olivia nearly burst. "We've been apartment hunting. Looking for our own place to bloom."

"Girls, that's wonderful." I wrapped my arms around their waists. "That makes my heart so happy."

I caught a glimpse through the young pine trees up the incline of Jack and Doc peeking out their window at us. From that distance they looked like two little boys. I waved, then motioned for them to join us. Jack disappeared. I turned around completely so there'd be no mistaking my intentions, gestured again, and waited.

Doc opened the door and held it for Jack until he stepped onto the deck.

"You don't mind if Doc and Jack join us, do you girls?"

"They're part of Nana's family, aren't they?" Sarah stated.

"Yes they are."

Olivia nodded in agreement.

Good thing. The men were on their way to the beach.

"You should serve Nana's almond slices at the tea room," Olivia suggested.

"Lemon squares too," Sarah shared her favorite recipe.

"Coconut custard pie," Doc and Jack said in unison. "You do have the recipe." They looked like a couple of panicked bears with an empty picnic basket.

"I baked one for tonight. After everyone leaves, we'll toast her with a slice."

"Hannah would have liked that." Doc spoke softly, an unchecked tear rolled down his cheek.

"Yes, she would." I agreed. He tried to say something else, but his words got choked up in his throat. Jack hung back with Doc. They walked behind the me and the girls until we reached the water's edge.

A wave rolled up and washed over everyone's feet, zories and all. A rush of cold splashed between my toes. Side by side we waded along the shoreline, silent. Shades of blue pocketed in our cove under the harvest sun and near cloudless sky. The lake spread out slate blue, cerulean, and sapphire in the volcanic depths where the intensity of blending hues mingled along the horizon.

Jack offered me a flat rock to skip. I accepted, pulled my arm back, and aimed.

I pitched, and it skipped seven times. Water rippled in a circular ring, widening from the epicenter, farther and farther into the body of the crystal-clear basin.

I entwined my fingers through Jack's. How small we stood before those majestic mountains. For the first time in many years. I knew we were not alone.

Chapter Thirty-Three

Emily's Correspondence

To my mother,

I never understood the pain in your heart. You seemed to be haunted by Beddie's death. I thought you blamed me. Nana told me you blamed yourself. I lost you when he left us.

How I wish you'd lived long enough to know my daughters. You would have fallen completely in love with them. Their names are Sarah and Olivia. It is a great loss that they never got the opportunity to know you as their grandmother.

I needed you when I was pregnant, when they were babies, when the first day of kindergarten arrived. I wanted you when boys started to notice them, called for dates, and drove off with them in their cars.

I remembered the day Beddie died. You were so young and carefree. That is how I am going to remember you. No more sorrow, sickness, and death.

I choose to remember the living.

For a long time I refused to forgive you for the lost dreams and hope I once had for a future together. I forgive you. For everything. Even for asking Nana not to tell me.

Nana's prayers for all of us were heard, and are still being answered.

I loved you so much, Mama. ~ Emily

One Year Later ~ October of 1996

A quick glance at my watch reminded me I had eight minutes to be on time. I taped the cardboard box shut, then
rushed out the back door and tossed the parcel onto the front seat
of my car.

Autumn had arrived early and in full splendor on the lake.
The aspens fluttered like butterflies spreading amber-edged delicate wings in flight, their slender white-bark trunks lined up
along the roadside in alternating groves inset among Jeffrey and
Ponderosa pines. Sunlight as golden as the fall foliage filtered
through branches bending in graceful dance with a zephyr bringing in the season's first lower temperatures from the west. Tahoe
Yellow Cress emerged upslope along the shoreline next to the
highway.

It was difficult to concentrate on the road ahead of me while
surrounded by the intensity of changing color. It helped knowing
my second destination was a hike at Taylor Creek on the south
shore, an outing Jack had been promising for weeks, includ-
ing the Stream Profile Chamber. Its windows offered a view
of the underwater world of Tahoe life, especially the Kokanee
salmons' annual ritual swimming upstream, turning the creek's
clear waters a coppery red and signaling the ushering in of the
quiet, end-of-summer tourist calm.

But first, I had a promise to keep. I almost missed a right turn into Hollister Home. The place my Nana used to call the "Old Folks Home for Wise Ones." The parking lot was empty other than Jack's truck and the employee section on the far left. With the package tucked under my arm, I entered through the front door managing not to set off the alarm like the last time I dropped off my delivery.

"Hello, Emily." The reception desk attendant's greeting sounded monotone.

When I opened my mouth to respond, I shielded my nose from the onslaught of noxious scents that had settled on my taste buds from the moment I'd crossed the threshold.

"Hello, Fred." He never so much as glanced my, or anyone else's way. He sat at the desk, head bowed to watch his mini TV, or blared his boom box throughout the place.

In the main lobby I found Jack tending to Harold, the oldest resident, a saxophone player from Cal/Neva's heydays. From the first time I visited the home, the elder musician was certain I was his Alma. I'd heard his daughter deserted him the day she signed him in here at the "Hollister Hotel" fifteen years ago. Harold claimed me every time I came, and there no convincing him otherwise.

These poor neglected souls didn't even know who they were half the time. Sewing bibs for the residents is one thing, but Jack spends several hours here twice a week, filling in for Doc when the volunteers were no-shows. I set my latest batch of dribble-and-drool creations on the table near the front door. The extra-large, double-sided, terry-cloth-and-cotton print bibs would only last until the Christmas holidays. Between the food and medications spills, and bleach machine washings, the fabric wore out fast.

Harold hadn't seen me yet so I could break away before he called me to his side and a waterfall of tears began flowing. Jack was combing a thick thatch of the old musician's hair, and he had a head full to contend with. The vintage bass sax sat in the empty wheelchair beside them, the polished brass gleaming under the bright rays of light shining in from the picture widow.

Every once in a while, Cool Cat Harold Richmond plays a blues tune from his earlier days in San Francisco, without a misplaced note. Other days he blows on the wrong end of the instrument until I just want to cry for him to stop.

Jack nodded as he got Harold situated in his wheelchair and handed him his sax. I motioned that I was going to head on out.

Tape ripped off the box behind me with a loud zip. I turned and saw a rotund woman, much younger than most of the seniors in the room, yanking out one bib after another and handing them to everyone seated nearby. A comical ruckus ensue, with snowy-crowned oldsters arguing from their wheelchairs and walkers, and whacking about with wooden and metal canes to get in on the only action in town. The normally over-medicated crowd exhibited far more strength and mobility than I'd witnessed before. Someone was going to end up making contact with a flailing limb or unprotected noggin. Sure enough, Mable Parker's sister landed a direct hit with the side of her cane on Mr. Lee's forehead.

Sighing, I knew what that meant. Jack wasn't going anywhere until he examined and treated the patient. I snatched the empty box off the floor. Jack assessed the situation, and wheeled Mr. Lee off to the treatment room down the long, smelly hallway leading toward the residents' living quarters.

"Alma, you came!" Harold had caught sight of me. He laid the sax in his lap and tried to get up out of the wheelchair. The brakes were still locked and as he struggled to wiggle free from the safety belt restraining him, the chair shifted to the left. Loose brown trousers hitched in the gears and his chair toppled to the floor. Attendants were nowhere to be seen.

Rushing across the room, I grabbed the right wheel and hooked it on the arm of a sofa where two distracted gentlemen sat trying the Velcro fasteners of a couple of designer-jeans bibs. Fred slugged over barely in the nick of time to help me drag Harold's wheelchair upright.

"Alma," the old man gazed up at me, his face piqued with anticipation, eyes wide.

"Are you okay?" I looked him over but didn't see any rising bumps or streaks of blood. I made sure the restraints weren't twisted or cutting into his flesh anywhere.

"I be okay now that you're here, baby girl."

"Fred, aren't you going to check him out?" Hands on my hips, I watched the receptionist already on his way back to his station, his faded green scrubs rounding the corner.

"Harold is fine." Fred yelled over his shoulder. "He dumps his wheelchair at least once a day." He stopped and glanced back. "Be sure to take the saxophone before he starts honking away on that thing."

"He needs help."

"Alma. I knew you be comin' back for me." Tears flooded down his cheeks, past the white chin stubble onto his pea-soup-stained yellow polo shirt. "Baby girl, I knew you couldn't be forgettin' your daddy."

Clear streams ran from both his nostrils. He grabbed my hand, squeezing tight.

I pulled away.

One of the men sitting next to me took his off his bib and placed it around Harold's neck.

"Don't worry. Don't worry." He tried to clasp one end of the Velcro to the other, but the cloth kept falling onto Harold's shoulders. "Oh. Oh." He sidestepped to the right and to the left, waving his hands in the air, then turning in circles, his baggy-hopsack olive slacks dragging on the floor. The tap, tap from his shoe heels clicking on the worn tiles in a nervous pattern. "Oh, Oh…"

"Alma, baby," Harold whined, "Why you be gone so long?" He swiped his hand across his nose and wiped snot on his pants. "I keep telling 'em my baby girl be comin' for her daddy." Harold reached out for my hand with the same one he'd just used to wipe his nose.

My feet froze in place, cemented to the floor with a stronger adhesive than any glue. Arms stiff down to my fingertips, I remained immobile.

"Alma, don't leave me here, take me with you." His outstretched hand hung suspended in mid-air, wavering, and faltering.

"Don't worry." A thin arm covered in purple-and-black bruises and red blotches extended a withered hand on Harold's bobbing head. A plastic wrist band was bound loosely around the arm of the distraught senior who tried again to fasten the Velcro tabs. He sat on the sofa, constantly repeating, "Don't worry."

Clasping both hands on the sax, Harold's torso slumped forward.

"Turn off the waterworks you old coot! Nobody wants to listen to it today." Fred hollered from his post, then turned up the volume on the office radio. A barrage of obnoxious rap blared through hallway and sheetrock walls, to the obvious dismay of many residents who ducked their heads and covered their ears.

I connected one end of the Velcro tab to the other behind Mr. Richmond's neck. His body rocked the wheelchair, shaking the floor under my hiking boots. I unstrapped and slid off my backpack, and dropped it beside his flannel slippers. Both of his little toes had poked holes through, exposing thick, long, curled-under nails.

With a slow steady pull his head rose. Whimpering, he gazed at me. His huge saucer-brown eyes stared deep speaking a language devoid of words.

Kneeling beside him. I used the soft terrycloth underside to clean Harold's face. The light blue turned dark from the soaked-up fluids draining down, streaking his cheeks and dribbling from his nose. With a final swipe, I sopped up a string of drool from his collar. I inhaled the familiar scent of Old Spice as I swept over his stubble one more time.

How could someone drop their parent off here and never come back?

"I'm sorry it took me so long to get here … Daddy, I could never forget you." I ran my other hand back and forth over his shoulder blades. I pressed my lips lightly on his forehead, near at the beginning of a receding hairline.

"Alma, Alma. He sobbed, those soulful eyes staying on my mine. He sniffled, trying to catch his breath, struggling for some semblance of composure.

I removed the saturated bib and accepted a stack of new ones from the man in the olive pants. He took the soiled cloth from me and disappeared down the hall.

Harold picked a lime-green bib from the center and tugged it out. I snapped it on and daubed his damp face again.

"I'm sorry, Alma. I didnst' want to go without you. Daddies aren't supposed to leave their baby girls behind." A pained expression cast a shadow on baggy eyelids and the sagging skin of his hollow cheeks.

"I know." My chest heaved, a lump lodged, and tears glazed over my eyes.

"Oh, Alma, don't you cry now, baby." His thick lips parted into a slow smile, showing white teeth tinged with faint brown outlines. "Ev'rything gonna be all right." His calloused palm rested on my hand and he patted with gentle reassurance. "No need to fret now."

He wiped a tear from beside my nose with the rosebud-print fuchsia bib on the top of the stack. I placed the bibs on his lap next to the saxophone and laid my head on the pile, trying to suppress the unexpected swell rising inside. My hands encircled his slender waist.

"You gonna be ok, child?" His arm wrapped around me. "Your daddy be here now."

The scuffle of shoes shuffled on the tile, and olive pant legs brushed beside me. Another pair of rubber soles followed: Jack's size thirteen cross-trainers. His boot-cut jeans stopped at my knees. I focused on gray shoelaces and the worn black penny loafers.

"You okay, Harold?" Jack asked. Not hearing an answer, he suggested Fred turn off the radio, immediately.

When the noise quieted a bit, Jack crouched beside Harold. "Old Percy here came to get me. Said you found Alma."

"She's here. My baby girl done found me." A grin brightened Harold's face, as he pointed at me.

Jack gave me a quizzical 'when did you become Harold's long lost daughter' look. To which I mouthed 'Just go along with me.'"

"Maybe I should give these extra bibs to your friends, Daddy." I stood and handed Percy the first one.

"How is Mr. Lee?" I glanced over my shoulder.

"No need for stitches. Just a lot of blood. Thin skin does that. I cleansed the cut and he's doing great. He isn't on blood thinners like most of the others here." Jack wore a surprised but pleased expression. He opened his mouth, closed it, and opened it again.

"What?" I smoothed out the wrinkled knees of my jeans.

"I should not be calling you Emily."

"Correct. Want to help hand these out?" I gave him half the bibs and pointed toward the crowd gathering near the epicenter of activity.

Jack walked over to a couple of ladies sitting on the sofa across the room and let them chose the color they liked. "I see you made progress with our retired nightclub disciple. Harold still has it in him. He can deliver a bluesy solo that will beguile your socks right off."

"He was worried his daughter thought he left her behind." I whispered when I got close enough for only him to hear. "How do you work here without it breaking your heart?" A few of the gents indicated they wanted a bib so I headed their way. Jack followed.

"Doc and I and a few others are the only ones who come." Jack shrugged. "Most people don't take the time to see the person shackled inside the aging body."

"Oh." I was thinking, well, that would be me too.

"Harold was one of the original members of the Black-and-White jazz bands from the 1920's. He started jamming with them after he moved out to San Francisco from New Orleans as a teenager. Jack glanced at the front desk, then lowered his voice. "Some folks only see the senile outer shell, the worn, decrepit form broken down by nearly a century of living." He shook his head. "It's a shameful loss of beautiful human beings."

Harold wheeled through the lounge, weaving around walkers telling anyone who would listen that his daughter wasn't lost after all. "See? My Alma found me."

"I've never seen him so happy." Jack sat on the sofa. "Or so interactive."

I squeezed in next to Jack before one of the little old ladies could claim that spot. "Does he just wait for Alma every day?"

"He spends all his time polishing that sax, cleaning the mouthpiece, and sitting in front of the window playing to his biggest audience, the lake."

"That is both sad and beautiful at the same time."

Jack said, "Tarnished people aren't always elderly, some deteriorate early on."

"I can see that." I clutched my bright-pink bib, an idea forming in my head. "I can design some flyers and put them up in my bookstore, maybe get some writers or homeschool groups to come and read the classics these folks grew up with. The children will love these oldsters right up."

"That would be nice." Jack's voice softened and he took my hand. "We should be leaving for Taylor Creek soon. But I want wait a little longer to be sure Mr. Lee doesn't have a mild concussion. Tess Parker smacked him a good one. I don't think he needs an X-ray." Jack peeked at the clock hanging across the room. "It's almost lunch time."

"Don't you stay and help feed them?" I knew he usually did.

"Yeah, but they can do it without me this one time." He drew me close. "We've got a trail to blaze and schools of spawning salmon waiting to be photographed."

"Woo-wee!" Harold whistled. "Jack is making a play for my baby girl."

The crowd hollered and clapped until the lunch bell rang. Then an instant assembly of appliance-assisted seniors hurried down a worn pathway to the dining hall.

"Watch out for the walkers, they move the fastest," Jack warned, a grin broadening across his face.

"Why don't we stay," I offered. "I can help out during lunch."

"Are you sure?"

"Yes." I grabbed the handles on Harold's wheelchair and steered into the troop of hungry diners donned in a colorful assortment of new bibs. My cheek brushed against his when I bent over. "What's on the menu today?"

He sniffed the air. "It's gotta be something good."

The hallway floated with a myriad of odors I couldn't quite identify. I crinkled my nose.

Harold's hand tapped mine. "You gonna eat supper with me?"

"Only if I can sit at your table."

"Ha! Jackson, you go get your own girl. I gots mine here now."

Jack placed a hand over his heart. "I'm wounded, my friend, that you'd think I'd try to steal her away from you." Jack winked, wheeling one of the more heavily medicated elders. Several uniformed attendants ushered the less mobile on ahead.

"Taylor Creek, this weekend," Jack promised. "Lake of the Sky Trail. Stream Profile Chamber."

"I'll pack the picnic hamper."

"What you two be talkin' about?" Harold asked. "Alma done found her way back home. You gotta sticks round a spell now." He clasped a hand over mine on the handle of his wheelchair.

"Yes, Daddy." I turned to look out the window at the lake. Blue spread from one end of the plate glass to the other, filling the now-empty room as if spilling over into one pool. The sky rolled out like an endless sea mirroring the infinite depths below.

I remembered Nana's words from that day we sat on the driftwood log as if we had all the time in the world to sit and chat, I asked her, "What do you see when you look at the lake?"

She answered in that mild Southern accent I long to hear every day, "I see redeeming waters bathed in grace from the winter snow melt cascading down from mountain-tops. Pine trees unfolding needled branches heavenward in simple praise to the Creator, who planted them deep as seedlings in rich soil. And I see the beauty of a holy God who saw fit to plant me here for a season."

Discussion Questions

For Book Clubs

1) Was there a particular character or several characters that you could relate to throughout the story? What drew you to this person or people?

2) What did you think was the main theme of this novel?

3) In the beginning chapter how does Emily's interaction with Doc, Jack, and Nana influence your first impression of her?

4) Did you think the relationship in *Language* between Emily and Nana was intimate? Do or did you have an intimate relationship growing up into adulthood with your parents or grandparents? How did it affect your later decisions in life?

5) Does the obvious friction between Jack and Emily in the beginning of the story change? How? Does one character try harder than the other to work things out?

6) Friendship is important in this story. Doc and Nana share a special friendship that weathers storms. What do you look for in a friend?

7) Do you see any similarities between Jack, and Emily's deceased husband David? Did Emily treat Jack with distrust because of her husband's betrayal?

8) How do survivors like Sophia deal with being spared?

9) What did you think of Jack's parents ~ Zack and Helen? How important is the example parents set?

10) Nana prayed almost as she breathed. Doc and Annie believed in prayer too. Do the prayers of people live beyond their human death? In what ways do you pray?

11) Is there a difference between someone being religious and someone having faith?

12) Why do you think Emily kept putting off telling her youngest daughter the secret? Was it necessary to tell Olivia about her father? Did you agree with Sarah and Nana, or Emily? Where does one draw the line when it comes to secrets?

13) Do you think it was important for Emily to remember the day her twin brother died, and how he died? How does the memory of his death change her behavior?

14) If she was so close to Nana, why did Emily avoid talking about Beddie with her? Why didn't Nana tell Emily about her first marriage?

15) Where was God in the middle of all the heartache these characters experienced? Did Doc's loss of his infant daughter Isabella, and later his wife Annie, deepen his faith or destroy it?

16) How was Emily able to forgive her mother? How hard is it to forgive someone you feel has abandoned you? How important is forgiveness?

17) When Jack leaves why does Emily change her mind about him? Emily blamed Jack for all her troubles, do you think she should have been looking at herself? Why did she finally ask Jack for forgiveness?

18) There is death in this story: the death of innocent children, of a cheating husband and father, of Doc's beloved wife, Emily's parents and her Nana. Is there a finality in death? What do you believe?

19) When a child dies before the parents, do the living children and/or a spouse sometimes feel abandoned if one person is consumed in grief?

20) What did you like or dislike the most about Language of the Lake? And what struck the deepest cord in you?

Who has Emily been hearing call her name?

Have you ever heard a still small voice calling your name?

Music Play List for Characters in the Language Story

Emily Maxwell Taylor ~ loves music and dancing. Much of her relationship with Jack is based on song and melody. She grew up listening to lullabies, and sang as a child when she hung laundry on a clothesline with her mother. Some of Emily's favorite songs: He's Got the Whole Word, Lavender's Blue, Scarlet Ribbons, These Dreams, Landslide, and All I Know. If Emily had the chance to listen to music of our day, she would love Rachel Wagner's songs, especially ~ Untold, and I Won't Be the One.

Jackson Luke Conner ~ Jack has played the guitar since he was ten. He spent his teen years strumming away, longing to write his own lyrics, but mostly playing other musician's songs. He keeps his favorite guitar in his office for when he needs to unwind. Simon & Garfunkel continue to inspire him. Jack's music: For Emily Whenever I May Find Her, Bridge Over Troubled Water, Comin' Back to Me, Who Will You Run Too?, You Look Wonderful Tonight, April Come She Will, I am a Rock, and The Boxer.

Doc John Walters ~ Doc waltzed with Annie through the decades of their lives with her size five feet on his shoes. Music was pure joy for them. It carried him through the grief and sorrow of losing both his infant daughter, and his beloved wife. There will always be a song in Doc's heart. These are the records he still plays on his hi-fi: What a Wonderful World, That Lucky Old Sun, Dear Heart, Be Thou My Vision, How Great Thou Art, Amazing Grace, Glenn Miller, Mills Brothers, and Duke Ellington.

Hannah Mae Harrison ~ Nana grew up back east. Everyone in her family played at least two musical instruments. The piano set her soul free. She cherished the old hymns, and sang Christmas music all through the year. Music that brought her joy: The Little Brown Church in the Vale, Go Tell It on the Mountain, Hello in There, Scarlet Ribbons, Ella Fitzgerald, Beethoven, Mozart, Bach, Count Basie, and George Beverly Shea.

Daryl Bannister & Hard Liners ~ started his band at fifteen, in Reno, Nevada. Lead singer, guitar, and keyboard. High school girlfriend Heather has played beside him since the beginning. At every gig he sings The Moody Blues ~ For My Lady, for Heather. Daryl's a big Eric Clapton, Steve Winwood and Heart fan, and plays all their songs. He jams with Jack a couple of times a month where they hang out at The Station.

Cool Cat Harold Richmond ~ such a gifted musician. He jammed on the east and west coasts with some of the best jazz men of all time. His saxophone was never far from his reach, and when he played tears rolled down cheeks. Surely when Carole King sang, Jazzman, she was singing about Cool Cat. Harold's beloved tunes: Goodbye Pork Pie Hat, St. Louis Blues, Strange Fruit, One o'Clock Jump, Mood Indigo, and Jelly Roll Blues. Harold's memory is fading, but he can still play. Some days, better than others.

Acknowledgements

I am grateful to my writer friends, beta readers, and fearless critique groups, for all the first drafts, rewrites, and revisions they read and offered thoughtful suggestions while honoring the voice The Language of the Lake story speaks.

Thanks to Amador Fiction Writers ~ John Clewett, Jessica Moore, Pam Dunn, Jo Sarti, Betty Weatherby, Sarah Garner, Victoria Collier, Bo Howard, and Jennifer Fellure.
Foothill Scribner Writers ~ Carolyn Bakken, Tonia Martin, Marilyn Rickabaugh, and Lynn Hallimore. Willow Glen Writers ~ Susan Nicolson, Janice Lawton, Al Van Hise, Fred Semken, Raoul Mowatt and Patrick Walker.
Mokelumne Hill workshop leader Antoinette May Herndon, who invited me to be a part of something special, and brought Language to the end of the story.

I spent years traveling between the Mount Hermon Christian Writer's Conference, and the Squaw Valley Community of Writers. These two literary homes influence each word and sentence I write. The late Oakley Hall, one of the SVCW founders, encouraged me when I attended the open to the public panels, discussions, and literary reads. Thank you also to James N. Frey, and the Hall family ~ Sands, Brett, and Tracy.

The late Roger Williams, and his wife Rachel, gave from their hearts at Mt. Hermon. Thank you Jerry B. Jenkins, James Scott Bell, Christine Harder Tangvald, and the late Ethel Herr. I continue to be blessed by the instruction from these MH mentors.

Research Help ~ PA Jerry Clevenger, Police Officer Daniel Rego, and Sheriff Mike Rice.
Readers ~ Original stinky boy-Chris Williams, Keith Earl, Joe Fellure, Amber Morgan, Lynn Cordone, Marlene Risse Johnson, Deb Klepic, and all the Language Influencers.

With a grateful heart I thank my agent, Wendy Lawton, from Books & Such Literary Management, for taking a chance on me, and for believing in the Language story.
The Language of the Lake was written to reach the deep places of hurt, loss, betrayal, and abandonment in the hearts of my readers. I hope that Emily, Jack, Doc, Annie, Nana, Abigail, Sarah, Olivia, and the little innocents ~ Isabella, Beddie, and Sophia are characters you can relate to whether through joy, grief, anger, hatred, or love.

If you read this book, I have prayed for you.

"You are born into this world and you probably never
know to whose prayers your life is an answer."
~ Oswald Chambers

To God be the Glory